Other *Leisure Books* by Max Brand:

TROUBLE IN TIMBERLINE
RIDERS OF THE SILENCES
TIMBAL GULCH TRAIL
THE BELLS OF SAN FILIPO
MARBLEFACE
THE RETURN OF THE RANCHER
RONICKY DOONE'S REWARD
RONICKY DOONE'S TREASURE
RONICKY DOONE
BLACKIE AND RED
THE WHISPERING OUTLAW
THE SHADOW OF SILVER TIP
THE TRAP AT COMANCHE BEND
THE MOUNTAIN FUGITIVE

THE WHITE WOLF

LEISURE BOOKS NEW YORK CITY

A LEISURE BOOK®

November 1995

Published by special arrangement with Golden West Literary Agency.

Dorchester Publishing Co., Inc.
276 Fifth Avenue
New York, NY 10001

Cover Art by Hermon Adams

Printed in the United States of America.

THE WHITE WOLF

CHAPTER I

In an upper box-cañon of the Winnemago River, Gannaway saw the big man first. Gannaway himself was big, and hard-muscled from wandering across the ridges of the Rockies whether in summer suns or through combing winter hurricanes. By the very face of Adam Gannaway, one knew that he could make himself at home in the heart of a blizzard one day and in the desert the next. And his work as meteorologist kept him busy year in and year out, wandering and never pausing. That deep and quiet soul of his, ever removed from the ways of other men, was more at ease up here and in the wilderness of the mountains, he could spread his elbows at the board; in all other places he was a self-conscious, clumsy fellow.

He was a great hunter, too, this Adam Gannaway, though he was fonder of hunting with a camera than with a rifle; but the result was that he knew the ways of the wild beasts as hardly any other in the length and the breadth of the mountains. But for all these qualifications, when he saw Tucker Crosden for the first time, he felt like some effete city dweller brought suddenly before the face and frown of nature.

Adam Gannaway was big. He was well above six feet, and he had a sturdy spread of shoulders, but when Crosden strode closer to him, Gannaway felt himself shrinking into the dimensions of a boy again.

And Gannaway had had his share of this world's troubles and its joys, but when he looked up into the face of the other, half brutal and half melancholy, it seemed to Gannaway that compared with the soul of the stranger his own was filled with nothing but remembered stuff—dead print!

Tucker Crosden walked with a staff which was heavily shod with steel, and such was its length that it reminded Gannaway of the rough-hewn spear of some early hero; such was its girth that despite the sinewy strength of his own arms, Gannaway would not have cared to carry it with him through a single march. Yet it dangled like a peeled willow wand in the fingers of the giant. The little burro which scampered along before him, the big man whacked with this staff, from time to time, and every blow raised a welt along the ribs of the suffering little beast; and compared with the bulk of its master it seemed rather like a dog than a beast of burden.

However, it was loaded with a heavy pack, and so completely spent by the long struggle up the steep cañons of the Winnemago that when they reached Gannaway the giant let it stop to rest on wide-braced legs.

Human society in the San Jacinto Mountains was rarer than sweet music and more deeply hungered for, but Gannaway had a shrewd conviction that had the burro been fresh the big man would have pressed on with never a word. As it was, he glanced twice at the scientist before he rumbled an indistinguishable word of greeting and then:

"Have you got the makings, stranger?"

Gannaway handed over a package of brown papers and a little Bull Durham in the bottom of a sack. Then he wondered at fingers so heavy and so thick employed in the nuances of rolling a cigarette. Crosden did not waste time in thanks. When his smoke was lighted, he went to the farther side of the burro's pack and took from an open hamper a big female bull-terrier. She was heavy with young and it was patent when Crosden put her on the ground that her hour was fast approaching, yet even so Gannaway wondered that such a man had burdened his single pack animal with the weight of a dog.

The giant followed her to the edge of the Winnemago and watched her drink, scowling thoughtfully down at her. Then, because there was a sharp pitch up the bank which she had to climb, he lifted her carefully under his arm and brought her to the top. She thanked him with a wag of the tail and lift of the ears. Then she went slowly off through the grass.

But Gannaway felt a wonder that deepened every minute. After all, what he had seen was not much more than any humane man would have done for a dog in the terrier's condition, but it seemed as absurd to attribute humanity to the giant as to attribute mercy to a mountain lion or charity to a grizzly. Moreover, it seemed to the observer that the care which the big fellow lavished upon the dog was not the spontaneous result of emotion, but rather the effect of carefully considered plans. As if, for instance, he had been offered a very great reward for bringing the bitch safely across the mountains.

"She's a fine specimen," said Gannaway.

The brute glanced sourly across at him.

"Is she?" said he, offensively, and continued to watch the maneuverings of the terrier with a gloomy eye.

Now Gannaway was no expert in bull-terriers, but he knew all animals well enough, and he knew not only dog standards in general, but something of the special type which the bull-terrier breeder has in his eye. Now Gannaway scanned the bitch again, carefully. He saw her from the front and the rear, the side and the back, and he found nothing against her. Here were legs splendidly straight and huge in bone, a great chest, a pair of shoulders to glad the eye with their cleanness and their fine muscles, a neck neither too long nor too short, and not covered with loose skin. There was her tail, too, set on low, thick at the butt, tapering beautifully—looking as straight as a string, with a spring set in the base of it. But perhaps the head was at fault. No, for it was a glorious head, with little triangular black eyes and a "fill up" clear to the eyes, like the back of a man's hand.

"By heavens," said Gannaway; "if that bitch hasn't championship stuff in her, I'm a fool."

"You ain't the only fool in the world," said the other.

He waited, glowering, expecting the other to take up the insult, but when Gannaway remained calm, the giant consented to add:

"But she's a champion, right enough."

Gannaway was much intrigued. Good bull-terriers do not grow on every bush, in these degenerate days, and one does not expect a champion to approach her hour to litter among the bleak heights of the San Jacinto mountains and expose several hundred dollars' worth of blind puppyhood to the tender mercies of a winter gale.

"Where did she win? And what's her name?" he asked.

The giant turned his back: "It's time to move, Nell. Come here, Nell!"

She came obediently, trotting with a heavy step, and stood before him waiting for further orders so that the heart of Gannaway was warmed in spite of the insolence of the big man. However, at this moment the other finished his cigarette and he half turned to ask: "Got another makings?"

"No," said Gannaway, "that's the last."

"All right," said the giant. "I'll take pipe tobacco, then."

"I'm out of that, too. Not a crumb of it left."

The big fellow stared, incredulous, but there was a world of honesty in the steady blue eyes of Gannaway, and Crosden burst out with an enormous oath.

"But," he growled, "you ain't been giving away your last smoke?"

"I can get on. I've gone without it before," said Gannaway.

The giant looked helplessly about him, as though he strove to find an explanation in the wind and sun and hard rocks around him, but discovered no way of interpreting such generosity as this. Then another thought struggled into his eyes, a conclusion against which he fought hard but which persisted in spite of him.

"Why, hell, man," he exclaimed suddenly, "you must be white!"

And he glared at Gannaway mutely, like another Balboa, "silent, on a peak in Darien." As though, indeed, this discovery of decency in a fellow man were a mystery which could not be comprehended, breaking down all preconceptions.

"Have you got a pipe?" he asked at last.

"Yes."

"Then—fill her up!"

He dragged out a well-filled pouch and offered it; but still while Gannaway gladly and obediently filled his black pipe, the stranger surveyed him with wonder from head to foot, writing down in his mind the distinguishing features of this new species.

"She's Barnsbury Lofty Lady II," he broke out at last, "and she got her championship right back there in New York, like the rest of my breed. I don't bother with none of the little country shows. The big stuff, or nothing."

"An expensive business, that—shipping the dogs so far," suggested Gannaway with respect.

"Oh—ay, it costs money, but I get enough for my dogs out of the traps. I sell enough furs to keep the dogs pretty good. The family don't like it. But—damn the family!"

Gannaway overlooked the latter half of these remarks, and he answered: "She's a good-looking bitch. By the way, my name is Gannaway."

"Gannaway," said the trapper, "I dunno what your business is but it ain't dogs. Well, she's good looking enough for most. They wrote her up when she went East. They give her cups, and they shook hands with me, and they offered me big money for her. Three thousand dollars, says a pinch-faced little son of a fool to me. Three thousand for her? No—nor thirty thousand—nor three hundred thousand—nor three million. Money ain't gunna touch her."

It was not madness, but the divine enthusiasm which makes good horses or dogs on the one hand—good statues and poems on the other. Gannaway understood and nodded in sympathy. His heart, too, was set upon a distant star.

"No, it ain't what she is," went on the giant more to himself than to Gannaway. "It ain't what she is, but it's the hope that's locked up in her. She's got the stuff in her; and maybe it'll come out. She's got the stuff in her!"

"And what is that?" asked Gannaway gently.

The giant looked at him in irritation, askance, but then his thought took hold on him and made him raise his head until his long, thick hair fell back and showed a smile of singular and pure beauty on his face.

"The King!" whispered he. "She's got the blood of The King in her, and maybe that blood'll come out—in this here very litter. I dunno. Nobody can tell—only God!"

CHAPTER II

THEIR way did not lie in the same direction, but Gannaway was glad to turn from the true course which should have led him across the valley of the Winnemago and across Mount Spencer and Mount Lomas in the southern distance; he travelled, instead, up the valley of the river until in the evening they reached the lower Winnemago hills and camped there among the pines. Beyond that range, over the broad side of Spencer Mountain, the stranger intended to hold his way until he reached the valley of the Seven Sisters. In the morning, therefore, they must part, but in the meantime, Gannaway determined to learn, if craft and patience could help him, the riddle which would solve the mystery of why a sane man chose to peril the life of a three thousand dollar dog among the cold winds of the upper mountains—and endanger all the lives of her cubs also, as a matter of course!

But it was not easy to draw information from Crosden. He responded to apparent curiosity as an Indian does—with silence. And what was chiefly clear to Gannaway was that the dog-breeder was a pure type of brute with one consuming passion—the desire to produce a perfect bull-terrier. But it was not until their supper had been cooked and eaten and their second pipes thereafter were fuming that the tongue of Crosden was loosened by chance.

"Whatever else they may say about her, she has a perfect head," said Gannaway, and took the head of Nelly in his hand.

Only one phrase of his speech seemed to come to the ear of the giant.

"A perfect head?" echoed Crosden softly. "Once there was a perfect dog. You hear me, Gannaway? You, being a white man, you might understand. There is crooks and sneaks and damned little else, and who would want to talk about a real dog to such as them? Them folks back East—worms! They ain't men! But you, Gannaway—you're white and you would understand, maybe. Suppose—should I tell you the story—why, here it goes, and why not? It'll do me good, or send me crazy—talking!"

He brushed the long hair back from his face, half melancholy and half brute, and with his walking staff gripped in his hand, he brooded for a time upon the fire until a flare of its light seemed to gather again in his own eyes from long staring.

Suddenly he raised his glance to Gannaway, and the latter shrank a little and had to steady himself.

"I'll tell you, back in the beginning there wasn't nobody much except Newton and me. The others had dogs, and they showed 'em, and they got their championships and they did their talking, but nobody knew the secret of putting a head on a bull-terrier. Nobody but me—and then Newton, he stole my idea. He seemed to understand, too. The bitches are what count. You can have the best stud dogs in the world and get nothing. But when you take a bitch that has got an eye in her head—and enough weight to—but here, you ain't a dog-breeder.

"Well, let that go. I knew, and Newton knew. I knew that he knew, and he knew that I knew. Sometimes we wouldn't get much. Just red ribbons or yellow, or such, but I would go and look at Newton's dogs, and he would come and look at mine. And each of us knew that the other fellow was coming pretty close to the real thing—a dog that would be a dog.

"We got our championships, too. We got them pretty

thick and fast, after a while. But still he kept waiting and watching me, and I kept waiting and watching him. And finally one time when I got to Madison Square Garden I seen Newton go by with a guilty look in his eye and I reached out and grabbed him. He's a little gent. He curled up inside my hand and put up an arm like I was going to hit him.

" 'Keep off of me!' says he. 'Who's been talking to you?'

"All at once, I guessed that he *had* it. I guessed that he had beat me out—and I come near to killing him—mighty near!"

He raised the steel-shod staff and struck with it a heavy rock—and the rock splintered like crumbled chalk.

" 'You take me back and lemme see it!' said I. 'It ain't on your bench yet.' "

"Because I had seen the dogs that he had on the bench. So he took me back and he opened a crate in a corner of the room and he snapped his fingers and out jumped—the perfect dog!

"I mean, when I seen her in the first flash, and her whiteness, and the sick sort of a feeling that I had in the bottom of my stomach, I figgered that Newton had turned the trick and he had beat me.

"I said: 'Newt, you've done it! This here is the dog!'

"Well, he looked up sidewise at me and he shook his head, God bless him! I loved him for doing that. And he said: 'I used to think that she might come to it when she was a pup. Her promise was perfect. But when you haul off and take another look at her, partner, you see what's wrong. And it's in the head and neck—but it ain't nothing that the standard'll tell!"

" 'Ah, damn the standard!' says I. For we've all seen the dog that lived up to the standard pretty near perfect but that would get beat by some ordinary cur, because the cur would have the fire in him. And I looked at the bitch and I seen that Newton was right. She was a mite off in the head and the neck. Just a mite wrong below the eyes.

" 'What is her name?' says I.

" 'The only name she's got,' says he, 'is The Queen.'

" 'Newton Queen?' says I.

" 'No, just Queen,' says he.

"Well, she deserved that name. She was only a ten month puppy, but she got best of the breed over a hundred bull terriers, and she went on and got best terrier in the show, too. And she would of gone higher—clean on up to the top. But when will they give best of all breeds to a bull-terrier? Not, by God, till a dog comes along wearing a crown—

"But that comes later!"

Tucker Crosden rose and began to stride back and forth, fighting hard to control himself.

"Newton, he comes to me after the show and he says: 'Crosden, damned if I ain't shot my bolt. There is something that tells me that I ain't gunna never get no higher with my dogs than what I've done already. The Queen, she's my best bet, unless I go outside and get new blood.'

"I guessed what he meant, but I shut up tight and I only said: 'Where could you improve her?'

" 'I dunno,' says he. 'But what about takine one of your dogs for breeding to her, old timer?'

" 'I hand fifteen years of work to you, and you pay me a twenty-five dollar stud fee and then you hog the glory?'

"He hated to do it, but he had to. He admitted that he would give me half of the litter and then I had to say that I didn't have any dog that was really anything to get excited about. But he says that the dog didn't matter—it was his pedigree that counted. So we picked out the best of my lot—Champion Barnsbury Moonstone, that had got his championship the year before and he bred The Queen to him. And a couple of months later, I was over to Newton's place in Colorado and I sat by and seen the litter born. The first went to Newton, of course, and the second to me. And five was born, and they was nothing to shout about, not none of them. And then there was a whole hour, and finally the last of the litter come, and belonged to me!"

Tucker Crosden lifted up his great staff and shook it at the stars and laughed.

"He was little, and he was weak, and there wasn't much to him. And Newton, he give him one look and then he said: 'Look here, old partner! I hate to see you let down this here way with two no-account bitches and one ratty little dog when you come so far to see the litter arrive. Here—you take this here first-born dog, and I'll keep the little rat—or drown him—one of the two!"

"I just looked at Newton and I laughed. 'You damn sneak,' says I, 'd'you think that I ain't been born with two eyes? No, old son. You can have the other five, but I'll stay by this here one!'

"And I done it. And when he was three months old he had the stand of a dog that was carved out of marble. And when he was seven months old it come time for the big show and Newton wrote to ask about the pup. I just sat down and I wrote out on a piece of paper: The King! and I sent it back to him, and the next train brought Newton over. He come to my house. He says: 'Well, lemme have a look. Lemme see the The King.' And he laughed squeaky and small and high.

"I says very careless: 'Oh, you mean the pup? Why, he's around somewhere.' I give a whistle—and there come The King walking through the doorway and standing against the dark, and he half-closed his eyes and looked us over.

" 'My God!' says Newton. 'Oh, my God!'

"Yes, he was that close to perfect that you could hardly of drawed a line between him and perfection. Newton and me, we took a special trip to New York for the show. We was in the cab together and the dog was in my arms when the crash come—going around a curve—we hit something—"

Gannaway drew his hand across his forehead, but without taking his eyes from the tortured face of his companion. After a pause, the big man went on: "I buried him and I come back and I tied up my dogs in a line and I shot 'em down, every one! I come into my house and I called my wife and my girl and I told 'em to go out and bury the mess. And they done it. But pretty soon Molly, which is my girl, she come in and she said: 'Daddy, there is one living.'

" 'I'll fix it,' says I, and I started out. It was a little two month old bitch. And Molly, she drops down and grabs it up, all blood where the bullet had cut it.

" 'Oh, Daddy,' says she, 'God don't mean you to kill it!' "

"I says to myself that maybe she was right. I got sort of superstitious, and I figgered that maybe there would be luck in that bitch. So, when the time come around, I bred her to Newton's dog—Champion Silverside. Then I got to thinking, and it seemed to me that what my dogs always needed was a more rougher life—out in the wilds, y'understand, like other animals. So I thought that I'd take Nelly up here into the mountains with me, and raise her litter during a spell while I was trapping. And that's why you see her along with me, now!"

"Perhaps there'll be another King?" murmured Gannaway.

"Nobody but God knows!" said the giant. "And he ain't telling!"

CHAPTER III

La Sombra was in a dreamy mood. She was not more alert, say, than a hungry dog, or a hunting cat, for though the snow lay banked beneath the trees and down the mountain side the white wind-riffles were frozen stiff, the sun of this April day was bright and warm and seeped through her rough outer coat, through the dense winter fur beneath and so to her skin. She was of a mind to close her eyes and sleep in that new and delightful heat, but nature had so adjusted the nerves of the mother wolf that in spite of herself she could not close more than one eye at a time. Now, with the one half-opened eye, she saw her husband on the mountain shoulder beneath twice stand stiffly erect with his nose pointed into the western wind, and twice sink upon his crouched fours with the long fur of his back rising and roughed into a great lion mane over his shoulders.

La Sombra opened both eyes and shivered a little, not with fear but because she felt that a period was about to be put to her sun-bath. Not with fear, for she was wedded to the king of his tribe, the great Black Wolf himself, equipped with a hundred and forty pounds of sinew, bone, and wire-haired muscle. No mountain lion would dare to trouble the pair of them, and as for the leisurely monarchs of the mountains, the grizzly bears, not one of them had risen from his winter sleep at this season of the year. So she opened both her eyes and shivered, and wondered what the danger could be; for the Black Wolf was not a creature of imagination.

Then, rumbling from the deeps of his throat, he spoke one dreadful word: "Man!"

La Sombra sprang to his side as the lariat leaps from the hand of the cowpuncher. With her nose raised into the same line of the wind, with her eyes closed, she took the scent, and at once the same thrill of horror rushed upon her. It was still faint and far, that odor, but she sped up the slope, making herself small like the squirrel which darts across the open in dread of the hawk that hangs in the sky above. Now she pressed through the narrow entrance of the cave and bounded to the nest. One by one she touched the soft, warm bodies with her nose, but so lightly that there was not a stir in answer. Then she hurried back to the mouth of the cave and crouched at her lookout.

Her eye travelled through the cleft of the first box-cañon beneath her, then a dizzy drop to the foothills, and so across the vague green blur of the cultivated lands of the valley, then on to the grey desert beyond. The green strip of the cultivated lands was what had always meant "man" to her. In this upper part of the world, what business had the strange demon that walks upon two legs—that plants steel teeth in the earth for the foot of the unwary—that slays afar with a great noise, only, and a keen-bitten stench?

Yet the Black Wolf, like a venturesome madman, remained at his post upon the shoulder of the mountain.

"Come back!" whined La Sombra.

He came with his head yet turned over his shoulder, bristling and speaking to himself.

"You will not leave me!" whimpered the mother. "Make yourself smaller—you will be seen!"

"Peace, little fool," said the Black Wolf. "There is another scent in the wind. Do you not taste it? It means great trouble, for the blind Devil has other eyes with him. Dogs, La Sombra!"

At that, she forgot her fear for herself and stood boldly up into the breeze. High and low, from side to side with her eyes closed tight she read the message in the air. Then she dropped down again, and the ruffled hair dropped on her back, also.

"You were always half blind in these matters of far scents," said she complacently. "There is only one dog, after all."

"Only one?" grinned the Black Wolf, lolling out his tongue. "In that case I shall go speak to the fool before it comes too close. Perhaps I shall not have to hunt far today!"

"Do not go!" pleaded La Sombra. "Where there is Man there is danger. Have I not seen my mother die before me?"

But he was already gone down the black trail. Presently he would circle around the edge of Spencer Mountain and slink through the pines towards the trail which came up with the western wind. La Sombra shuddered again and stole back into the cave. They wakened this time at her coming and she lay down to give them food—lay in the velvet blackness of the cave, nosing and licking them fondly—a double fondness now that danger was driving towards them up the wind. Who could tell what this day would bring?

But when the litter had eaten their fill and curled for sleep against the warmth of her breast and her belly, she disentangled herself with a swift and gentle dexterity and went again to the mouth of the cave. The worst was true! The thick smell of woodsmoke rolled up from the hollow at the side of the mountain and rank through the smoke was the odor of man and the things of man. Twice she started to crawl to the edge of the rise from which she could look down on the place; and twice her spirit failed her and she slunk back to the cave.

With the dusk the Black Wolf came to the mouth of the cave and spoke; she went to him instantly and sniffed the rabbit which he had dropped—then the feet of her husband.

"Phaugh!" snorted the mother. "Your feet, your whole body stink with it—Man!"

"He is making a smoke and a fire in the hollow," said he. "You may smell it as plain as day. I lay as close as from here to the three pines on the edge of the hill; I lay and watched until the red heads of the flame got so big that I felt fear in my belly. So I killed and ate, and killed again and brought to you."

She left the meat untouched.

"The dog?" said she.

"It is a white thing," said he, "so utterly covered with the man-stench that it has hardly an odor to call its own. There is no heart in it. It sneaks at the heels of the man with its head down and its tail down. It makes no sound. Twice it came on the scent of me, as I could tell by the bristling of its hair; but it made no sound and went on at the heels of the man. Even for a dog, it is a shameful, spiritless thing. We will have no trouble with it. Ah, the little ones are awake and speaking."

"Let the little ones be," snarled La Sombra. "If I trust you and your teeth nearer to them than the mouth of the cave, I am not La Sombra, but a coyote that eats carrion. Be off! The stink of man on you chokes me! Be off, and keep watch!"

So she picked up the rabbit and went back to her young. But it was a wretched night for La Sombra, and brought her no rest. Dim and far on the horizon of her mind, she heard the human voice speak again and again in the hollow; and every sound of it made her cower to the cold ground with a weight of dread on her heart.

In the chill of the dawn the Black Wolf came with a fat rabbit in his teeth. But even with her appetite working in her, she would not eat until she had heard the news.

"The dog has whelped and is surrounded by naked little white things like herself. The Devil who owns the dog leans over her and feeds her, and she licks his naked hand. Fah! How my gorge rose at the sight of it!"

"They will grow big—those little ones!" moaned La Sombra. "And then what will come of me and my children."

"Do you fear that?" said the Black Wolf. "I tell you that if the Devil will only turn his back, I shall lay them all dead!"

But ten days of agony followed for La Sombra, and every day from the mouth of her cave she read the stronger news of "dog" mingling with the old horror of "man." Each day the Black Wolf when he brought food to La Sombra brought her news, also, of how the Devil stayed close by his fire, or at the most made only small excursions into the forest to set little traps in which he caught rabbits and birds. It was not until the tenth day, therefore, that the Black Wolf found the thing which he wanted. The trapper left his fire and placed on his shoulder the thing of iron which speaks and kills and went far off. But not until the last noise of his steps had died away through the forest did the marauder stand up and slink to the edge of the camp. In a spot where the sun broke through the trees and fell upon her, and where there was warmth from the fire also, the bull-terrier lay in a nest of softest inner bark with her brood around her, gambolling on rickety legs. So dulled were her senses with warmth and content that the danger was almost upon her before she whirled to her feet and faced the dark monster.

He was thrice her weight, or nearly so, and clad in bristling fur, he seemed a giant of dread indeed. She had time for that one glimpse only before he was upon her. The blow of his shoulder spun her on her back but the slash of his teeth missed the throat and only opened her side as a sharp knife slides through naked meat.

She twisted, bleeding, to her feet. It was not too late even now, perhaps, to call back the Devil her master with a howl of fear, but it was not in her nature to call for help. She bared her teeth in silence and met the second charge; and as he struck her, her grip was on a foreleg.

Five times in his glorious young life the Black Wolf had been chased by the pack, and five times he had slain the leaders and escaped; but their manner of battle was his own manner. They bit, and reached for a new hold, and bit again, working towards the throat; and at that game his mighty jaws were ever the master. But this was strange and new. A painful vise was clamped upon his leg with teeth that worked deeper through fur and skin and flesh to the bone. An exquisite agony held him and ground deeper still while the bull-terrier twisted and jerked and strove to snap the bone. She was a white, snarling demon—no, a red demon now, for the chisel edges of his fangs had ripped her to bits, but still she clung with a greater power to her hold and the muttering voice in the deep of her throat was like a chant in the ears of the Black Wolf—"Death! Death!"

In his writhings he swept her across and across the clearing. They struck the tent. It went down with a crash. She was whirled against a tree with a thump that took half the life from all of her except those locked jaws. Then, in the sheer ecstasy of pain and fear, he snapped at a puppy striving to scamper out of the way and the soft young life went out between his teeth.

That instant her grip relaxed and he leaped away, limping, but free, and saw her stagger to the small dead thing and lick its body. Then the Black Wolf charged again, and this time he found the throat.

CHAPTER IV

HAD they been creatures of the wilderness, the litter would have been deftly hidden here and there in every nook and crevice long before the mother was dead; but they had behind them only long, dull generations in which Man stood between them and the problems of existence. So they scampered and tumbled here and there, yelping faintly with their terror. Only the first-born, the eldest and the strongest and the biggest of them all, had wit enough to flee straight away. Terror inspired in him what instinct could not.

La Sombra lay on the ledge above. She had heard enough to bring her to the battle-ground and now she watched her mate at work and lolled her long red tongue and laughed with a quivering belly of delight. She did not see the tottering puppy that struggled up the crusted snow of the mountain side. The sun had gone out; a fine drift of new snow was falling; perhaps the greyness of the air kept her keen eyes from spying the tiny creature that fled straight to the sanctum and crouched at the door of the cave, and then passed inside.

It was the warmth that led the puppy; and the farther he went the greater the warmth became until he reached a huddle of softly-furred bodies. Among these he snuggled, lay for a time quivering and shaking with dread, and then closed his eyes and slept!

Faster and thicker fell the snow and drew a soft, early twilight upon the day; then the Black Wolf strode back to his home and his mate was at his side as he limped along. Twice he paused, and twice she licked his double wound with a solicitous tongue. So they came to the mouth of the cave at the same time that a great man's voice began to thunder and rage in the hollow. They shrank instinctively.

"But," said the Black Wolf, "what can follow a trail through the new snow? Least of all Man, for the Devil is blind and has no nose! They are dead—they are all dead —but it is a day's work which I shall never forget!"

He sniffed the deep wounds in his leg and hobbled on.

"All dead?" cried La Sombra from the mouth of the cave. "All dead? I tell you that one has come into our home! The trail is as rank as the smell of a new kill!"

And with a moan in the deeps of her throat, she sped to her litter of young. Feverishly she searched among them in the blackness of the cave until the tip of her nose touched a soft warm body, smooth as silk—a different feeling from the well-furred offspring of La Sombra. Her fangs were bared that instant, but they did not drive home. For the stranger had so buried in the litter that their rank body-smells had quite drowned any native odor of its own. And what her nose told La Sombra was the book of unfailing wisdom to her. Thrice she tumbled the little creature over and over; but the scent was still the same. Then she searched every nook and angle of the cave, but the trail of the dog had gone out. So she returned to the Black Wolf.

"If it came," said she, "it is gone again. For a breathing space, when I found that trail, I saw my own children dead and mangled like the litter of the dog. But they are safe. There is no danger. All is well!"

Oh, blind, blind La Sombra!

But the terrier was already asleep, as though nothing of its concerns were being mentioned; and for another fortnight the white puppy slept more than it waked, and never waked except in the deep blackness of the cave. But then, on a day, the litter was routed out by the nose of Mother Wolf until they took the alarm and scampered bravely forth until they stood quivering and blinking in the sun. They were amazed for an instant only. Then a thousand odors rushed upon their nostrils—things which in the depth of the cave they had sensed only dimly and far away, a dreamlike vagueness. Now the naked beauty of the world flashed before their eyes.

And what a world it was on this May day, with the whole San Jacinto range shouldering out of its white cold blankets into the warmth of the spring. Everywhere the slopes were misted or stippled with wildflowers; and a dozen watercourses, thronged with waters of the newly melted snow threw varying notes upon the thin mountain air, which makes all noises seem distant, from the muttering bass of a great fall to the soprano chimings of the nearest brook. But La Sombra, after the first instant, paid no heed to the rollings and the tumblings of her litter. She sent up a sharp call which was instantly answered from a group of lodgepole pines, and the Black Wolf bounded up to the terrace before the mouth of the cave.

"Look!" said La Sombra. "Here is such a thing as I have never seen before. I have heard of white wolves and found them only faded yellowish things; but we, my dear, have brought into the world a white wolf in very fact!"

The Black Wolf arched his neck and the fur ruffled about his shoulders and up the ridge of his back.

"Wolf?" said he. "Wolf? La Sombra, this is a dog which you have raised—a dog like those which I killed in the hollow!"

His voice was so deep that every one of La Sombra's cubs squatted flat against the ground with their sharp ears flattened in the soft fur of their necks.

"Wolf?" repeated the father of the family. "No blood of mine is in a wolf like that! Let me take it away, La Sombra. If this thing should be seen in your family, you would become the laughing stock of our people! Let me take it away—very gently—and put it down in the soft grass, yonder, where it may run away—"

La Sombra sat down and put her head upon one side in thought.

"You talk like a man and a fool," said she. "Do you think that a mother could be deceived in one of her own children? While all the others cower and quake, see how bravely the little thing stands up before you and—Back! Stand Back!"

The last was a harsh warning to the Black Wolf, for as the terrier started on wobbly legs towards the great shadowy creature, a glint of green battle light appeared in the eyes of the monster. But he shrank from the snarl of La Sombra; he had felt the sharpness of her teeth before this in their family debates.

Behold, the little white dog lifted his head and, his tail shaking from side to side with the violence of his efforts, he began to bark a furious challenge. La Sombra jumped as though a trap had closed over her paw.

"Do you hear?" growled the Black Wolf, licking the great scar in his foreleg. "Is that the voice of one of our kind?"

La Sombra reached out a tentative paw and turned the puppy on its back; then she sniffed it from head to foot.

"It is very strange," said she, hesitant. "But—"

"It is not half the size of the others, for one thing," remarked the father.

"Its hair has not yet begun to grow," argued La Sombra.

"Look at its little triangular eyes and—phaugh!—see the pink nose of the creature, like the nose of the pig that I killed last summer."

"There is no charity in you," said La Sombra, growing angry with herself because she found that she was half-agreeing with her spouse in her heart of hearts. "Everything is different while it is young. Give the white wolf time to grow into himself and he will be a cub that I shall be proud of. And—look!—see how bravely it plays with the largest of my other sons!"

The white dog had selected the largest of the entire family for its sport.

"The largest of your other sons is about to eat it, you see!" grinned the Black Wolf, as the cub laid hold on the puppy's throat.

"Ah, ah," murmured the mother. "That tender white skin—but it must learn by experience. There is nothing better than experience to teach children and—look! the little thing has turned the tables already!"

For the terrier, having endured the sharply scratching teeth of its foster brother in silent torment, now wriggled loose and laid its hold upon the first target that offered—the broad, soft, delicate ear of the enemy. There it clung, while the big cub ran here and there, dragging the white leech with it, and whining pitifully for help. The Black Wolf stood up with a snarl.

"That reminds me of another day!" he said. "It puts a tickle in the muscles of my jaws to see that thing, La Sombra!"

"Peace!" snapped the mother, so sharply that the puppy relaxed its grip and tumbled head over heels in the pine needles. "Do not come an inch further forward, my dear. I know you! You would like to make a mouthful of my white son. Come, little scoundrel!"

She scooped the puppy to her with a lightning paw and then lay with her head stretched forth, resting lightly upon it. And instinct made the terrier lie still.

"In these matters," said the Black Wolf, "your word is the law; but as for hunting for you and your brood so long as this detestable little creature is one of your—"

"Do as you choose to do," snapped La Sombra spitefully. "But I tell you once for all that this tender little son of mine with such a brave heart is dearer to me than all the rest—tush! see what he has done!"

And from the ear of her eldest son, she licked away two pin points of blood where the teeth of the terrier had sunk home. As for the Black Wolf, he wheeled and stalked away with his mane still erect in anger and horror; and from that day forth, not a morsel did he contribute to the welfare of that family! Neither was he seen for weeks at a time, except as a looming outline on some sunset hill, or a drifting shadow through the underbrush.

It would have been a bitter time for La Sombra with eight mouths to fill beside her own, and in fact she grew starvation thin; but the spring was peculiarly pleasant this year and the broad bosom of Spencer Mountain swarmed with small game. It meant frightful labor, but while her own ribs thrust out from her sides, she kept her tribe in raw meat. There was little time left her, however, to teach her family the necessary laws and lessons of the wilderness, and therefore the wilderness took toll. Yet the first tragedy came under the very eye of mother wolf.

She brought in a quarter of a deer and lay sleepily at rest watching her eight savages tear at it, when a shadow slid from the sky above and the steel talons of the great bald eagle whose nest was at the craggy top of Mount Spencer sank into the body of the last born of La Sombra's litter. La Sombra sprang as a cat springs, but far too late, for the marauder was already beating off through the void of air while a dying cry trailed down to the ears of the mother.

The second blow fell, however, when she was far away.

CHAPTER V

In the center of his camp, Tucker Crosden leaned upon his great staff and stared at the dead. He had gathered them into a line, and now he studied them gravely.

"Wolves," said Tucker Crosden, "are a sort of connoisseurs in dogs, all right. They pick the good out from the bad. And here's all of 'em lying dead in as straight a row as a gent would like to see, but the best of the lot was eaten. This here wolf, he says to himself: 'The rest of them is good enough for killing, and this one, it's good enough for eating.' And so, it was swallered!"

At this, he began to laugh. He had done his raving, his cursing and his storming, but no man could have guessed how close to madness was this laughter of his.

After that, he saddled the burro, and laughed again at the thought that the wolves had chosen to kill the dogs, and yet to leave this ten dollar slave alive! But when the pack was built, he started out on the long back trail.

Had a wise man been there, he would have advised Tucker Crosden to stay where he was, and to work out the passion that was in him, but there was no seer to give counsel to the giant, and had it been attempted, indeed, it would have required the very thunder of heaven to daunt the ears of the big man. And the result was that he embarked on a nine day march towards his home in the lowlands, nine days of monotony, nine days of silence, during which the bitterness fermented in his soul. As he started down the Winnemago, Gannaway, returning from the south, wearily, had a sight of the giant beating the burro before him, and something in the mere stride of Crosden gave the other a premonition of disaster in the past and disaster in the future. He did not even attempt to overtake Crosden, but watched him out of sight with vague forebodings.

And so the one man who might have given Crosden a chance to express the misery of his soul in words failed him and left before him nothing but deeds.

He finished his journey through the broken country of the box cañons which descended to the green farmlands, and he turned south toward the home place, driving the burro until it reeled and staggered with weariness.

Crosden Farm lay on a bit of rippling land where the very trees grew small, and where crops were never good. It had been a sizeable place, long ago when he first settled here and poured his money into the soil as a young man, but it had shrunk and shrunk. Mortgages had eaten away one bit of it and then another, until now he could call his own only the little shack and the sheds around it, besides a bit of pasturage for the horse and a few cows.

The kitchen window was lighted, and when the long, yellow ray came through the night to Tucker Crosden, he stopped and asked himself why he had come back. The death of Nelly and her puppies had not made any essential difference to that part of the original plan by which he was to go into the mountains and trap in order to make money for the sake of his family. They needed that money, God knew. And what would Caroline say when she saw him coming back, with never a pelt to show for his effort and his absence?

He actually turned towards the mountains again, but as he did so, it seemed to the giant that all of his hopes rose up like ghosts before him. It was worse than facing death itself, for it was death in life to big Crosden. So he swung heavily around and lurched on towards the house.

It was a dark, warm night, the first true night of spring, and though the snows were finished melting, the earth was not yet done drinking the moisture. All the roads over which he had tramped for the past three days had been inches deep with mud and each step was weighted with whole pounds that clotted around his boots. But this warmth which brooded over the fields meant that life was coming there, and the green would be spreading rapidly before long. The thought brought no joy to Crosden.

There was only one thing which had contented him during all his march and that was in beating down, cruelly, the sense of fatigue that weighted him, and forcing his tired muscles ahead. When he reached the shed, he dragged the packsaddle from the burro and let the little animal into the pasture. There it stood with hanging head, too spent to even seek for water, while Crosden swung the heavy saddle over his shoulder and went on to the house. And even now he took a grim pleasure in the knowledge that two men might have staggered under the weight which he was carrying...

At the misted kitchen window he paused and looked through, but he could not see into the interior. He could only make out the voices of his wife and Aunt Abbey. And when he heard the latter, he scowled.

"Now go to bed, Caroline."

"It ain't eleven, yet."

"And what different does that make? What's there to sit up for?"

"I dunno. When Tucker's out at night, I mostly sit up for him till eleven. It sort of peeves him to come back and not find somebody setting up to pour his coffee out for him."

There was a snort from Aunt Abbey.

"Well, Tucker ain't here—thank God!"

"Oh, don't be sayin' that, Aunt Abbey!"

"You baby! Are you still scared of him, and him away off in the mountains?"

"There ain't no getting rid of him. This here house is all drenched with him, as you might say. It's just chuck full of Tucker. There ain't a minute when he ain't sort of behind the door, as you might say, no matter how far away he may be."

"Ay," said Aunt Abbey. "Like a nightmare, he is! It was a weary day when you come to take such a man for a husband!"

Crosden, in the outer night, waited with held breath to hear his wife deny it. But the denial did not come, and the truth struck a hammer blow upon his heart. Sometimes, he had wished with a cynical smile to know what his family really thought of him. Of the hatred of the rest of the world he was convinced, of course. But those who lived beneath his own roof remained a problem to him. Now, however, that the solution was presented to him, he shrank from it.

And he wished with all his heart that he were any place in the world except here.

He heard Aunt Abbey say in her acid voice: "You won't say it, but you think it. And thinkin' is the same as saying. Only it don't get it off of your mind. You have et yourself away, fearin' and hating that man."

"Not hate, Aunt Abbey!"

"Call it by another name. It don't mean no different. Ain't I seen you set watchin' him, like you expected him to hit you the next moment?"

Tucker Crosden had seen the same thing—like a shadow hanging in the eyes of his wife, and it sent a fury through his brain to know that others had seen it, too. He strode to the door and kicked it open, and bowed his head enough to enter.

Aunt Abbey turned white. But after all, she was a Crosden, and whether men or women, the Crosdens did not blench from danger. She stood up to face the monster, but poor Caroline shrank in her chair.

"You're glad to see me, ain't you?" sneered Crosden. "Both of you is glad. I can see that."

He dropped the pack, and it crashed heavily upon the floor.

"Tucker!" gasped his wife. "You'll be waking her!"

"What of it?" said Tucker Crosden. "Ain't she got a right to wake up and come to see her own father?"

But his voice had lost its assurance. He stepped softly to the inner door and held it a bit ajar; bare feet came pattering; yes, he had awakened her. So he went and stood with his back to the stove as little Molly ran in. She went to him with a happy cry and with her arms thrown out, but when he made no move to meet her, she merely clasped one of his great hands in her two thin ones. And she bent back her head and looked up at him.

"It's bad luck again—" said Molly. "But oh, ain't I glad to have you back here with me!"

"She's catchin' her death of cold," said Aunt Abbey's iron voice.

Crosden leaned and gathered his daughter with the sweep of one thick arm. He looked at her brown feet, knotted and deformed from going bare-footed so much of the time, and he looked at the spindling brown shanks of her legs beneath the nightgown, and then to her skinny throat, where every cord could be numbered, and the thin face above, like the face of Caroline but prettier even now, and finally, there were the courageous brown Crosden eyes.

She was not beautiful, but she touched something in the heart of Tucker Crosden, and she always had since on a day in her third year he had disciplined her with a cuff of his hand, and she had flown at his face with beating fists. He could always see the tiger in her, and he loved it. That was his blood speaking back to him and it always made him want to laugh out loud.

She was ten years old, now, growing hardly more feminine with the passage of the years.

"Now, look at you with your feet dirty," said he, "and you might of stopped to put on your slippers, I'd say."

She reached up and rubbed the knotted frown from his brows.

"Would you smile, maybe?" said Molly.

The smile broke through, like lightning. He trembled with joy at her knowledge of him.

"Your hand is dirty, too," said he. "Is that blood?"

"Hush!" said she. "Mother'll hear!"

He carried her from the kitchen and put her back into her bed.

"Now tell me!" said he.

"I wouldn't wash it off last night, because I wanted to see it in the morning, Daddy. It's Sammy Maxwell's blood. I punched him good."

"You didn't do that!"

"Right on the nose, I did. He give a howl and run off up the road."

"How old is Sammy?"

"He's past eleven."

"Ah, Molly, wouldn't you of made a grand boy?"

"Wouldn't I, though? Wouldn't I, though? And

wouldn't you and me of had the times together, Daddy? Why can't I be changed, some ways? Why can't I be a boy?"

She straightened and stiffened her body and screamed suddenly: "I *will* be a boy!"

He began to stroke her head, not knowing what he did, but feeling the hair blindly in the dark.

"You're right enough the way that you be. I dunno that I would have you changed, much. Your ribs is pretty much sticking out, though. Ain't you been eating enough? You got to fight less and not climb so many trees, and you got to eat more. Now, I'm gunna ask you something!"

For the great question surged up from his soul and choked his throat.

"All right," said Molly, "blaze away and ask me."

But he stood up and shook his head.

"I guess I won't ask you, after all."

"So long, Daddy."

"So long, kid."

He stopped at the door.

"Look here, Molly, what these here women might be saying, it ain't always the gospel, you know!"

"Don't I know it?" said Molly. "Aw, don't I, *just!*"

She added quickly: "I ain't asked about Nelly."

He managed to say huskily: "Why not, honey?"

"Because I'm saving the good news for the morning. I'm saving it for then!"

CHAPTER VI

WHEN he had closed her door, he stood for a moment with his hand on the knob listening to the beating of his heart and thanking God for her. They would never pull the wool over her eyes, he decided then. She would always have a mind of her own and know how to use it for herself. And no matter what her face might be like, her eyes were the right color—and so was her blood.

He went back into the kitchen and looked at the bright, nervous eyes of the women.

"You been letting my girl run around here like an Indian," he said, scowling at Caroline.

Caroline parted her lips to speak, but fear stopped her. And Aunt Abbey put in, sharply: "Who started her going wild? Who taught her to box instead of letting her learn how to sew? Who started her to riding and swimming instead of cooking and sweeping?"

"I'm sorry that I done it," said Tucker Crosden. "Maybe it is my fault. Now she runs all around the neighborhood getting callouses on her knuckles from knocking down the boys! She's a trial to me, she is. She pretty near breaks my heart grievin' over her bad manners!"

He tilted back his head and broke into a roar of laughter that made the room quiver and when he ended, the pans which hung in black rows along the wall were still chiming softly against one another.

Now that Caroline saw that his humor was better, she

gained enough assurance to come up to him and reach up towards his hat.

"Lemme have your hat. And set down here while I fix you a cup of coffee. I got some of that yaller cake with the raisins in it that you like so well, too. Oh, my land but ain't you muddy, Tucker! Look at him, Aunt Abbey; I never see such a man!"

He sat down at the table, dazed, and reached one enormous arm towards the stove and slowly seized upon handfuls of the heat. But he was filled with wonder at himself. Now that he was confident that this woman did not love him, he marvelled to find himself in her kitchen, allowing her to minister to him. He was struck with astonishment to discover that the coffee simmering on the stove smelled as good, and the cake looked as appetizing as ever it had done. He tried a crumb of it, and then a great wedge. The taste of it softened the eyes which he cast at Caroline. Perhaps it was the fault of Aunt Abbey. She was a devil, not a woman. She might have been putting ideas into the head of Caroline.

"Abbey—" he said, with his mouth still full of cake.

"Well?" said Aunt Abbey, sitting up straight, her lips set in distaste at his full-mouthed mumbling.

"Funny name—Abbey."

"Is it funny, Tucker?"

"Never knowed a married woman to wear a name like that!"

He grinned maliciously as he saw the flush dart across her wan face.

"There is things which you ain't never been able to find out—good manners being one of 'em, Tucker," said she, "except when you got your dogs around you!"

He was much irritated by the point in this rejoinder, and looking blankly around him, by the merest chance his glance fell upon the portrait of The King, where it hung against the kitchen wall. He stood up and went to it. And it operated like a charm upon him. It was only a common enlargement of a snapshot, so that it was dim and lacked proper crispness of outline, but still there was an air about it. The camera had caught more than the flesh something of the spirit also when it was snapped upon the terrier.

"Seven months!" said Tucker Crosden with a sigh. "Think of what he would of been at—"

He stopped short and went back to his chair. And there he sank down and was lost in his thoughts. The coffee was ready, now. He consumed the cake and drank the coffee noisily, unconsciously, like a feeding beast. And Aunt Abbey bit her lip in disgust.

"Might it be that you've had a mite of luck, Tucker?" asked Caroline Crosden at last.

"Would you think that?" he asked.

"I pretty near know it!" said she, leaning forward. —except you had found—I dunno—maybe—a couple of silver fox, Tucker?"

He grinned at her lighted face.

"Or, maybe—a bit of high-pay ore, Tucker?"

He grinned again.

"Or, maybe," she admitted sadly, "it was only because one of the puppies looked almighty fine—and you wanted to bring it back—where it would have a better chance— Was it only that, dear?"

Between her face and his a reddened mist swept in, and in the mist, small white bodies lying dead, while the blue-jay fluttered in the sun above.

"All of them are dead," said Crosden.

Caroline closed her eyes, but Aunt Abbey snapped: "The puppies? Up there in that cold mountain air, no wonder. Who but a fool would of took them up there, I ask you? But Nelly is all right, of course?"

"You wouldn't worry about her, would you?" asked Crosden. And it amused him, still, to toy with the agony in his heart, just as he had toyed with the frightful weariness of his march home. It was a mystery that he could reach so far into his vitals, he felt, and still find there another and another strength to endure.

"I never cared about the nasty, narrow-eyed things, myself," said Aunt Abbey, "and I never cared to pretend that I did. Particularly, when I seen them ruining lives!"

And she sent a meaning glance towards Mrs. Crosden.

It was the very sorest point in the soul of the giant. He knew that when he married Caroline she had been a pretty girl. He knew that she was only a weary woman, now, with haunted eyes, and although he could not tell exactly how it had happened, he knew that people accused him of having worked the change. And in his own soul there was sometimes heard a sudden voice of accusation speaking too quickly to be drowned.

Now Caroline looked across at him in alarm, and started when she felt his glance upon her.

"Don't say it—don't talk about such things, Abbey!" she murmured.

And in her eyes there was that familiar shadow of dread, as though he were raising a hand against her. *His* hand—against a woman! He drank mingled rage and horror—an exquisite draught of poison.

"He ain't gonna beat you, Carrie, you little fool," said Aunt Abbey. "The man is a Crosden, after all. Only, what I do wonder, Tucker, is that you won't sell that dog. If she'll bring in three thousand—it's a heap of money!—why won't you sell her and set up your family like decent folks?"

"Ain't they decent?" asked Tucker.

"Look at that patch on your wife's dress. And look at the color of it—it was blue, once, but it's been wore and washed to a dirty white. Look at your girl, without one pair of shoes to her feet! Look at that table with one leg wired into place because there ain't the means or the wits or the industry in the men folks of this place to nail in a new wood one. Look at them things, Tucker, and then ask me again if your family ain't kept decent. And then I'll tell you some *more* reasons why you had ought to sell the miserable dog! I could keep on telling you new ones all the night long!"

He leaned back in his chair until it crackled with his weight, and he nodded and smiled at her in restrained madness of wrath.

"You got to excuse me, Aunt Abbey. Or maybe I better say that you had ought to excuse Nelly. You see, she up and died on me, and the market on dead dogs, it ain't the same as the market on live ones."

"Dead!" gasped Caroline. "Oh, Tucker! Three thousand dollars worse than wasted! Oh—"

He leaped from his chair. And when he swayed his giant fists above his head, they struck against the ceiling with a crash.

"Ain't there nothing in it but money that's lost?" he cried at last, and his voice was like the blast of ten bugles blown in deafening harmony. "Look here, Caroline, don't you see what else there is?"

She shrank from him, but he stood above her and bellowed:

"I'll tell you what else that there is—there's blood, by God! There's blood! There's blood! There's my blood and hers. And there's all of them years that I've been working and hoping and praying—and now you say—three thousand dollars—but I tell you, not three millions would make the difference, you hard-hearted—look up here to me!"

He caught her arm. He was forcing himself to be gentle, but how could he judge the power which was in those enormous paws? She looked up, indeed, but it was a face white with pain and with dread, and her voice piercing his ears:

"Don't kill me, Tucker! Oh, God, lemme live—I don't mean no harm—I wish that Nelly was back—I wish—"

He threw her arm away from him. The weight of that gesture flung her whole body with it, and she crashed against the wall. There she sank upon her knees with that dreadful, that soul-tearing scream again.

Tucker Crosden beat his hands against his face. The devil, it seemed, was conspiring to make it appear that he had struck his wife—struck a woman—he!

And so, with a stifled yell, he rushed from the kitchen into the black of the night.

Caroline could not move. Terror paralyzed in her all but the power to whisper: "Lock the door. He's gone out to the shed for a gun. He'll come back to—to murder—the both of us!"

Aunt Abbey was only a woman, but she was also a Crosden. She was not a giant in stature, but she was a giant in courage, and she said now: "A pile of good locks would do. He would kick in that wall like it was the side of a match-box. We got to do something else. We got to fight fire with fire."

She ran to the telephone box and whirled the bellarm around and around.

Then for three age-long seconds she waited for a response. It came at last, and her calm voice said:

"Hello, Central. This is Miss Abbey Crosden. I'm speaking from the farm house of Tucker Crosden, my nephew. Tucker has gone mad. I've just seen him beating his wife. He's gone out to get a rifle and come back to murder us."

The scream of central seemed merely an annoying interruption to Aunt Abbey.

And she heard behind her the muttering voice of Caroline: "Oh, tell 'em—come quick! Come quick! I'm gunna die—my heart is choking to death!"

"Central, will you listen? We depend on you. As fast as you can, you ring up the Morelands and the Burtons and the Charlie Heeney places. They're the closest. You ring them up, and tell them—for God's sake to send over quick all the men that they've got. Tell them not to wait to saddle—to come bare-backed. You can get them here in five minutes—and nothing *but* you can do it—Goodbye!"

"It's a lie!" cried a piping voice behind her, and she whirled about and saw Molly in the doorway. "There ain't a *word* of truth in it. My Daddy, he wouldn't hurt a *flea!* I—I hate you, Aunt Abbey, and I'm gonna find him—"

"Keep her back, Abbey."

"Child, Molly—don't run out. If he was to come across you—I dunno what he would—"

"Would you try to make *me* scared of him? I'll go out and get him and bring him back here—by the hand!"

And Molly darted out into the night on her quest.

CHAPTER VII

Beyond the shed there was a series of small kennels, with long, narrow runs arranged before each, and fenced in with powerful and closely meshed wire, nine feet in height. For one cannot use ordinary wire with the bull-terrier. He climbs like a creeping vine, if he chooses, and he jumps as though he had wings. And all of that wire was brought down a foot below the surface of the ground, because if a terrier makes up his mind that he will get out, he probably will stick to his problem until he has solved it. Yet in spite of all of the precautions of Tucker Crosden, sometimes a dog would burrow out and the first warning of his absence would be a frantic summons from a neighboring farm—

"One of them damned white dogs of yours has been over here and killed our Rex—right out under our eyes, and we couldn't pull the white devil off—and—"

Well, such were the runs for the bull-terriers which had been built with such care by her father, and whenever there was trouble in the house, Molly was sure to be able to find the giant by going straight out to the runs and searching for him there. But tonight he was not there.

However, the second best bet was where the bridge arched across the little creek. He was fond of that place, and day or night he might be found there with his broad, fleshy chin dropped upon a fist studying the whirl and the flow of the waters. At night, it was a living, writhing, ominous force. In the day it was a pleasant green mystery.

But when she went to the bridge on this night, he was not there. She herself sat down, as she had often done before, and studied the snaky curlings of the stream and wondered where her father might be. And so she remained, wondering and guessing, until the time had passed when she could have met Tucker Crosden and saved him from himself.

He had not gone to the runs of the dogs, for all the dogs were dead. He had not gone to the bridge, for he wanted no further mysteries to occupy his brain. But he ran straight forth across the fields which he had once worked with such labor and gained such a bitterly small return—over those very fields where he had learned for the first time that to honest effort there is not always an honest reward—and where, at last, he had felt that he discovered Fate in her proper form—a shrewish cheat.

He ran until some of the fury was dissipated in his brain, and then he turned slowly back. He had done exactly as a child does, or a savage. He had worked the poison a little from his system. And as he came back there was a comforting thought which he repeated over and over to himself.

"Mostly, women are all fools. Mostly, women are all fools!"

He had not gone half the distance to the house when he heard three horses gallop at full speed down the road. And before he reached the fence, a close cluster of four more came with a rush and turned in to his house.

At that, he hurried on a little, wondering what could be wrong; at least, by this time Caroline had had time to right herself and see that it was only her own hysteria which made her think he was attacking her!

He went round to the rear door—the kitchen door, amazed at the sound of excited voices murmuring inside the house. And there, in front of the kitchen door, he found two men. They leaped back when he loomed before them, and he heard the voice of Sam Watchet, thin and strange in fear and excitement, crying:

"You keep off from me, Tucker Crosden. You've raised enough hell for one night!"

"Look here, Sam," said the giant calmly, "there is something wrong with the brain of you. A body would think that the house was on fire, the way that you're acting. Now, I don't mean you no harm. And I'm simply gunna walk into the house."

"You're not!" cried Sam. "I got a gun, Tucker. I warn you to keep off. Because I got a gun, and I'm gunna use it if you come a step nearer."

"Sam," he answered, "you're crazy. What have I done?"

"Maybe wife-beating ain't nothing in your part of the country," said Sam Watchet, "but around here—look out! Keep back, Tucker, or by God—"

But a wave of madness struck through the brain of Crosden as he heard. Lurching forward, he heard the explosion of the rifle, and there was a tug at the side of his coat. Then he reached the gun and plucked it from the smaller man as though it had been from the hands of a child. Sam Watchet was of a fighting breed. He sprang in and locked his arms around the giant's body, as around the trunk of an oak. And the second man, with a shout, swung his clubbed rifle for the head of Crosden.

The big man struck with the back of his hand into that desperate face; and man and rifle pitched backward into the dark. He dropped his fist upon the back of Sam Watchet's neck, and that gallant fellow crumpled upon the ground.

Then Crosden tried the door. It was locked and bolted, so he smashed the rifle through it, stripping the butt from the gun as though it were made of paper. He kicked open the wreck of the door. Before him, he saw men and the glitter of guns, so he flung the tangled wreckage of the door in their faces and the shriek of a woman, far off, stabbed through his brain.

The men were gone from before him. They had slammed and locked the second door; their excited voices, shouting advice, orders, were all far away, and Crosden looked helplessly around him.

Now that he was here, what was he to do? He could smash down the second door as he had the first, but this would be no gain, except perhaps to bring one of the fools into the grip of his hands,—and that would be called murder. But it gradually dawned upon him that they were not here uninvited. That woman's scream, and now the hysterical laughter, told him that they had come by request to save his wife from his hands.

It cleft his very soul, swordwise. It sheared away all his life that had gone before, and staring about him, he saw the only thing from his past that he cared to take with him into the future—the picture of The King hanging on the wall.

He stripped the frame from it, folded it with care, and placed it in his breast pocket. Then he went out through the yawning doorway again. Two men were groaning on the ground, but he had no word for them. He carried with him the heavy pack which he had recently stripped from the burro. In the pasture, he found the grey horse, strapped the pack upon it, and looked vaguely about him. All was level blackness except where the outermost bulwark of the San Jacinto range rose against the eastern stars, and towards the mountains he turned, reached the road, and began to retrace the last stage of the long journey.

Below the hips, his body was numb with fatigue, but he was not conscious of it, for every instant of what had happened since his return home was flashing before his mind in swift pictures, lighted with red fire. Then he heard behind him the one voice for which he would pause. He waited until the small figure hurried to him through the dark.

"Oh, Daddy Tucker," cried Molly, "it ain't true what they say—that Nelly is dead?"

"Her, why, I've forgot about her," said Crosden. "But lemme tell you the thing that counts. There was one in the litter that looked like The King, when The King was little. He looked like The King, only better. There wasn't nothing wrong with him. I used to sit by the campfire and hold him in my hand and he would lay hold of my thumb and bite, it, pretty fierce. I would say: 'If there is anything wrong with him, God, tell me what it is!" But there wasn't anything wrong. He was perfect. Well, Molly, *he's* dead, along with all the rest!"

He waited. "Three thousand dollars gone!" his wife had said to him, when she knew.

But Molly?

"Poor Daddy Tucker!" said she. "Oh, poor Daddy Tucker! How your heart must be just bustin'!"

"Molly, God bless you! I'm gonna be gone till I can come back with enough to keep you like a lady, clean and fine. Will you believe that?"

She caught the flaps of his coat and tugged at them.

"D'ye hear me, Daddy Tucker?"

"I hear you, honey."

"What would I be doing at home, with you away from us for a long time?"

"Look here, Molly, would you want to be fool enough to go trapping with me?"

"I got my heavy coat on. What more do I need? Couldn't I cook for you and mend for you? Couldn't I do anything better than sit at home and watch mother cryin' and foldin' her hands?"

"What would become of her?"

"Nothin' but that she'll go home with Aunt Abbey."

"It ain't right, Molly. I ain't good at finding the rights and the wrongs of things, but me with these here hands of mine—are they made for bringin' up a girl like she should be brought up?"

"There's no hands in the world that could bring me up like I would want to be, excepting yours!"

He was too filled with doubt, with grief, and with joy to answer her. But presently he found that he had walked a long distance, leading the horse and with her hand clasped in his. She was very tired but fighting hard to keep up with him through the mud.

So he raised her to put her on the horse, but instead, he set her on his great shoulder and marched on steadily through the black of the night. He had a guilty sense of joy, but to the soul which was locked in the giant's body, it seemed that if the thing which he was doing were wrong, the stars could not shine so bright. A frown would have been placed, instead, across the broad, bright face of the heavens.

When she sank into sleep, he placed her on the pack and walked slowly on beside the horse, one arm about her, riches of grief and joy in his heart.

CHAPTER VIII

UPON this fatal day of days, Mother Wolf had risen early, for yesterday had seen hard hunting and short fare. She raised her head and looked back along her flank where the little ones were stretched close by, in sleep. Instantly the short ears pricked and the bright eyes opened; only the body of the "white wolf" between her forepaws did not stir except for a tremor that shook him in his sleep. She dropped her nose to him again, fondly, and wondered vaguely how he could face the dangers of that dreadful world beyond the cave and for which nature had equipped him with senses how dull, how sluggish! Even when her muzzle touched the soft velvet of his skin he did not move, and when she moved her fore legs gently away from him, he merely turned in his sleep and snuggled closer against her breast.

La Sombra opened her red mouth and laughed in joy and in sorrow, silently. She stood up, and the white wolf opened his eyes at last and blinked drearily at her, as she walked to the mouth of the cave. Lop-ear, first born and strongest of the litter, followed her at once, but she turned and nipped him just hard enough to make him whine.

"Keep here in quiet," growled La Sombra. "Do not stir until the sun is hot and then see to it that you do not go more than ten jumps from the mouth of the cave, for there is a danger in this morning air." She lifted her head again to scent it. "It is coming up the valley of the Seven

Sisters, I think," said La Sombra. "But if you are quiet, as little wolves should be, no harm will come to you."

She made a step from the entrance and the terrier whined. So she came hurrying back with a rumble in her throat, but when she stood over him, she melted, as she had so often melted in the past, for she felt for him that tenderness which a mother always has for the stupidest of her children. A look, a lifting of the paw, the slightest baring of her teeth was enough to herd the rest of the litter into the right path, but with the "white wolf" it was sadly different, and now, though she made the sign for silence, he persisted in cowering and whining beneath her, and instead of nipping him soundly, as a good disciplinarian should have done, she began to lick his face and mutter in the deeps of her rough throat:

"What is it, little fool? In your heart of hearts, what is it you see that the bright eyes of the others cannot make out. Oh brave little coward, oh wise and silly, did ever another mother have such a trial as you are to me?"

Presently he consented to curl up in a ball to sleep, but she noticed that he did not seek the warmth of the rest of the litter. He was ever a trifle aloof from them; while they romped with one another, he was apt to be playing with a stick or a stone by himself; and when they rolled themselves up against her flank at night, he would always creep up to his accepted place between her forepaws. Her heart ached as she looked down on the sleeper now, but because she could not understand the reason for this sorrow, she growled again, no louder than the hum of a bee, far off down the wind. Then she left the cave.

The eldest son, Lop-ear—for the set teeth of the strange white brother had marked him for life—watched his mother slink away across the clearing, and at the margin of the trees he saw her leap spitefully and futilely at a squirrel that barked at her from the branches. Then she was gone without a sound, and he went back to his fellows.

After that, there followed a cold time for the terrier, for the wind out of the south and east combed the chilly ridges of the San Jacinto mountains and slid icy fingers through the recesses of the cave. His foster brothers, robed in downy fur, paid no heed to this prying current of air, but every touch of it went through and through the terrier like an invisible sword. He curled himself into a harder, tighter knot, and he endured, shuddering, wrinkling his very nose in his discomfort.

And at last, he forgot the warning of La Sombra. He crept to the mouth of the cave and lay there half in the cold shadow and half in the kind warmth of the morning sun. He could sleep, now, and the tremors that ran ceaselessly through him were the pricks of conscience, which torments us when it cannot subdue us.

At this example of brazen-fronted daring, the little wolves looked on in amazement and glanced at one another—until Lop-ear stole also to the front of the cave and stood beside his white brother. There was danger in showing oneself. A chord in his heart which the growl of his mother had started vibrating was still stirring, but now as he looked about him his soul grew warmer. If the eye could see no danger, no danger existed, surely.

He ran back to the huddled litter, touched noses with a frolic sister, and in another moment the lot of them were gambolling in the joyous heat of the sun. Not without some caution. For now and then, in the midst of a wild chase, unknown scents blew to them from the undiscovered world to the east and the south where Mount Dunkeld and the San Jacinto range harried the sky with the bold array of peaks, and far south and east Mount Lawrence rose like a monstrous, round-sided pyramid, with a great white cap pulled far down upon his head; and when the wind brought them sharp and startling scents from the valleys between the crests, the playing youngsters would drop suddenly upon their haunches and point their noses into the air, overwhelmed with silence and the ten thousand centuries of knowledge which were locked within their brains.

The White Wolf did not join the play. In the first place, he needed sleep more than his fellows, and when he was slept out he still did not join the frisking. For he was not popular among his companions; by mutual assent he was ruled from their society as an unwelcome member. In the first place, there was no real pleasure in including him in their games of tag, because he was never "it." Nature had supplied him with four legs which were four quivering bundles of steel wires and nerves, and if he could not run faster, he could dodge ten times as deftly. Sometimes, when they mobbed him in the universal strength of their dislike, it was as though they tried to put their teeth in a fluttering butterfly, or a dead leaf that whirls in the air from the hand that tries to beat it down. Yet again, if he were indeed permitted to frolic with them, they could never tell when evil would come of it. Their own well-padded bodies could take many a vigorous nip and pinch without real harm, but the least touch of a tooth was apt to bring blood upon the silken coat of the terrier and transform him into a raging young fiend. Neither did he howl or whine to show that he was hurt, but in a devilish silence he flew at the foe and laid hold—it mattered not where—and set his jaws, and worked his teeth in, and in, and in, while his eyes closed in hearty enjoyment of his work! So, on the whole, they let him alone. Or if they paid him any attention, it was in a troop of three or four, come to bully and mob him. Even then he was apt to give work to them all, until he fled to a little crevice at the back of the cave where there was just room for his body, and no more, and where they could not come at him except one by one.

So he lay on this morning watching them, his heart aching to make one of their game, but turning his head sadly away in assumed indifference towards the mountains, and the forests like thick shadows on their sides. And it was now that a squirrel screamed at the edge of the trees—screamed in a mortal fear that made the wolf litter flatten against the ground.

They saw the streak of a silver squirrel dash along the ground, gain a tree, and dart up its side, and just behind it rushed a creature that was composed of ten pounds of silky deviltry, built long and low, with something snaky about the carriage of its head. When it came to the tree it did not pause but darted up the tree as easily as the squirrel itself had gone. A rush and a rustling higher up the pine—a scream that died before it was half begun—and all those awestricken midgets knew that a murder had been done.

Lop-ear was the first to recover his wits, and rising from the ground he began to steal back towards the cave;

the rest one by one followed that example, but oh, how far it seemed to the safe shadow of the cave! One other saw, and understood. The little brown devil in the pine tree had not killed the squirrel because of hunger. Already the softly furred body had fallen from its bloody jaws and was tumbling towards the ground with a muffled shock against every bough, while the fisher stared out through the branches at the scene beneath.

He had very little time. The cave was close, and there might be secure shelter there for all these small lives, so the pekan did not wait to run down the trunk of the pine; he merely launched himself straight out into the air, in a wide-arching leap, and dropped twenty-five feet to the ground. He landed without harm. The very shock of the landing coiled his muscles into springing position, and in an instant he was among the flock.

He did not use his jaws alone, but as he ran he struck to the right or to the left with forepaws which were garnished with five murderous daggers each. He ripped the very ribs from the cubs with the power of his strokes, and he entered the cave with all the litter lying dead or dying behind him except Lop-ear.

A flash of white before him showed Lop-ear where to go, and as the terrier gained his favorite crevice and backed far into it, Lop-ear flung himself into the same retreat. Pressed against his white foster brother, shuddering with a dread too great for utterance in whimpering, he smelled the foul stench of the breath of the fisher as the cat sniffed. Then a knife edge slit the skin along Lop-ear's back; he sank farther against White Wolf, with a moan, but still he was not safe, for the sides of that crevice were crumbling soft stone and the stout paws of the pekan could widen the passage in five minutes' work; but here Providence stretched out a hand to save the two shivering little fugitives. A mellow, deep, and ominous note came faintly on the wind, blown from the head of the Dunkeld hills—the cry of a hunting wolf, and the fisher listened and recoiled.

Then, crouching in the darkness of the cave, he breathed the deep scent of the wolves, and the warmth of motherhood that was in it. It awed and appalled him. He was not one to take a back step for the fiercest wolf that ever stepped a mountain trail, but the thing that made him tremble now was grief-stricken, furious motherhood.

He gave a final glance of savage desire towards the mouth of the crevice. Then he slunk out into the bright day; the dead and bleeding bodies lay before him; and he slipped like a guilty thing into the all-covering shadow of the forest.

CHAPTER IX

THERE was this rich kindness in nature, that the heart of Mother Wolf swelled only once above the bodies of her dead ones, and then she led the two who remained to her to a cave among the brown rocks in Dunkeld Cañon and devoted herself to them with a full content which was only marred, now and again, when she looked westward towards the looming blackness of Mount Spencer in the sunset time and remembered, dimly, the tragedy which had happened on its broad bosom; but past and future were to her narrow and dreamy margins and the broad page of the present day was all that truly mattered. Besides, she had a great work of education on her hands, greater, perhaps, than ever a wolf undertook before, for the white foster child was a heart-breaking problem.

His nose was "blind." That was the first and the greatest handicap, no doubt. Again, he was not armed with a million generations of suspicions, and unless she whispered a thousand times: "Hush! Hush! Softly, White Wolf!" he would walk through the brush with as much careless noise as a prowling grizzly. Furthermore, his legs were sadly short, and his wind was short also. But as Mother Wolf was fond of saying: "A wise brain is teeth to a wolf, and legs also!" So she spent her time cramming the head of the bull-terrier with her teachings. She was in the prime of a young life, crowded with experience; she had hunted from the western desert to Mount Winnemago in the far northwest; and she gave to her strange son all that his brain would hold. As for Lop-ear, nine-tenths of the lessons were already at the tips of his claws, but White Wolf had to be taught to find mice and dig for them, to hunt rabbits by patience and craft rather than speed, to map the woods and the waters and all their havens in his memory, to learn that the porcupine does not rattle his quills for nothing, and that the skunk has his own reasons for fearing nothing under the wide heavens.

Moreover, there was a brain in White Wolf that could learn, and he had these special gifts to set against his disadvantages. He could sprint a hundred yards faster than a greyhound; he had the courage of a lion; and in fighting he possessed a strange dexterity and an ability to find a paralyzing hold, as Lop-ear had learned over again during their family arguments.

That summer and the early autumn was a time of joy for the terrier. He did such work as would have killed a man-raised dog a hundred times over, but in spite of that, he grew big and strong and hard of muscle. And all the valley of the Seven Sisters was theirs to roam through until there came a day in October when Lop-ear was reaching towards his full height, though he still lacked many a pound of his promised bigness—a season, too, when the young wolf began to manifest a certain unruliness, and a desire to travel according to his own lights.

On this day therefore, he had broken into the lead ahead of Mother Wolf, and through the trees towards Pekan Lake, the fifth of the Seven Sisters.

"Your place is at my heels," panted Mother Wolf as she ran. "Have I been eating rocks? Are my teeth too dull to teach you still another lesson?"

But the youngster bounded on ahead.

"There is rabbit in the air!" said he. "I feel the kill coming in my bones—"

And here, as he leaped up to the top of a small rise of ground, he dropped flat upon the ground with a grunt of surprise and fear. Mother Wolf, coming into the line the next instant, dropped also, but the terrier ranged vaguely ahead, studying the wind curiously until he, too, found the scent. He did not drop to the ground, then; he stood straighter to examine it. For a thin breath of woodsmoke wandered through the trees, and tangled in the smoke there was a riot of new things—food, and the scent of an unknown animal.

"Get down!" gasped Mother Wolf.

"Down, down!" breathed Lop-ear. "It makes my belly cleave to my back and my mane bristle. I have never smelled such a hateful thing."

"You are wrong," said the terrier. "It brings me nothing but happiness, not fear. Ah, what is that?"

For through the forest came a pounding, ringing noise.

Mother Wolf spoke through her bared teeth.

"Do you feel no fear? I tell you the thing you listen to now is the monster sharpening his claws. Hush!"

A sound like the brushing of a great wind, far off, then a crackling, and crash that shook the earth.

The terrier jumped stiffly to the side and pricked his ears.

"What is that?"

"He has clawed down a tree. Do you fear him now? Ay, crawl back to my side and whine, if you will. But is there no sense born into that foolish head of yours? Did not Lop-ear know? Did not I know, also, when I first took that scent, long, long ago? Now come with me, and let us leave the curse behind us. Only I tell you this—that the last day of happy hunting in the Valley of the Seven Sisters has come to us."

She led them back like the wind to the hills of the Dunkeld. There they lay in a little grove of young poplars, and licked the dew-drenched grass, for it was twilight. Before them, the golds and the crimsons of the autumn colors were fading into the deep blue-purple of the night.

"It is a thing of which I have never spoken," said Mother Wolf, "because to speak of it before it is seen or scented means nothing. But I tell you that my mother before me died by that same monster, caught by the teeth which he plants in the ground, and he stretched her skin before the entrance to his cave and dried it in the sun. I, La Sombra, have crawled to the edge of the trees and seen his face!"

And she shuddered from nose to tail tip.

"It is strange," murmured White Wolf. "I would have run down that trail to the smoke. It seemed very good to me. It made my mouth water and my heart light!"

"This it is to be born a fool!" sneered Lop-ear.

He leaped from his place just in time, as the white teeth of his foster brother snapped at the spot where a leg had been.

"No time for nonsense," said La Sombra. "Look up, little son. Tell me what you see!"

"Only the eagle who lives in the crags at the top of Mount Spencer."

"If he had those wings, and the strength of a grizzly in his talons, and the armor of a porcupine, and the stench of a skunk, and the poison of a snake—would you fear him, little one?"

"Ay," said the dog, "if there could be so many terrors in one creature."

"I shall tell you one thing," said the wolf. "I have seen him stand far off—farther than from here to that fallen tree—and with a flash of fire and a thunder-noise, kill a grizzly at that one blow."

The terrier licked his thin, pink lips.

"That is the strangest of all!" said he.

"Iron is the slave of this devil, whose name is man. Where he carries iron, he carries death also. And when there is a sharp and a bitter scent that makes the throat dry and stings the nose—that is a sign that he carries with him the voice that kills far off."

"Tell me, if you know," said Lop-ear, "is he much larger than a grizzly?"

"He is no larger than your father, my son, if your father were to stand up and only walk and run upon his hind legs."

"Do his quills rattle when he walks?" asked the terrier.

"He is not armed with them. His body is as soft as a rabbit's, or the body of a farm pig, which you have never tasted. His flesh is foul. His walk is slow and his run is nothing. But he has slaves, and there is a devil in him!"

"Have you seen him close?" they asked in one breath.

"There was a dreadful day when I was running a hot trail down the wind and I jumped out suddenly before a man! He did not carry the voice which kills, or I should have been dead that instant, but he had the tooth which fells trees, and yet that was the least thing that he had with him!"

"Mother," said the terrier, "you are looking from side to side as if you were afraid."

"Watch your own nose like a well-bred wolf," she snapped, "and let my eyes alone! I tell you, that when this man-beast looked at me, something went out of his eyes and entered mine, and it turned my heart to a stone. I could not stir. I could not speak. And the weight of his look turned my eyes aside as the current in a stream turns a dead leaf. I was sick. Then he made a shout, and my strength came back enough to let me run away. But I have never forgotten! And I had rather stand in reach of a mountain-lion's claws than of the eyes of a man!"

"Hark!" said Lop-ear, dragging himself forward on his belly. "There is a stir in those bushes. What is that?"

A deer stepped into the vale and Lop-ear darted off with a whine of frantic eagerness.

"Come back!" cried Mother Wolf. "You may as well chase a hawk, as that creature at this season of the year."

But Lop-ear merely wavered, and then went on again.

They waited for a long time, and then they heard his far-off cry. Mother Wolf rose instantly to her feet.

"That is the voice of a wolf who kills for himself only," said she. "He will never come back. And it is time. How long, my son, before you go also?"

"Why should I leave you?" asked White Wolf faintly, and he would have crowded close to her, with head abased, but she snarled and sprang aside.

"Because you need the world, and the world needs you, to teach you such things as even La Sombra does not know and chiefly this, White Wolf—to kill alone, or to be killed! Walk far from me! There is a tingle in my blood to-night!"

CHAPTER X

For a dog, the sleep of the terrier was a light, light sleep, but for a wolf, it was a heavy slumber, and when White Wolf wakened in the morning he found that La Sombra was gone. For that matter, she was often away early in the dawn; for a rabbit which has the wind to feather its heels at noonday may be a sluggish creature in the chill of the morning. However, White Wolf remembered what he had heard the day before, and this absence of hers gave him a thrill of instant dread.

He hurried out to the edge of the ravine and looked up and down. Beneath him, the river ran through the shadow, fringed with creaming white upon either side; its voice rose in a sad murmur to his ear, and White Wolf turned from the empty ravine and hurried at his full speed north across the Dunkeld hills to the edge of the valley of the Seven Sisters. He was weak with fear when he sat on the edge of a gentle eminence and scanned the flaring autumn colors of the valley, dashed with the seven silver places of the lakes. An October land mist lay between, all gleaming rose and amethyst with the dawn lights upon it, but White Wolf had no eye for natural beauty upon this day.

Where had Mother Wolf gone? Or could it be that she had intentionally deserted him? As Lop-ear had gone yesterday without a warning, could it be that she was going to-day?

At the broad base of Spencer Mountain there was a little creek where the rabbits loved to troop for the sake of the tender cresses which they could eat in that spot, and where the deer often came to drink, so that a wary stalker might often strike them while their gleaming muzzles were still in the water. That was a favorite hunting place for Mother Wolf, and if a yearning for venison had stirred her heart in the night, she might have stolen here in the morning. Towards the Rabbit Creek, therefore, the terrier took his course, and nearly came on grisly disaster before he had run half a mile, for a low-moving grey thing stirred in his path and backed clumsily towards him. By the tenth part of a second, White Wolf saw the danger and side-stepped it with a speed which a true wolf could never have managed. He smelled a rank stench, he heard the light clicking of the quills, and then he was by the swishing tail of the porcupine with hardly an inch to spare.

He gained the Rabbit Creek and hunted it recklessly up and down, but there was never the familiar sign of Mother Wolf, let alone the sight of her! He went out on a heap of rocks, therefore, and squatted on the topmost one, with his nose pointed at the sky, and his eyes closed with anguish. His belly heaved, his neck swelled and bristled, and there issued from his mouth a cry which was a dog's best effort to imitate the dreadful howl of a wolf. And it was very well managed, except that the final note of ghostliness was lacking; among ten thousand, Mother Wolf could surely have detected the cry of her foster child.

But when he listened to the death of the echoes which he had raised, he heard no answering signal, and he knew that she was gone indeed. He lay for a time on the rocks, his heart breaking. He felt that he was going to die, there was such an ache of sick sorrow in him, so he started down the valley of the Seven Sisters again, blind with grief, running across and across the wind in the desperate hope that he might find a trace of her in the air; but there was no trace for White Wolf.

He let a rabbit jump up under his very paw and leap frantically to safety; for there was no appetite in White Wolf on this day. He would hardly pause to drink, until the dryness of his throat tormented him.

The noonday shadows shrank close about the trees,

huddling to their feet. The afternoon grew hot, and the golden evening sank again to melancholy twilight, while the puppy roved hopelessly, wearily through the woods.

Once a hungry lynx, crouched on a conveniently low branch, grew tense at the sight of the flashing white thing that moved beneath the trees, but then to its nostrils the wind flung up the taint of wolf, far stronger than the smell of dog. And the lynx sheathed its claws again and shrank back to its place. For wolf was a difficult kill and a tough dish after the killing. For winter meat it might serve on grim occasions, but not for October diet!

And the White Wolf sped beneath the hanging danger and ranged on.

He left the woods for a brief detour and blundering among a patch of rocks a hiss and a burr of rattles made him swerve stiff-legged to the side. "Softly, brother!" whispered the rattlesnake. "Your foot is harder than my back. Heed your footing here, or else you will foot it no more!"

He shrank from the warning towards the trees again.

It was a monstrous wood of many varieties, but most of all the giant silver spruce rose in green mountains of foliage to a sky of which the White Wolf had only broken glimpses, and saw the planets beginning to burn thinly down towards the earth. But under the trees it was almost full night, and the terrier was saved from running into the open mouth of danger only by the happy chance that he saw it move against a background of the white waters of Lake Preston, now shining through the trees like burnished metal. It looked to the puppy at first as huge as the grim silhouette of a grizzly, but what actually sprang into the clearing before him was a great wolf, dark as the night itself—the Black Wolf, with his hundred and forty pounds of massive strength now magnified by the raising of his mane.

The terrier flattened himself instantly upon the ground, and with his tail beating in conciliation, he whined: "I am your good friend. There is no harm in me. I have no wish except to remove my miserable self from your path if you will permit it!"

"Ah," snarled the giant, "are you not that sneaking bastard child of La Sombra? You are, for I take her scent from you as truly as coyotes make hard catching. She calls you the White Wolf, and makes herself ridiculous through the whole San Jacinto range with her nonsense. She has ways that are taking enough, but at heart she is like all other women—a fool."

"I am going, if you please," breathed the terrier, and he rose a little to his feet. "I am waited for. La Sombra will be in a rage and she will punish me."

"Stop!" growled the great wolf. "Do you think that I have wasted these many hours watching you and waiting for you, and biding the time when I should catch you at a safe distance from the teeth of that sharp-eyed vixen; and now am I to let you go? No, little one, have no fear! La Sombra shall never punish you again. I, the Black Wolf, shall leave nothing but a patch of blood for her to mourn over."

"Alas," whined the terrier, "am I not your own kind? Is not La Sombra my mother? Will you murder me here in the dark of the forest when I have never harmed you?"

"You are not facing a woman, now," said the monster. "And if my nose tells me that you are a wolf, it tells me also that that is only a borrowed scent, and under the skin it says that you are dog, all dog, and will never live for my good. Now, you rascal, will you stand up and fight for your life, or shall I take you by the nape of the neck and break your back?"

He made a stiff-legged step or two towards the crouching puppy. The heartbroken whine of the youngster could never touch the cruel soul of Black Wolf. He leaped, and his teeth flashed like a dim lightning above his foster son.

There was no excuse for it. Nothing but the rankest carelessness. He whose bite could tear pounds of flesh from the straining flank of a bull in full gallop, or sever the hamstring of an elk at a single cut—he whose leap was a proverb for surety among all the lobos of the range, now sprang so carelessly that when he descended the white dog had turned into a white streak, and the fangs of the giant merely slit the back of the puppy as it fled for life, with a yell.

White Wolf ran blindly. He put a hundred yards behind him before the enemy had time to fairly turn and gather his speed, but the wind of the puppy was not yet hardened to what it was to become, and presently he could hear the heavy, lurching gallop of Black Wolf swinging up behind.

If he stayed within the forest, he was not better than dead. So he turned to the side and struck the waters of Lake Preston with a resounding splash that scared every fish in the place into the safe and secret pits of blackness. Black Wolf, lunging from the forest to the open bank, saw his quarry cutting the water like a knife for a little island a stone's throw away, and the big fellow was instantly in pursuit. He did not like water in this fashion. It clogged his fur and chilled him to the soul, it weighed and weighed him down in most deadly fashion, but still he had taken to rivers more than once when the dog packs chased him, and now a lust for blood was raging in him, and he slavered with hate and eagerness as he swam.

He gained fast, but not fast enough. And as he neared the shore, he saw the puppy clamber out and stand trembling in the starlight. Here, however, was satisfaction delayed, but not removed. He lunged on through the water, driving along with the strokes of pads as bulky as the hands of a man. Close to the island, he reached for bottom, but he found none, and if he pressed on here was an enemy transformed above him.

With water flowing on all sides of the little island, even a rat would have known itself cornered here, and the terrier had no intention to die without a struggle. He had tried submission and he had failed. He had tried flight and he had found that his short legs were no match over a distance for the stride of the big fellow. There was nothing left but battle, and battle was what the puppy intended. The very expectation had thrown him into an ecstasy. He danced up and down. He shuddered with dread and with delight. And in the pale starlight his eyes turned green as he followed Black Wolf along the water's edge, snarling shrill and high.

Twice the king of the San Jacinto Mountains lurched bravely for the shore, and twice he shrank from the staccato challenge of White Wolf. For, in spite of his bulk, he shared the nature of his kind. A wolf, like an Indian, is brave enough; but he does not like to face loss. That warrior is most praised who slays in utter safety. And the sparkling teeth of the white dog looked to Black Wolf as keen as knives.

So he circled the island. Only at one point was there footing but at that point it was deep, soft mud into which he sank with alarming ease as he strove to poise himself and fling out of the water at his foe. In the meantime, his strength was sliding out of his very soul; he turned back for the other shore and when he regained it he stood on the bank, shook his loose flanks until the water flared far away from him, and sent a long, dreary howl quavering up towards the stars.

White Wolf chattered in his ridiculous soprano barking: "You great black coward! You cutthroat and sneak! Behold, I only wait for my strength and then I shall hunt you, son of a coyote, as you have hunted me. You will wish for longer legs when you hear my voice. You will sneak into the mud and wallow there like a sick bear and hope that I shall go by without seeing. But do not doubt that you will die with my teeth on your throat."

So spoke White Wolf, dancing in an ecstasy of triumph on the edge of the little island, until the sting of his speeches brought a veritable yell of rage from the dark-coated giant on the farther shore; but out of the distance that cry was answered by a long, smooth howl.

"La Sombra!" cried White Wolf.

"La Sombra!" echoed the giant gloomily.

"She is hunting fast!" said White Wolf. "She is hunting for me, and if she finds you here, I will take your hind legs and hold you down while she fumbles for your throat. It will be a pretty game. Wait for her, father. I beg you to wait. I shall call to her to hurry."

He squatted on his haunches, lifted his nose high, and raised a wailing call. It winged far away and brought quick response from La Sombra. That call of hers was much nearer. She was coming fast, at the full speed of her tireless legs, and Black Wolf knew perfectly well that if he lingered here much longer he was apt to have his former mate and her half grown youngster at him tooth and nail.

"I shall see you again," he snarled harshly at the white dog. "Beware of me! The thought of me shall never sleep in your mind. I shall be in the shadow behind you, and the thought of me will hunt you up and down, until I make the kill, little pig-eyed one. Faugh, snake's head! Wait for that day."

He backed reluctantly into the shrubbery, and he was hardly gone before the waiting ear of the terrier heard the body of La Sombra breaking recklessly through the brush. And now she came with a bound to the edge of the water, gasping:

"Speak to me, little white son. Has the lake eaten you? Ah, here is the scent of Black Wolf on the shrubbery. Oh, murderer and traitor! Do you live, my child? Can you speak to me?"

He was so excited that he could barely whine: "I am here—I am unharmed. It was the Black Wolf himself! He has gone that way—through the trees!"

He dived into the water and swam towards her, and La Sombra waded belly deep to meet him, lapping the cold water greedily.

"So!" panted La Sombra. "You defended yourself on the island. You made the water into your friend. What? What? At such an age have you done such a thing? Then no matter for the short legs and the shorter wind, the dull eye and the stupid nose, for you will live and grow great, my son. By wits and wits alone we must prosper. I, your mother, prophesy. The joy and the sorrow with which I have ever watched you takes hold on my heart and on my belly and I prophesy—you will be great."

A prophecy indeed, and one which White Wolf never forgot in the days of his greatness when he was more than a name from Winnemago on the north to Mount Lawrence on the south, from the western desert to the eastern end of Dunkeld Valley.

When he came to La Sombra, he reared and would have smothered her with caresses, but she slid her long nose between his forelegs and flipped him dexterously upon his back in the lake. He rose, spluttering and gasping, but very happy.

"I thought you had left me forever," he gasped.

"Let us not speak of that. All that matters is—your voice reached me in time."

"But do we not follow that black-coated murderer while he is near?"

She merely grinned at him.

"Men will be men," said La Sombra. "You must learn their ways, which are more fighting than peace. But ugh! what a cut he has left on your back."

And she licked it clean.

CHAPTER XI

It seemed as though La Sombra now wished, by special tenderness, to make him forget the manner in which she had left him, but desertion he knew that it had been, and he vowed that nothing should make him lose sight of her, now that he had regained her again.

"Have you eaten?" said La Sombra.

"I am hungry as a young bear," said he. So they hunted together, and on the edge of the woods, all dappled with moonlight, they came upon a fawn so young that as yet it gave out no scent; but the sharp eye of La Sombra marked the tender morsel, and they feasted riotously until they could gorge no more. They were too filled with meat to travel back to the cave in the Dunkeld Cañon, so they slept for a few hours in a thicket and when La Sombra stood up, silent as a shadow, and stole away, the youngster wakened suddenly and leaped out behind her.

At this, she whirled upon him and showed him all her fangs with a grin of devilish malice.

"Lie down and sleep again," said La Sombra. "I am only going across the meadow, because I heard the voices of mice, there, like little birds in their sleep."

But he knew that she was lying.

"I could not sleep again," said White Wolf, yawning until he trembled. "I could not sleep again for a day, at least. I shall walk along with you, since there is nothing better to do."

The moon was high, covering the earth with a cold, false day, and La Sombra turned her eye askance. Truly, she had become like a stranger to the puppy.

"Well," said she, "come if you will. But I am running fast to-night. Come!" And she was off instantly at a pace that made the lungs of White Wolf burn.

Between a grove of poplar and a wood of ash she paused and dropped her head towards the grass.

"Read the trail! What does your nose say, my son?"

He studied the grass with careful sniffings.

"Blood has been here," said he at last, "and good red meat has passed this way on foot!"

"Is there nothing else?"

"There is nothing else."

"Follow me."

She led a little way farther and then turned over a broad leaf with a flick of her nose.

"What is here, my son?"

"There is a print on the soft ground."

"What manner of print?"

"A long, broad print, unlike anything except the foot of a little bear."

"It is not a bear. It is man. And he has made the sign of the blood on the grass! Follow on!"

A little further, they came close to the silver water of Pekan Lake, fourth of the seven sisters of the valley. Here, in the way before them, they found a narrow pass between young saplings, where the ground was covered with soft, deep sand.

"And now," said La Sombra, "tell me what is here?"

The dog stopped short. With head low he studied the trail. With head high, he studied the air.

"Ah!" said he, and started forward, "there is the meat of which I spoke."

The sharp snarl of La Sombra drove him back.

"There is the meat!" said she. "But where are the legs to carry it here?"

"I see none."

"And do you smell man?"
"There is nothing."
"Your nose is blind, blind! He is still in the air, and on the ground, and he has brushed against that bush, yonder. Faugh! What a stench of man is here. But you, my son, read nothing with your nose except great print that even a rabbit could notice. I say that the tall wolf-hounds with which man follows us have noses as good as yours, or better. And all the forest folk know that to be a dog is to be a fool! And a slave also. Now listen to me, and take witness by my mother who died before me in a place even like this! This Devil, Man, plants teeth in the ground, and they close on a careless foot and hold one in pain until Man comes with the Voice that kills in the distance. And where he plants his teeth, he puts such meat as this to bring us closer, so that the teeth can leap on us."
"It is strange!" said the dog. "Even the ground helps Man, then, to fight us?"
"All things help him, if he wishes! Walk round the place with me, but carefully, carefully! Make your feet delicate. Make them as light as blowing thistle-down! for where men have been, who can tell what danger is near? If it were not for your sake, little white fool, nothing could tempt me so close. There—walk yonder on that side—and I on this—and study it from all sides. I tell you, I would not for the price of a fat bull touch that meat, yonder, with the poisoned scent of man around it!"
The youngster did as he was bidden. Lightly, lightly he stepped around the forbidden strip of sand, staring at the bit of raw meat as though it were equipped with a dozen yawning mouths, well-armed with fangs. The wind, long asleep among the trees, came to life and whirled a great dead leaf behind La Sombra. At the noise, her tensed muscles reacted automatically. She leaped far to the side, and White Wolf heard a dull chopping sound, as when snapped teeth bit through flesh to the bone. There was a howl of anguish from La Sombra.
"Man! It is man! His teeth have caught me!" she wailed. "Help me! Help me, oh my son!"
He came to her, shuddering with fear.
"Mother, mother!" he whimpered. "Teach me what to

do. And do not call so loudly. For if you call, every beast in the woods will know that La Sombra is here in pain. And Man will come with that Voice which kills. Speak soft—and tell me what to do."

She was straining back against a chain that would not give, and moaning as she struggled. Wise she was, but all her wisdom seemed to leave her, now. She began to slash at the chain with all her might.

"Help me to bite through this thing that holds me!" said she. "Use your strong teeth——"

He lay down and gripped it tentatively, than shrank from the strange taste and the hardness.

"Aye," whined La Sombra. "It is iron. But still work for your mother in pity. Work for her, and if you free me——"

He worked, patiently, until his jaws ached, and the rusted chain was polished by his chewing, and his teeth were chipped. Then he stopped, and La Sombra stopped, also. Her muzzle was frothed over with blood, so savagely had she been chewing.

She sprang up, the prisoned foreleg dragging.

"Listen!" said she. "Listen! What do you hear?"

"Only the wind walking through the trees far off."

"Ah, if that were all. No, there is another thing walking —man, man! And he is coming here—Save me, White Wolf!"

She fell into a frenzy, the chain clinking as she tore and worked at it. But still the trap held, and the cruel steel teeth worked deeper and deeper into the bone.

And then, falling silent, White Wolf himself heard a noise hurrying towards them—a reckless trampling through the brush as of some big animal which moved through the forest as carelessly as ever skunk or porcupine stepped. La Sombra heard also, and the next instant her terrible white fangs were sunk in her own leg below the trap, where the pressure of the great spring had made her flesh almost senseless with numbness.

She leaped back again, and this time she leaped to freedom and turned to flee, but oh, with a stride how changed from her long and joyous gallop of the old days.

There was no struggle now for the bull-terrier to keep pace with her, for she hobbled upon three legs—holding one pitifully stumped foreleg high in the air.

The puppy turned terrified eyes behind him, for it seemed that a monster so cruel and so mighty, which planted teeth in the ground and sank them home while the owner was far away—it seemed that a creature so marvelously gifted as this would be granted speed like the windy falcon, also. But all that he heard from behind was a hoarse shouting that died instantly upon the wind. And the puppy settled down to travel on at the side of his foster mother. In spite of her agony and the weakness caused by her loss of blood, she resolutely held to her work and put whole miles and a pair of creeks between her and the danger which lurked behind on the banks of Pekan Lake. But at last even her nerve of iron gave way, and she took cover in a thick brush. When he would have gone in with her, she turned on him with a dreadful snarl and a blow of her fangs that slit the tight skin over his shoulder muscles.

So he lay down, whimpering, in the outer edge of the brush, and spent the gloomiest night of his young life. There was no sleep for him. It was the first time that he had spent a whole night away from the shelter of a cave and the wilderness lay like a dreadful weight upon his heart. Dark and tall, the solid ranks of trees nodded gravely to one another, waving their graceful tips across the stars, but theirs was not the only life that stirred. The wind hung in the southeast, and the mountain lion that ruled the Dunkeld Cañon sent his bloodcurdling cry up the breeze, for he was hunting late, and complaining to the stars for his empty stomach. What could have suited him more for supper than a lamed wolf and a puppy?

Then a soundless shadow drifted over the tree tops—a monster owl that stooped suddenly towards the dog and showed him a pair of broad, pale-blazing disks for eyes. The bull-terrier shrank deeper in the grass with a gasp of terror, and at that broad wings waved, and floated the owl up and away across the trees.

What other dangers, silent as this but more dangerous by far, stirred abroad through the blackness?

The dog closed his eyes for dread, and yet he dared not

keep them closed. And he wondered for the hundredth time how Lop-ear could have found in his soul courage and strength to wander far off of his own free choice, to hunt and work out his own destiny?

La Sombra, stirring in her sleep, hurt the stump of her mutilated leg and howled quick and short in agony, but though the terrier felt a tremor of sympathetic pain run through him, he was almost glad of her wound. For she could not leave him now, as she had threatened to do that very day. She must perforce depend upon him to hunt for her and for himself.

Just before the dawn, she came slowly through the brush, snarling terribly when, in spite of herself, the dangling leg touched some obstacle. She gave the terrier a growl of bitterest hatred and then she hunched herself down the slope, a weird caricature of her former grace, her back bowed, her belly drawn high, her head sinking almost to the ground. When she came to the bank of the creek her foster son heard her lapping the water long and feverishly. But when she attempted to climb back, she missed her footing, rolled—and the short quick howl of agony went knifelike through the heart of the young dog.

There on the bank of the stream he found her stretched out, lying flat on her side, breathing with a rattle in her throat, and he made sure that she was dying. Yet when he had waited a long time, she was still breathing. Food might help her—he was off at once.

No, not hunting selflessly for her sake, but for his own. Far away to the south and the east he saw the great head of Mount Lawrence capped with dreary hoods of white, and as cold as those snows was the dread that was in the dog. If he were left alone in the wood—with the bitterness of winter coming upon him—with what La Sombra called a blind nose, and a half-grown body—no, it meant wretched death for him, he was sure. He hunted now to bring the food which might save La Sombra—save her keen wits and her long experience to help him in the struggle for existence.

CHAPTER XII

MAN did not come near them while White Wolf taxed his wits morning and evening to kill for two, but when the leg of La Sombra had healed, November winds were blowing. November snow was falling, and she knew with one look up and down the valley that in the bitter winter to come there would be hard hunting even for four-footed Wolves. And since Man was here in the valley of the Seven Sisters, she made a desperate resolve to go to another place where there were men also, but where there was much game, easy to find, easy to kill. Already her flanks were drawn, the ribs of White Wolf thrust out terribly, and she turned her head west at once.

They travelled for a fortnight by easy stages, while she gathered strength and learned to run wonderfully well on her three legs. They passed between Mount Lomas and Spencer Mountain, dropped down the box-cañons, where all was a world of rocks, slippery with frost, and on an evening came out on a hill-shoulder above a broad and rolling plain. Here, there and again, little yellow rays of light shone at them and White Wolf crowded suddenly close to her side.

"What are those eyes, Mother?"

"They are the tamed fires of men which they burn in their caves."

"But what beast is this which you call fire?"

"There are more questions in you than thorns in a blackberry bush. Ask no more, but follow me and watch;

for I am about to show you things that are new. When I was young and rash, I hunted this country and grew fat. Come!"

They descended to the lowlands and reached three strips of iron, each strip armed with spurs, but Mother Wolf jumped it, landing with a stagger on her single front leg; and the white dog sprang instantly beside her. Before them, in a corner of the field, there was a tangle of huddled grey forms, easily visible through the night. Mother Wolf dragged herself forward on her belly, whispering to her foster child:

"When I growl, they will jump up. They are like little deer, without strength. Therefore seize by the throat and tear—and you will feel the life go out with the first rush of blood. Now, my son!"

She rose with a growl, and three score white creatures bounded up before her with a pitiful clamor. Their number and their strangeness sent terror to the heart of the dog, but he had learned the first great lesson of the wilderness—to obey. And now he drove for the first throat that swung towards him. It was all as La Sombra had said. One eager grip, a tearing of the soft flesh, and as the hot blood poured into his mouth, he felt the life of the feeble creature go out.

Here was La Sombra beside him, tearing at the warm body, while the sheep fled bleating to the farther side of the pasture.

"Quickly!" said La Sombra, between mouthfuls. "These great rabbits—did you ever taste such tender flesh?"

"Not since we killed the fawn at the edge of the forest. How much noise the foolish things make!"

"Therefore, be quick. Ha, my son, they are already come!"

Three or four forms were darting across the field towards them, raising a great yelping noise.

"More wolves!" cried the terrier. "And yet they bark as I bark, and not like you and Lop-ear!"

"Not wolves, but dogs," said she. "They will not stand to us. These are the slaves of men—noisy fools who speak ten times before they act. Do they not talk as though they were grizzlies, lords of the mountains, and with nothing to fear? Take the dog which runs in front and I shall take the one next to him if they dare to close. Remember, my son—the shoulder first, hard and low—and then your teeth for the throat!"

For, of course, he had been raised to fight in wolf-fashion, which is a terrible fashion enough for dogs which have not studied the mysteries of that science. As the four dogs came, a raging battle lust burned red before the eyes of White Wolf. He darted forward as though launched from springs and running low, his compacted weight struck the foremost sheepdog fairly on the breast.

That was a wise and formidable warrior whose flashing teeth were dreaded by every village dog within many miles. He struck with his own fangs, wolflike, but he was dealing with a white streak which struck him a hammer blow that knocked him into the air and flat upon his back. A perfect and wolflike maneuvre was this, but the terrier finished the battle after a fashion which La Sombra had never taught. He checked his rush, caught the fallen dog by the throat, and locked his grip, worrying his teeth deeper and deeper, and closing his eyes in soul-satisfied bliss.

"It is done," said La Sombra, panting beside her foster child—for she had scattered the rest of the pack with a slash or two and a single rasping snarl—"it is done, and this dog is dead. Let him be!"

He stood up, licking his bloody lips.

"This is a very pleasant game!" said White Wolf. "It is better than any I have ever played before. Let us run after them and play it again."

"So?" said La Sombra. "I am tired. Let us go at once."

"Start back," panted White Wolf. "I shall run after them—and be back instantly—"

She cut him short with a snarl.

"Have you forgotten the Valley of the Seven Sisters and the teeth in the ground? These dogs are the slaves of Man, and the sheep are his, also. Did you not smell man's stench upon them? I tell you, it is wiser and safer to steal the cubs of mishe mukwa, the grizzly, than to trouble the slaves of man. We have been bold enough already. By my mother who died before me, we have done too much! Now come back with me!"

So White Wolf trotted obediently at her side out of the field, and angling back towards the hills. Another fence rose before them. They leaped it side by side, and in the starlight great monsters heaved up from the ground.

"Mother! Mother!" cried White Wolf, dropping to his belly on the ground. "What are these creatures?"

They had gathered in a circle, heads lowered and pointing out, brandishing their armed heads and panting forth great clouds of steam on the frosty air. They were huger by far than even mishe mukwa, the grizzly, himself.

"Stand up," said the mother, "for these are more slaves of man, and therefore they are fools and cannot harm us if we keep our wits. Come closer and you shall see."

"The very pads of my feet are trembling!" breathed the terrier. "But I obey. Ha—will not this monster swallow us?"

For, as they came closer, a young bull started impatiently from the circle and raced after the two foemen.

"Away with me!" cried La Sombra. "I will show you a trick worth knowing!"

Even on her three legs she was fast enough to keep ahead of the charging bull. Far off across the field he pursued them.

"Now!" cried La Sombra. "You to that side and I to this—quickly, quickly, my son—leap wide!"

He was not too shaken with fear to hear and obey. He sprang wide, and as the bull thundered by, head down, he saw La Sombra leap in and slash at the tendon of the hind leg. She cut long and she cut deep, but the hamstring was almost as big as a man's wrist, and she did not slash it through. Moreover, she staggered with the effort and fell headlong—and lay still!

To White Wolf it seemed that she must be playing a game, but when she dragged herself up and sat stupidly blinking, he knew that she had been stunned in the fall—and here was the bull charging widly home again.

And now, if he had been any other living creature unless it were perhaps a grizzly mother fighting for her young, White Wolf would have turned to flee for safety from that charge. But he did not turn and he did not flee. He was desperately, horribly frightened, but out of the deeps of his heart spoke suddenly the voice of a hundred ancestors whose courage had ever been greater than their fear. He flung himself straight in the path of the monster!

There was a picture for one who could paint it—the bull so huge, so black, moving with thunder; and the dog so small, so white, and so still!

Three strides away, the head of the bull went down and the polished horns drove level with the ground. And there was the last of White Wolf, be sure, had not instinct laid a hand upon his back, as it were, and crushed him to the ground. Suddenly he was flattened upon it—as many a one of his ancestors had dropped in the old days of the bull baiting in Merry England. The deadly horns drove over his back, the broad, iron frontlet of the bull passed, but at the broad, tender nose of the monster he gripped.

Not with teeth, but with two jaws of fire the bull was held. And fifty or sixty pounds of twisting, dangling, wrenching muscle were rending all his tenderest nerves. His bellow boomed far off through the night; it swept through the soul of little White Wolf like a glory of a hundred bugles chanting the praise of battle.

But, blind now with pain and fear, the bull reared, the wrenching weight of the terrier flung him just far enough to the side to spoil his balance, and the monster lurched down upon his side. Something flashed close to the head of White Wolf—the teeth of La Sombra slashing the throat of the bull across and across. Then: "Let him go. He will bleed to death and then we will eat till our bellies are in pain."

They stood back, and the doomed bull rose to its feet and stood on braced legs, dying slowly, while La Sombra licked the face of her foster son.

"There is none other in the world of wolves like my son!" said La Sombra. "I say it, who speak the truth, and the truth only! Have I not seen Black Wolf kill? Have I not seen the bull elk go down before him? But who is like my white son? He takes the giants by the head and throws them on the ground so that his mother may have food."

She paused to take breath, and then she added softly: "If I forget how you came between me and my day, little son, think no more of me than of a rattlesnake—and call me dog!"

CHAPTER XIII

It was a full year and a half since Adam Gannaway had been south of the Winnemagos, and now he hurried by long marches, because he was anxious to get to the lowlands before the last warmth in the autumn air was gone, and before the days of misty gold had vanished completely. His mind was far before him as he descended into the valley of the Seven Sisters, and of course all woodsmen know that it is always in our absent-minded moments that we see the wonders of bird and beast. Adam Gannaway, coming to the edge of the pine forest, looked down to the long river and the seven shining lakes. And then something passed between him and the view—a great grey wolf running with desperate bounds, the loose pelt shaking up around his shoulders at every stride. From the brush behind broke three monsters far more terrible to the eye than the wolf itself. They were built like greyhounds of enormous stature and huge beam, and they were covered with disordered mouse-colored hair in an ugly tangle.

Plainly the wolf had come for the broken ground in the hope of shaking off these pursuers, because a wolf does better than a dog over the rough, but these long-legged devils continued to gain with every leap. The exhausted wolf attempted to double back, and flying towards Adam Gannaway the meteorologist could study the straining eyes with the nightmare of fear in them. But he felt no pity, for of all things that are crafty and cruel, he hated the wolf the most.

Under a tall rock which promised some security at his back, the lobo turned suddenly at bay, and Gannaway settled himself to watch a long battle. He had seen one wolf scatter half a dozen fighting dogs. He had seen wolves handle four and five trained canine warriors with the most perfect ease; he had never seen two dogs which could pull down a lobo; and though these strange monsters looked formidable enough, he felt that three to one made about equal odds.

In half a second all the preconceptions of Adam Gannaway vanished. To the right and the left one of the monster dogs feinted at the cornered wolf, and his teeth slashed the air as they crouched back from him; but the next moment the long jaw of the third hound was clamped in the throat of the lobo and then all three swarmed up on it.

They did not tear or rend or snarl. In a few seconds they stepped back, licking their lips and glancing at Adam Gannaway out of their suspicious little eyes until he felt distincty uncomfortable. There was something professional in the manner in which this killing had been accomplished. It was unlike anything he had ever seen before, and he did not wish to see it again. It seemed uncanny, unnatural. As though the fighting soul of the wolf had been dissolved before the battle actually began.

A shout from the trees below, then two men hurried out and coming to the dead wolf they had taken its scalp before they noticed Adam Gannaway. And still what impressed him in the men was that which had amazed him in the dogs—the utterly calm fashion in which they accepted this slaughter of a full-grown lofer wolf. They had brought three more dogs with them—two of the type of the hounds he had already seen in action, and one an odd shaped beast which might be a cross between a greyhound and a foxhound. They marched with heavy packs upon their shoulders, and no matter how far the chase might have taken their dogs astray, it was apparent that the pair of them had not hurried. One would have thought that the possibility that a wolf might rip up one of their dogs had not occurred to them—or that he might distance them in the rough, broken country. And indeed, it was not hard for Gannaway to guess that this was the simple truth of the matter.

They did not bother to skin the victim. The scalp was enough for them, and one of them was scraping it clean when Gannaway came up to them. "Strangers," he said, "will you tell me that there isn't so much as a scratch on any one of those three dogs that just pulled down the lobo?"

That question had found the straightest road to their hearts. Wolf-catching might be an old, old tale to them, but their pride in their dogs had never died.

"Ay," said the taller of the two, "there's a mite of a scratch on the off shoulder of Lefty. But that's all. You take a look over the rest of them and see for yourself!"

"I'd rather handle painters than those dogs," smiled Gannaway. "I'll take your word for the scratch. As a matter of fact, I've seen dogs run wolves before, a good many times, but I've never seen such a professional air about it. You weren't here to see, but I can tell you——',

"You don't have to," grinned the elder of the two. "Because we know. Lefty, here, he come up in the center, with Pete on his right, and Tiger on his left. Tige and Pete, they made a feint on each side, and while they were drawing the eye of the lobo, Lefty dived in and got a hold on the throat, or somewheres near to it, and then the other pair just slipped up and finished the job with a flank hold and a foreleg hold—to steady the lobo down while Lefty was feeling for his windpipe."

"You trained them for that?"

"Very particular."

Adam Gannaway produced that never-failing power with men of the wildnerness—a well-filled pouch of tobacco, and he offered it. It was an invitation well-understood since Indian days, at least. He who accepted the gift must sit down until he had smoked out one pipe at least. But there was no hesitation in the owners of the dogs. That tobacco had a rich, black look that spoke directly to their hearts, and while they filled their pipes, Gannaway surveyed them in more detail.

They were cut with one stamp. The elder was the

larger of the two, but here his dissimilarity from the pattern ceased. Each had a thin, brown face, dusty-looking eyebrows, a small head poised awkwardly at the end of a forward-jutting neck, high, narrow shoulders, and feet and hands disproportionately large. Through the Nebraska plains such men grow from the soil as naturally as weeds.

Once the tobacco began to work, their tongues were loosened. The elder did the talking, turning to his brother from time to time for confirmation.

Thus: "They're mainly Irish wolfhound stock. That is, except Grampus, yonder."

Here he indicated the creature with the body of a clumsy greyhound and the head of a foxhound.

"They're mostly Irish wolfhound, with one outcross. Only one."

"And what's that?" asked Gannaway.

"Ay, you ain't the first that's asked!" grinned the speaker, with a sort of malicious secrecy, nodding to himself. "You ain't the first, nor you won't be the last. But that's the secret. Ain't it, Tom?"

"Ay, Dan," said Tom Loftus, with equal complacency. "That's the secret."

"Where we was raised," said Dan Loftus, "there was always enough lobos to make trouble. They would pick off a lot of calves and colts every season, and when we hunted them we drew a blank. Unless we got the dogs out. The dogs could find them and catch them, but we noticed that most generally before the party was over it had cost a hundred dollars' worth of dogs and horses and men to get ten dollars' worth of wolf. So we aimed to find a breed that could run fast enough to catch a lobo and fight fast enough to make a kill without getting themselves ripped to bits, while the party was going on. We worked for a good many years, but finally we turned the trick, I guess. Eh, Tom."

"I guess we turned the trick," said Tom, closing his eyes with bodily and spiritual enjoyment as he dragged deep on his pipe.

"But," suggested Gannaway, swallowing his distaste for these fellows in his curiosity, "it seems that you've come a long distance from nowhere to run your wolves."

"We're just nabbing what comes in our way," said Dan Loftus. "But mostly we're bound for the place where they have the White Wolf. He's the meat that we want, and I guess that he's worth the trip. Eh, Tom?"

"Twenty-five hundred is about worth the trip," agreed Tom with his usual smile of secret enjoyment.

"Twenty-five hundred dollars!" cried Gannaway. "You mean to say that you are expecting that much bounty for a single wolf? A white wolf, did you say?"

"*The* White Wolf," they answered in chorus.

"I never heard of him."

"Never heard! Where you been keeping yourself the last year, then?"

"Mostly in the tall timber," smiled Gannaway, waving towards the peaks.

They looked at him with ill-disguised suspicion; but he had learned long before this that it would not do to attempt to explain his profession. A man who declared that his purpose was to study *weather* in the higher mountains was generally regarded as little short of a plain maniac. So he held his peace and let their thoughts take their own course. But he could have smiled as he saw them stiffen and draw closer together.

"Well," said Dan Loftus at last, "all I know is that for a year down on the lower Winnemago there's a three-legged wolf and a white wolf that's been raising so much hell that they get in the papers regular. They've killed enough sheep and cattle to stock a ranch. Then they take a day off and raid a hen roost or a duck pond, and when they leave off there ain't much but blood and feathers left. They've trailed 'em with bloodhounds. They've scouted for 'em with horses. They've run 'em with dogs. But they ain't never got 'em. They're a foxy pair. They ain't been caught. But when we come swarming down there, it's gunna be a different story. Wolves that nothing else can catch is the favorite meat of these here babies, and you can lay to that. Eh, Tom?"

"You can lay to that!" said Tom Loftus solemnly.

"Hello!" said Gannaway suddenly. "What's that smoke, yonder?" Someone else is camping in the valley of the Seven Sisters!"

The two looked evilly upon one another and smiled

one of their secret, evil smiles. "Do you know who it is?" asked Gannaway.

"We got a sort of a suspicion," said Dan Loftus, knocking the bottle from his pipe and rising. "We been there before. It's a trapper and we knocked on his door about an hour back. But we didn't stay."

"He wasn't home? Why, my friends, you're not in the plains, now. The rule of this country here is that you make yourself at home whether the owner is in or out!"

"Don't we know that's the rule?" said the elder brother. "And didn't we try it?"

His face grew black as he spoke.

"What happened?" asked Gannaway.

"You go and try for yourself," said Dan Loftus. "There ain't no mother like experience when it comes to teaching. You go and try him!"

"I certainly shall!" said Gannaway calmly.

This announcement brought a burst of sardonic laughter from the two, but when they saw by his gravity that he meant what he said, Tom Loftus suddenly broke in: "When you see him, you tell him that after we catch the White Wolf, we're gunna come right back this way, and that when we do, we're gunna be carrying not just a rusty old Colt, but *rifles!*"

They said it with such an eloquent conviction that Adam Gannaway paused to mark them out of sight as they continued their march westwards, with the troop of six long-legged dogs mincing along at their heels; and though he was no seer, he felt that he could prophesy first-class mischief when the pair came back that way from the hunting of the White Wolf.

CHAPTER XIV

WHOEVER the trapper was who had dared to refuse hospitality to two such fellows as these, backed as they were by such a devilish troop of fighting beasts, Gannaway was consumed with curiosity to know him better at first hand, no matter what the risk. For the laws of hospitality are as rigid in the mountains as the laws of chivalry were ever a constraint upon young knight errant in the golden days of romance. And he wondered what species of outcast had dared to break the rules of the game?

So he went forward with a cautious step towards the smoke column which drifted low across the thin November woods towards Lake Pekan. He came first on sight of the glimmering surface of the lake, and then the squat outline of a log cabin against the shining of the water. And on the edge of the clearing he paused. He was a man whose very profession depended largely upon his ability to note small differences with his eye and draw large deductions from them.

He scanned the clearing and the cabin in minutest detail. By the axe marks on the stumps of the trees which had been felled to build the cabin and to supply firewood, he knew that the trapper was a man of great physical power as well as craft of hand. For science and skill must combine to flesh the blade of an axe so deep: The walls of the cabin, too, were straight at the outer corners—another eloquent sign that this was a man who knew his business. And the birch-bark canoe which lay bottom up on the shore of the lake was a thing of delicate beauty which would have delighted the heart of the most fastidious Indian, in a matter where Indians are fastidious indeed. The cabin was equipped with two capacious sheds to its rear, and these, again, were the token of industry and providence on the part of the owner. Moreover, those sheds were not flimsy lean-to's, but structures as solid as the main body of the shack itself. No casual hunting grizzly could rake down those walls following the scent of a side of bacon! But the crowning touch of all was that inset among the logs there was a large window of oiled silk, no doubt, for it was plainly not glass. The oiled silk was no marvel, but it needs the dexterity of a carpenter to fit a window in airtight soundness into the wall of a log cabin.

What Adam Gannaway concluded was that he had to do with a powerful and clever man who had thoroughly mastered the art of building a home in the midst of a wilderness. And when such a man was a surly scoundrel, he was apt to be formidable indeed. So that Gannaway could be excused for loosening his Colt in its holster before he advanced towards the house.

A rabbit jumped up before him. But it only scampered a long-legged leap or two. Then, descending on the top of a broad-face stone, it sat up and looked at him with bright, fearless eyes and wobbled its nose with much curiosity. It amazed Adam Gannaway more than all else. For it seemed that this strong and crafty trapper who was brutal enough to refuse hospitality to two mountain-bound travellers was yet foolishly tender enough to tame rabbits for his amusement!

It gave him heart to step to the door and rap. It was a ponderous door, so thick and so well hung that his knock descended as upon the solid wall of the house. He thought he detected a soft stir within the house, but that was all. There was no voice that spoke to him in answer, and he was about to rap again when the long, bright barrel of a rifle was slid out through a hole in the wall and exploded.

He jumped back with an oath. He would have fled to the woods, if he had followed his first impulse, but on a moment's reflection he decided that the bullet had been sent forth on a blind errand—simply to warn him that the owner of the house did not take kindly to conversation and was not in the humor for a visit at this particular moment.

All wise deliberation moved the meteorologist to leave that clearing, however. It was only the sight of the little rabbit on the stone that detained him. A man who wasted his time in taming and training rabbits—

He said calmly: "Stranger, I've come here to do you no harm. My name is Gannaway. I'm what you might call a mountain-tramp. I've never pointed a gun at a man in my life, and I don't intend to point it at you. But I have to tell you what you already know: that to turn a man away from your door is—a damned shabby trick! Do you hear me? A damned shabby trick!"

He paused. The rifle was removed from the loop-hole, but the mysterious silence continued unbroken, except for the sudden chattering of a bird through the autumn silence of the woods. He said again:

"What I want is a handout in the shape of a little bacon, if you can spare it. If not, any smoked meat will serve my turn, and by the look of your place, I know that you're the sort of a fellow who puts up his winter supply a long time before November. As for the—"

Here he paused, for the ponderous door of the cabin, without any sound of a drawn bolt, now began to stir and slowly yawned open before his expectant eyes—and in the darkened doorway stood an eleven year old girl with a pig-tail down her back, and dressed in a roughly made deerskin garment. A fawn-skin, dappled beautifully with color like a September sun falling in a pattern through the trees. He saw a freckled face and a pair of wide, bright eyes.

"My dad," said the girl, "he wants to know if the smoked meat will rest you?"

"Of course," said Gannaway.

The door slowly closed again—mute testimony to its weight. After a pause, it was opened once more and a ten-pound package, bound in tough bark fibre, was thrown out at his feet.

"I reckon that's as much as you like to pack along with you," said the girl. "So long, stranger!"

"Look here," protested Gannaway, "if your dad is a fellow who doesn't want his face seen—you might tell him that I'm blind in my near eye, and in my off eye I can see nothing but friends!"

The flash of her smile made her almost pretty.

"You *look* all right," said she. "But my dad—he ain't fond of strangers, particularly."

Inspiration descended upon Gannaway.

"My dear," said he, "your father is nowhere near the place. You're alone in that cabin."

He heard her gasp of fear—saw the door thrust almost shut—and then it was pulled slowly open again. Gannaway had made no move to advance.

"You got a nerve to stick around like this," smiled the youngster, "after you've had a slug shot over your head. What you want to stay for? If dad was to catch you here, he'd just bust you in two! You better mooch along."

"You're afraid of me, then?"

"Me? I guess not! Nor of two like you."

"If you're not afraid, I'll come in, then."

"If you was to come in—and dad was to find you here—"

"I'll take a chance on that."

"All right," said she, defiant. "Come along!"

She pulled the door to its greatest width, and Gannaway stepped into such a cabin as he had never seen before. The inside of the big logs had been planed as smooth as plaster—there was hardly the mark of the adze to be seen so deft had been that work. Instantly the well-fitted window became a lesser miracle. Here was a table which it seemed no art but that of the turning lathe could furnish, and yonder was a great stove built of square stones. Upon the floor, the great skin of a grizzly and another of a fine mountain-sheep; and on the wall some feeble attempts at decoration—a few calendars in bright colors, a grinning wolf's head nailed into the logs, and opposite it a framed picture of a bull-terrier.

"I see," said Gannaway. "Your mother did the arranging of this."

"Ma?" laughed the girl. "Nope. She wouldn't be able to stand it up here in these winters; she gets chilblains too terrible bad. But now you've seen the way things are fixed, ain't you better to move along? My dad—"

"I'll take my chance with him," smiled Gannaway.

"This looks like a proper place to sit down." And he lowered himself into a home-made rocking chair!

At that, with a squeak of fear, a small thing scurried across the floor, darted up the leggins of the girl, and here was a great, fluffy grey squirrel perched on her shoulder with its marvelous tail arched, barking a challenge at the stranger. She raised her brown hand, and the squirrel was stilled.

"All right," said the girl. "I've warned you—and I sure do ache for a talk! It's been a whole year since I've seen anybody but dad!"

"A year!" echoed Gannaway. "A whole year? If you were to tell me what makes him keep—"

He saw the coming of the lord of the house in her face as in a mirror, for she turned white with apprehension, but before she could speak, a shadow lunged from the doorway and a great hand seized on the back of Gannaway's neck.

"You damn rat!" said a huge, thick voice. "Are you come here to pump the kid? I'll talk for myself!"

Gannaway felt himself raised as by the arm of a steam derrick, and whirled, and above him, clothed in deerskin like the child and masked with a heavy beard, was none other than his giant of the year before—Tucker Crosden. Recognition dawned in the face of the big man, also—the fierceness melted—and suddenly he was booming: "Gannaway! Damn my hide if it ain't Gannaway. Man, man, you come near to getting your neck twisted. Why didn't you speak your name? Molly, come here and shake the hand of a white man. Take both hands and give him a grip, because there ain't so many white men in this little old world!"

Never, thought Gannaway, had the price of the makings of a Bull Durham cigarette reaped such a rich return a year from the date of investment!

There was no need for him to ask questions, for the big man talked freely enough when supper was ended and Molly was asleep in her bunk, and the mystery was explained with all the fullness of a sinner to a father confessor. It seemed wonderfully strange to Gannaway, but all that was locked in the heart of the giant was placed freely before him. Bits of that confession burned into the mind of Gannaway, never to be obscured thereafter.

"When I seen the first puppy, I didn't care much about the rest that might be born. It looked like only one thing. It looked like The King!"

He turned his head to the picture on the wall.

"Not like the way he is there, but the way he was when he come into the world. But bigger than The King. Stronger than The King. More head on him, and more behind the head!"

"The rest of the litter was good. And Nelly gave them all a good chance, because she was a fine mother. But there wasn't nothing to it! I used to sit and laugh to see the ghost of The King working in that pup. He would walk along at feeding time and root the rest of the family out of the way. He was a lion!"

"I tell you, his nose was sort of blue when he was born, and it begun to turn solid black faster than any nose I ever seen before in a bull-terrier.

"I knew he was real when I seen him born. And when he got his eyes good and open I was sure. He looked like he was a month old. His favorite place for sleeping was on his ma's head!

"When I come back that last day, I found the rest of them dead. But The King, he wasn't there. D'you see? The wolf hadn't been a fool. He killed the rest of 'em. But he *ate* The King.

"It left me sort of done up, like I had been hit with a club. I started back for home, not knowing what else to do. When I got there, there was nothing but trouble. My wife was scared of me. She sent for help, and the neighbors come and tried to keep me out of my own house. I knocked a couple of them out of my way. Not using my full strength on them, I swear to God! But before we got to the foothills—the kid and me—the news come along that one of them two was dead!

"And since then, I've been waiting for them to come to get me. I keep out of the sight of men. I know an Injun down on the Dunkeld. A halfbreed. I turn in my pelts to him at the end of the season and he gives me about half what they're worth, and he carts up the stuff that I need for the house. And that's the way that we've got on for a year or more. Just setting and waiting, you see?"

It was later, much later in the evening, that the giant leaned forward and laid a great hand on the shoulder of Gannaway.

"If The King could know what I've suffered from the women, Gannaway! If The King could know—he'd come up out of his grave, where I laid him all solemn and proper. What turned me out of my home? The women, Gannaway! What put a murder into my hands? The women, Gannaway! And all because of The King. My wife, she never forgave me. When The King was a puppy, she would come and watch the two of us. She would say: 'Tucker Crosden, you love a dog more'n you love your wedded wife!" She never forgave me for it. She *wished* for the death of him. I tell you, she prayed for it! But they're bad, Gannaway. They're all bad. There ain't any women that's got decency and kindness in them. And the kid, yonder, when she grows up she'll be like the rest of them!"

He rose from his chair and stepped to the side of her bunk with a soundless, stalking tread. There he raised the edge of the blanket and peered at the child's face; she was sleeping peacefully. So Tucker Crosden came back to his guest.

"You'd think it was an angel," said Crosden. "I ask you, looking at her, would you think there was the sort that would some day turn her husband out of his house and put a murder in his hands? But she's a woman, and she's got her mother's blood in her! She's got the blood in her, and she'll do the same thing all over again!"

The blood grew cold about the heart of Gannaway, and yet how that heart of his ached in pity for the big man whose sorrow was too great to be explained away by his simple mind!

"But there's one thing that I would like to ask your advice about," said Crosden.

He drew his chair closer. There was desperation in his face and a wild glitter in his eye that made the very flesh of Gannaway creep.

"If The King was to know the way I've suffered for

him, Gannaway—if he was to know—and what can keep him from knowing? I say, if he was to know what a dog's life I live up here, would he come back to me?"

He gripped the hands of Gannaway.

"Tell me fair and square," breathed Crosden, "him being true-blue and loving me like he did—wouldn't he come back to comfort me, Gannaway?"

Adam Gannaway strove to speak, but his lips were numb. He closed his eyes, and prayed for strength, for he felt a faintness coming over him.

"That's right," said the trembling voice of the giant. "It's a mighty hard question. It's a question that would stagger most folks. But my God, it's a terrible comfort to me, to see how serious you take it—to see how possible it looks to you. Because some folks, they would say that death having come in between him and me—you understand what I mean? Some fools would say, him having died once, that I'd never see him again. But it ain't right, Gannaway. Because I've told you the whole story, and you know as well as I know that he *did* come back once!"

"He—came back—once?" echoed Gannaway faintly.

"Ay, of course! Because the minute I seen that first-born of Nelly's I knew what had happened!" He sank his voice to a whisper, and that whisper thrust like a sword through the soul of his companion. "Some might of said that it was only a likeness, but I guessed the truth right away, and every day that I watched him, I knew the fact better and better till finally I was sure. It wasn't no likeness. It was The King himself, that had come back to the earth and to me!"

Gannaway drew a long, slow breath. He struggled with all his might, but he could not meet the brilliant, mad eyes of Tucker Crosden.

"And look how logical it is," said Crosden. "The King knowing how I loved him and how sick I was for the lack of him, wouldn't he of made the try? The soul of him would of made the try. It *did* make the try, and it did come back to me in the puppy that the wolf killed! All I want is your honest opinion, but I want to give you all the facts, first. If he could come back once, now why couldn't he come back agin?"

He glanced guiltily over his shoulder as though he

dreaded lest the very air might listen to the secret; his whisper sank fainter than before, and again the soul in Gannaway turned to ice.

"It was a wolf with a track like the hand of a man. A hundred and thirty or forty pound wolf. With a chopped toe in a forefoot. The second toe from the inside on the left forefoot. I've seen his trail since. And I've seen the wolf himself! A black giant, that's what he is. A black devil! I've seen him, but the shakes came into my hand when I drew a bead on him.

"Oh, it ain't for nothing that I've come back to this here valley! It's because the black wolf is here, too! And if I was to kill him, Gannaway, might you not think that it would make it a lot easier for The King to come back to me a second time? I ask you all open, and man to man—might it not?"

There was only one answer to give, and with all the courage and the strength in his nature, Adam Gannaway said gravely: "There's nothing more reasonable. Of course since he's come back once, he'll probably try to come back again, some day. And it might help a lot—to get the black wolf out of the way!"

Tucker Crosden threw his enormous arms above his head.

"God bless you, Gannaway!" he cried.

He crossed the room with a single leap. He snatched the child into his arms.

"Molly, Molly, wake up and listen to me! Here's Gannaway. Here's a scientist and a gent that knows pretty near everything that there is to be known. He agrees with me. He agrees with the both of us. He says that there's a good chance. That there's almost a certainty—The King is gunna come back to me!"

The wide, sad eyes of the child stared at Gannaway in perfect understanding, perfect sympathy. And he knew by the pallor in her face that it was only a feigned sleep which she had been having.

It struck him full of horror.

For how many, many times in the long evenings of the winter, had she sat alone with her giant father and seen the madness rising in him; and how many times had she been forced to soothe the insane fancy?

It made Gannaway think of a child's hand at the helm, guiding a great ship through storm and danger. He saw his own problem stand up and stare him in the face, though he would gladly have shrunk from it. But Adam Gannaway was an honest man and he knew that his conscience would never be clear to his death-day if he left this slender girl in the power of the madman. In some manner, by wit or contrivance, he must manage to take her away.

And in the meantime, Tucker Crosden was walking up and down the cabin, laughing and shouting drunkenly, with Molly still in his arms, letting the unregarded tears stream down her face. As though she knew that her father would never see them now.

CHAPTER XV

THE sun was out of sight before it set, for the instant that it entered the thick November land mist, the world was lost in a common greyness. That instant, La Sombra opened her eyes and yawned. All was so pitchy black in the cave that she could see nothing except the wan eye of light which marked the entrance; but she could hear the breathing of her foster son and now she touched him with the cold tip of her nose. He leaped to his feet with a growl.

"An empty stomach makes evil dreams," said La Sombra. "What is it now, my son?"

He crouched close to her, as though he needed the warmth of her body.

"I dreamed that we came back to the cave, and when we entered a hundred dogs rushed out at us, and I was choked with the scent of man!"

"Ah, ah," murmured the wolf, "have I truly taught you to hate that smell? But it is time to be gone. It is two days since we have had food and by this time they are not watching the bank of the river so closely."

They crept out into the dimness of the late afternoon. Their refuge was apparently nothing but a huge and naked rock which thrust up from the waters of the Winnemago River with a constant turmoil of the foaming current around it. Sheerest chance, on a day when the dogs pressed them hard, had showed the wolf and her foster son the one landing on the rock after they had taken to the water, and chance, also, had led them into the narrow crevice which expanded downwards into a comfortable sleeping place. But, once found, mother wolf knew what a treasure was here, well worth braving the current to gain and leave. She made it their home, and for almost a year the frantic ranchers and even their trained hunters who came for the sake of the constantly rising bounty offered, had found that the trails of the wolf pair stopped on the bank of the river. Higher up and lower down the river there were broad and wooden islands which had been combed from head to heel, but not even the most imaginative had ever thought it worth while to examine this little point of rock.

La Sombra, on this evening, peering up and down the brush-clad banks of the Winnemago, saw nothing dangerous, but when White Wolf said at her side—"All is well! Let us swim, now, mother!" she growled in answer: "All is well that the eye can see, but what does the truer eye that sees around corners tell you?"

White Wolf obediently sat back on his haunches and scented the wind which combed straight across the river towards them. He scented it high and low and to either side.

"There is a mink—and it is hunting up the bank of the river; and far, far away there is a skunk—"

"A mink and a skunk!" snorted La Sombra. "Have I asked you if the mountains are still in their places? May I never call my best beloved son a fool, but the mink and the skunk are scents which I read plainly long before we left the cave, and do you sit here now with a wise look and tell me about them? Tush! it is ever the same with you. A blind nose! May it never bring you to danger!"

White Wolf yawned and lay down. His feelings were terribly hurt because that dullness in the nostrils was his most sensitive weakness; therefore he pretended a sleepy indifference to all that was around him.

"You, then, read the signs in the air, mother. I am still filled with sleep. Besides, what is there for us to do except swim ashore and start the hunt?"

"We shall see," said La Sombra.

She closed her eyes, as a good wolf should do when it studies the silent voices that live in the air and send thronging messages to the wild.

"What!" said she presently. "Does my nose deceive me, or is there really a raccoon on the hunt at this time of the year? He should be at his winter's sleep long ago. But perhaps he will not walk very far to-night, for there is a mountain-lion near him. It is that lame beast from Table Mountain, I think. He was nipped in a trap and since then he could not make a living in the mountains, so that he has come down to the lands of men. But the fool will take to a tree when the dogs run him, and then Man will make an end of him. However, there is nothing else worth talking of to-night, except a patch of sour grass that makes my mouth water; and beyond that—even at this distance I think that I scent the folded sheep, my son. Come, let us go. There are no men on the shore, in hiding to watch for us. Faugh! How cold the water is to-day, and how swift it runs!"

She paused on the edge of the stream, having touched the current with her forefoot, and watched the water curl high around her leg. Her foster son rose also. He was far other than the puppy which first descended onto these man-hunted lands a year ago. That year of hunting and battle and ample food had brought him to his full self, and such a self as never a bull-terrier had grown to before. La Sombra, in her fluffy coat, looked twice his bulk, but there was hardly an ounce between them. Compact of bone and muscle, cat-footed, sleek, with knots of iron strength about his jaws, there was eighty pounds of this young giant, coated in a pelt like silk and of the purest white. He, too, touched the edge of the water and a shiver rippled through him. However, the thing had to be done; and between winter and summer there was not much choice of temperature in the snow-fed waters of the Winnemago.

He dived with the skill of an otter and came up in a flurry of foam, heading straight for the nearby shore. But even so he was swept two hundred yards down stream before he reached a shallow and waded to the land. There a convulsive shake rid his oiled hair of most of the moisture and he trotted along the bank to watch La Sombra struggling in. The missing forefoot was a sore handicap for such work as this, but she was accustomed to the labor. The stream bore her another furlong beneath the landing place of White Wolf, but presently she had waded to the shore, sent a wide spray flinging from her coat, and then touched noses with her companion.

"All is well!" said she. "This double bath each day keeps our pelts clean, and there is no blessing greater than that. For a clean pelt makes a clean cave, as every good wolf knows. Come—the chill is biting at my bones!"

And she struck away through the woods with White Wolf running behind her. In a mile they were warm, in two miles they were dry, and presently they came out of the trees upon the broad pasture lands of the valley, with the narrow shafts of lamplight driving at them through the dark—half a dozen houses in more or less distant view.

They leaped a fence into a level field, heading towards a carcass of a young cow, killed three days before, but they had not gone a dozen jumps before La Sombra stopped and jerked her nose into the air.

"Iron, White Wolf!" said she. "They have planted the teeth about the dead body, and we must hunt elsewhere."

"Ay," said White Wolf, "for even I can read that scent a little now. They were bunglers who set those traps, for their man-scent is mixed with the iron, is it not?"

"See if my son has not learned to read the truth—even though a little dimly! Yes, the man-scent is also on the buried iron."

"There is another message of a dead beef coming across the wind. Let us see."

"I have scented it long ago, but there is something unpleasant about it. However, we will look! But carefully, carefully! Do we not know that man will lie out to wait for us near the dead bodies?"

They ran for half a mile, and in a tree-shrouded corner of a field they found the body of a dead calf. White Wolf made straight for it, but La Sombra, coming well into the wind that blew from the carcass, stopped him with a gasp of horror and disgust.

"Poison, my son! Do not come a step nearer!"

"There seems nothing wrong—nothing to me, at least."

"I tell you that I know the scent. I have told you so before. Men will put in dead meat an enemy which cannot be seen. But I remember seeing a young wolf—in a starving winter when wolves must hunt together or die apart—eat of such a carrion, and die in horrible pain, biting his own flesh. It was a terrible thing to see, and the same strange odor was in that dead body. And the wolf, as he lay dying, breathed it forth also. Let us go on!"

Whatever were the doubts of White Wolf, he had learned long ago that his intelligence in such matters was as nothing compared with the wisdom of La Sombra. They journeyed on, and crossing to the leeward of a ranch house, La Sombra couched herself on her panting breast to take wind and observe.

"See what a vile air blows from that cave where the man-devils live!" said La Sombra.

"I smell man and iron and woodsmoke and food, also."

"But no fresh meat?"

"No."

"He eats no meat except what he has tainted with the smell of fire, first. I, lying in the brush in my youth, have seen man do this foolish thing. It was to marvel at, White Wolf!"

"I shall marvel at them no more," said the terrier. "Have we not lived under the very nose of man all these many moons almost past counting?"

"Peace, child! You speak who have never seen his face or felt his eye, except at a great distance!"

"He has his slaves. He has iron and the sharp voice that kills from a great distance and he has poison, and he has dogs. Are there not dogs in that same house, mother? I, the White Wolf, shall speak with them."

"Oh, my son!" moaned La Sombra. "You will find your death in these terrible games of yours."

"I shall not so much as bare a tooth," said White Wolf plaintively. "I go only to speak—or to look. Then I come to you again safely—"

And he vanished through the shadows.

CHAPTER XVI

FROM the hedge beside the back yard of the house, White Wolf saw the tangle of dogs. Most ranches had such a conglomeration. There were two or three indescribable mongrels, as well as a big brute of the mastiff type, a greyhound, and two foxhounds. White Wolf knew the type of each. He had spent every opportunity during the part year in testing the methods of various dogs and in perfecting his own style. For it is written in the wilderness: By the edges of their teeth they shall live! And besides there was in White Wolf a professional enjoyment of battle for its own sake. It was in vain that Mother Wolf assured him that all battles except those of necessity are foolish beyond description. The instinct burned in the terrier like a consuming fire and would not down.

So, with a thrill at heart, he lay on the leeward side of this group and studied them, wondering if the odds were too great for his purpose. On the whole, he had an immense contempt for dogs. He could handle them in two ways. When they were in numbers, he could use the tactics which he had learned from La Sombra and Lop-ear, two experts in toothplay after the school of the grey wolf, which teaches that one should strike with the shoulder and slash with the fangs as with a knife. He had the great advantage in this work of being infinitely nimbler on his feet than any wolf, and of having his weight more compacted and closer to the ground. He had the disadvantage of never being able to rip and cut with quite the effectiveness of a true wolf. As for his other system, he used it when he had only a single enemy and he did not need anything but practice to make him perfect in the art, for it was born in him as truly as his color. That instinct was to drive at the head of the enemy and get a jaw hold, if that were possible, a throat hold as a next best offering, and at the least a purchase on a foreleg, after which he worked his teeth into the bone or to the life. With that double equipment, where dogs were concerned he felt himself beyond so base a thing as fear. And now he watched and waited for his chance.

Here the kitchen door of the house opened—a flare of light shot across the dusk—and a great bone was thrown to the snarling pack. They closed over it with a rush, and their sharp, barking voices raised a great hubbub until there arose from the corner of the yard the massive form of the mastiff. He waded through the tangle, gripped the bone, and with a single growl he scattered the rest. They stood at a distance and slavered with impotence and with hatred, but a step closer they dared not take.

White Wolf stood up and looked more closely at the victor. He was tawny as a mountain lion, heavy with his own bulk, obviously slow of foot, but he had a jaw as wide and potent as an iron vise and that, no doubt, was the reason that the rest stood aloof and trembled with helplessness. Perhaps that jaw had been clamped upon one or two of their number and they had never forgotten the lesson of pain.

And, in the meantime, there was the bone, enriched with ample shreds of meat and with store of yellow marrow at its core. The bull-terrier endured until he could endure no more. Here were great odds. Here was the house of man looming just beside the place. And the central figure was one worthy of respect in hand to hand encounter. But here was also a prize worth fighting for and a battle eminent for its own sake.

He launched himself like an eagle dropping from its crag. The flash of his body was in the eye of the startled mastiff and out again as the teeth of White Wolf gripped the end of the bone and tore it clear.

He could have gone on freely with his prize, but though the taste of the cooked meat was strange and sweet to him, he had no desire for food alone. Battle was what he wanted, and presently it offered itself. He was still on the lee side of the group of dogs and they, staring at him, made no offer of a universal attack. And that was always strange to White Wolf. Once they had the wind of him, the dogs were sure to fly at his throat with the cry of "Wolf! Wolf!" But when he stood in the lee of the wind from them, they looked on him as one of themselves, it seemed. And this was a mystery which he could never solve!

However, dog or wolf, the mastiff was not inclined to give up this pleasant tidbit without a struggle. It lurched to its feet and charged. White Wolf sidestepped like a boxer and laid the hip of the monster open with a single slash.

"Wolf!" gasped the mastiff, as he rushed into the full scent of the terrier. And he whirled like a mad thing and charged again. Once more he struck thinnest air; once more he received a punishing cut; then all discretion left him. His head rose as he flung wildly in again, and this was the very moment for which the terrier had been waiting. He dived under and up like a swimming seal, and his long punishing jaw locked on the throat of the larger dog.

"Wolf!" gasped the mastiff, as he lay on his back, struggling futilely. "Help!"

"Wolf?" snarled one of the foxhounds, making use of this moment to seize on the neglected bone. "Wolf? No, but a dog like the rest of us—and your master, you fat-sided murderer!"

"Wolf!" choked the mastiff. "I am dead unless you help. Wolf! Do you not smell him?"

His eyes bulged and his tongue lolled far out as the bull-terrier shifted to a deeper grip and wriggled his teeth home. But here a mongrel, dancing with excited yappings to the windward of the struggling pair, stopped short and threw its nose into the air.

"Wolf! Wolf!" he cried. "It is true!"

And his teeth were instantly in a hind leg of the terrier. That was the example. The rest, with a chorus of startled cries, flung themselves in a heap upon White Wolf.

He had already turned from the exhausted mastiff. His first stroke tore the mongrel from eye to ear and made it loose its grip with a howl. His second split the ear and the jowl of a foxhound. And he rose like a white but evil spirit out of the tumbling heap just as the back door of the house opened and a woman cried: "Jerry—Mack—stop your noise, you fools—holy heavens, it's the White Wolf!"

She was a sensible woman and with a bit more light she would have known better. But it was the dusk of the day, and all that she knew was that a white form boiled out of the center of the dog-pack which shrank away as from a demon. The wraith-like creature paused to scoop up the beef bone, and then fled through the hedge. And all of this in a trice.

"Dad!" screamed she at the door of the house. "The White Wolf, do you hear? He's killed Champ, and he's laid out two more—and—sic him, boys! After him, Jerry! Hey, Mack, take him! Oh, you fools! You cowards!"

For the injured dogs lay whining, licking their hurts. And the ones with whole skins had seen all they wanted to of this lightning destroyer who carried teeth on all sides of him, apparently.

So they stirred in blind circles through the yard and howled eloquently for their master to come and lead them, when they would all prove themselves as valiant as lions.

Sid Harter did not pause to pick up a rifle. When he heard the word "White Wolf" a sudden golden vision of twenty-five hundred dollars crossed his mind's-eye, and he reached the back door in a bound, revolver in hand.

It was too late for even a chance shot, and all that he saw was all that most others had seen of the famous destroyer—a grey streak glimmering off through the dusk of the day.

"If I'd been here to see!" he groaned. "But it's too late. The devil will probably butcher a couple of beeves for us before the morning comes unless we give him a run. And we can't run him with a beaten pack! Get to the telephone, Mary. Get quick, and ring up Chick Parker's house. The Loftus brothers are over there with their dogs —the Loftus brothers that have done so much talking about what they'll do. Here's their chance to pick up a red-hot scent—and then we'll see what comes of them and their hounds!"

Under the three fir trees, White Wolf stretched himself panting at the side of mother wolf, and though the rich bone lay before her, she first sniffed the wounds in his leg.

"They are nothing," breathed he. "Only scratches that barely broke the skin. He came from behind while I had another down. But in the meantime, I am a little too hot for more work. Do you crack the bone, mother?"

"Ah ha!" grinned La Sombra. "This is the way of it, then? For all your fighting and for all of your grown-up ways, there are still things in which you need me? You cannot crack a bone so big?"

"Nonsense," panted her foster son. "It is only because I wish to save my strength of jaw in case there is more work to-night. Crack the bone and say no more."

"I say no more," said La Sombra, well pleased, "but I am not deceived, my white son! I am not deceived! However, all is as it should be, and the young must learn from the old—now watch me—even so!"

She held an end of the bone between her paws, so that the other end was well off the ground and then she snapped at it with a darting movement of her head and the full play of her powerful jaws. The heavy shell of the bone crunched beneath the stroke, and White Wolf wondered. No matter how he tried, no matter how he struggled to learn, he could never acquire quite this incisive power of jaw and this knack of using it.

However, here was the marrow bared to him, and they ate it side by side; and it came dimly into the mind of La Sombra that she had never before heard of wolves who could share such a prize in peace.

CHAPTER XVII

THEY hunted further west towards the desert than they usually went. The desert itself she had no liking for, because now that she was lamed, she knew its great open spaces were dangerous in case of pursuit, but they came close to its verge, studying the scents that greeted them.

"There are cattle on that hill, my son."

"I am not in the mood for killing a bull."

"There are geese in the pond to our right."

"Let them be. They are wallowing in mire and stinking muck."

"There are pigs, too, close to that barn which gives out the sweet scent of the hay."

"Ah, that is better!"

"Shall we go, then?"

"Wise La Sombra, you show me the way like sun in the middle of the night. Go first, and I follow."

They came to the verge of the rank pigsty when La Sombra paused.

"What is that?" said she.

"I hear nothing."

"Clear your mind of this strong scent and listen to something that is not half as loud as the wind."

He listened again, and on the far horizon, half-vanishing and half-heard, he made out now the baying of a dog.

"It is a hound at work," said he.

"And after what quarry?"

"How shall I tell? That same racoon which you scented before we left the river, perhaps."

"No dog ever cried in such a voice for a raccoon. There is a larger game than that. Listen again, oh my son!"

"I hear it more clearly; it is only a single voice."

"You hear it more clearly, because it is coming in this direction."

"Let us eat, mother. Do you fear a single dog?"

"When a dog hunts at this hour there is apt to be a man with it. Let us wait before we eat. There is much time, and it is not easy to run on a filled belly, as you know."

"Bah!" snorted White Wolf. "Life to you is one unending suspicion. It is a long misery to doubt every moment. I say that my very heart is aching for pork."

"Let it ache—let it ache. Ha! Do you hear it now? And every moment coming closer! What would you say if I told you what you should know already? That dogs give tongue in just that key when they run on the trail of a wolf!"

The terrier pricked his ears and listened with his head close to the ground.

"It is true!" said he. "They are running the trail of a wolf."

"And we are very far from the river. Come, my son. We must start back. And first we will run through that pig pen. There is enough odor there to kill our scent."

They leaped in and out of the pen before the startled porkers had time to open their drowsy eyes.

"How easy, how easy it would have been!" sighed white Wolf as they leaped on, side by side. "That white boar who slept on his side with his throat held out for your teeth, mother—! How easy it would have been!"

"An empty stomach makes a light foot and a sharp tooth, my son. And it is better to live hungry than to die fat. Let us cross this creek, and then have a look at our own trail which we made coming down and see what we may see. How fast that hound is coming!"

The baying of the dog was running fast upon them.

"And horses, too!" said La Sombra. "Which means men also."

For now they could distinguish the crackling of underbrush as horses galloped through it.

They took cover in a clump of shrubbery from which they had a clear view of an open space across which they had travelled on their way down the farmlands towards the desert. And they had hardly settled down before the bay of the hunting dog broke on their ears loudly and here it leaped into the clearing—a gaunt creature with the body of a greyhound and the grotesque head of a foxhound set on the long neck. It ran swiftly, nosing the ground only now and again, and behind it, like a flight of level-driven javelins, ran five great, dark dogs—bigger than wolves, with long, sinister heads. What made them seem more terrible was the silence in which they ran, and their long bounds carried them easily over the ground. They were travelling so fully inside their speed and their strength that their mouths were not opened.

They were gone at once among the farther trees. Two horsemen swept into view and out again. And La Sombra stood up and stepped forth into the twilight with a shudder.

"It is well that we are not heavy with food?"

"It is well, mother. Nothing can keep them from catching up with us unless it be for the cunning trail which you know how to leave behind you. Only your wits can beat them, and if they reach us I think that we shall find them different stuff from the packs which we have run through before like so many rabbits."

They headed not straight for the river above their den on the rock, but winding through the farmyards that stretched in a loosely drawn and circuitous route before them. For in every farmyard their scent would be drowned for a moment, at least. And in between these pausing places, La Sombra ran as hard as her three legs could carry her.

The voice of the hound died out down the wind. But presently it came again. The six dogs had reached the furthermost point in the trail and now they were turning back it and travelling with uncanny speed. Truly, as the terrier had pointed out, mere speed could never have saved the fugitives. But time and again the noise of the pursuit rolled swiftly up the wind, and time and again the dogs checked and paused while the wise-headed trailer deciphered the sign.

And so, at last, the two who ran in front came to the last ranch house and then had to shake free for the long drive across the fields and through the woods to the river. But La Sombra in this time of need was already far spent. They were not half way to the edge of the woods when they heard the yelling of the hound break into the open and La Sombra gasped:

"They are coming fast, oh my son. Now, if ever my wits were of service to you, if ever my nose has solved a problem for you, if ever my strength has guarded you, if ever my milk has cherished you, be true to me now and do not leave me!"

Her foster son ran half a stride in her rear.

"Do not think of that," he panted. "Save all your power for running, and remember that I am here to save your heels if they *can* be saved. Run hard, run true. I shall never leave you, mother!"

And that seemed to give her greater confidence, and confidence is strength. The one shoulder which had to take the jar and thrust of her lunging weight ached as though every sinew in it were parting, but still she kept at her work while the bloody mist of exhaustion spread before her eyes.

They reached the woods, and she took the straightest course for the water, where the Winnemago swerved in its line for the western desert. But oh, how fast the danger sped up from behind! There seemed no weariness in the flying legs of the hunters, and La Sombra sinking each moment lower on her staggering legs, and her bushy tail dragged and loaded with mud and wet and tangled leaves.

"I can go no farther," she breathed. "Let us make our last stand and die together."

"On and on!" cried White Wolf. "The river is near. Is not that the gleaming of the water that I see just ahead?"

Ay, it was the first sheen of the water, but now behind them arose a savage yell not from the hound's throat alone, but from all six of the monsters. They had taken their first view of the double quarry.

How fast they closed now! White Wolf, glancing back over his shoulder, saw the five dark monsters glide past the hound and leap into the lead without effort. Like flung spears they came—and still the water lay well ahead!"

"Go on!" gasped White Wolf. "Go on and on, mother! I shall give them one check—and do you find the water in the meantime. Faster!"

"I have nothing left—my loins are breaking—it is death, White Wolf!"

"No, it is life! Faster, La Sombra!"

He whined out the last in an agony of dread, for he felt the shadow of pursuit sweeping up on him and the panting of the leader just behind him—

No long-legged wolf or hound could have managed the maneuvre. It needed hair-trigger nerves and a compacted body. White Wolf hurled himself about and flattened himself to the ground at the same instant. He saw a great gaping of long teeth above him, but he had crouched too low for the teeth to flesh themselves home in his body. They merely skimmed his back while the grip of the terrier fastened like a hand of iron on a foreleg of the big dog.

Something had to give. Living flesh and sinew could not stand the sudden, jerking strain, and as the wolfhound pitched into the air and heavily down again upon his back, the strong bone of his foreleg burst fairly across.

So fell Tiger, the fleetest of the pack, and the oldest of them. He lay howling on the ground, snapping at stones and moss in his agony, while the terrier rose among five enemies instead of six.

The yell of their leader and the turning of the white quarry made them forget the lame wolf who ran ahead of them for the river; they jammed against one another in wild confusion in their eagerness to get their teeth in the bull-terrier.

CHAPTER XVIII

White Wolf, dashed to the ground by the somersault of Tiger, had half his wits knocked from him by the blow, but his instinct was still with him, which taught him ever to fight low, low—as close to the ground as his own bulk permitted. So it was that he rose under the long legs of big Sneaker and gave him a wolfish slash across the belly in passing. It twisted Sneaker into a knot—a dreadful wound, but one that still left him fighting strength, and when he straightened again, he was a pain-maddened dog—which is a mad dog indeed.

Four monsters rushed at White Wolf. It was like charging a fluttering moth. The ground turned to strong springs beneath the dancing feet of White Wolf. He was in and out and away before a single tooth was fleshed in him, and he heard the convulsive splash of La Sombra as she flung her exhausted body into the river.

He himself could never reach the river in a single burst, and he knew it well. But there was a high knot of rocks near the bank and for it he made, and leaped to the side and then to the top of the heap.

There was no permanent security, of course. But he had a chance to meet them one by one, more or less. So when Doc sprang at him, he gave that veteran a punishing cut across the face that blinded one eye. And the hound, Grampus, leaping craftily in from the rear, took a cut across ear and neck that toppled him to the ground with a yell.

The heart of White Wolf rose high. He had made good his ground, it seemed, and all was well, when two riders broke through the trees and the ringing voices of men sounded like a knell in the ear of the terrier. He heard them shouting:

"There's Tiger down—a broken leg, by God! Where are the two devils?"

"I see only one. I think—ay, yonder on that rock—just a white glimmer—the White Wolf, Tom! Take him boys! Pete, Lefty, Sneaker, Doc, Grampus—take him, boys, all together! Tom, where's your rifle before the white fiend gets away! The twenty-five hundred is ours."

It seemed to White Wolf that the sound of the man's voice transformed the dogs. They clambered up the steep face of the rock and charged him with a mad carelessness that made him wonder. Tiger was done, and done forever. Sneaker had rushed the rock for the last time and now lay bleeding and gasping at its foot, with his life blood draining away fast enough. But here were four raging devils, without fear of death, so it seemed! They came from behind—he drove them back with a snarl and a flash of teeth, then turned to face front again only in time to receive the long gripping jaw of Lefty in his throat.

There was such power in that grip as a wolf might have envied, and the terrier knew the meaning of the hold all too well. It was for that same purchase that he himself maneuvred in all his battles, and now writhings and straining would be all in vain to break that hold.

There was only one thing left. Another pair of jaws slashed at his flank and missed a deadly hold by a fraction of an inch, and in one moment all four would have their teeth fleshed in him.

White Wolf dove outwards from the rocks towards the lower stones thirty feet below. He saw the blur of stars above him as he whirled underneath. He saw the stars go out and the black faces of the stones beneath as he whirled to the top again, and then they struck the rocks. There was force enough to knock the wind from the body of White Wolf and send him rolling helplessly over and over, down the slope towards the swift current of the Winnemago, as the teeth of Lefty relaxed their grip.

They would never close on an enemy's throat again, for

the full weight of the two heavily falling bodies had struck on the ridge of Lefty's back and shattered the vertebrae like brittle chalk. He died that instant, and Pete, Doc, and Grampus lurching down the slope to the water's edge, saw the white dog seized by the current and jerked down the stream as though by a strong hand.

"God help us, we've lost three dogs!" screamed Dan Loftus. "Call back the rest before them damned wolves murder 'em in the water. Gimme your rifle! Who'd of thought that this could happen? Shoot, Tom. My nerve's all gone—"

"I don't see nothing!" groaned Tom, rifle in hand at the edge of the water—"nothing but the streak of the riffles, yonder, where they're foaming around the rocks. Dan, we've lost this trick. Help me look to the dogs! My God, what a night—and one wolf has gone through our pack like a knife through butter—and not a big one, at that. I seen that much—a runt of a white wolf, with all the devils in hell turned loose inside of him!"

White Wolf, weak with labor, weak with loss of blood, and half-stifled by the water which had entered his throat when he first rolled into the Winnemago, managed to reach the landing place on the rock, but he would never have had the power to clamber to the safety of the cave had not his foster mother waited for him there and, standing knee deep in the current, laid her grip on the nape of his neck and helped him in.

On tired legs he dragged himself to the cave and lay just within its mouth, his eyes closed, his body stretched helpless upon his side while the tongue of Mother Wolf licked his wounds and she murmured above him:

"There is no other but one, and he is the White Wolf. Other mothers have brought forth sons, but none like mine. Lie still. Breathe deep. You shall not die. It is weariness and not the wounds that makes you faint. Oh my son, if you owe me the life which I brought forth to the light of the day, you have paid me twice with the dead bull and the beaten dogs. Why have they not torn you to bits? Is your flesh iron? Can it take no wounds? Peace,—do not speak—all is well—you must sleep, and when you waken, the wounds will be already closed!"

They were not closed, to be sure, but they were wonderfully better in the morning. La Sombra ventured ashore in spite of her own weariness, and she came back shortly after dawn with a rabbit. She herself would not touch a bite of it, though her belly was as empty as a collapsed balloon, but she sat up and watched with eyes of fire while he consumed and presently fell asleep. All that day she watched over him and licked his wounds. It was not until night that she left him in order to hunt again for herself and for him, and when she returned, he had come to meet her at the edge of the water.

For he was almost iron in very fact, and a mauling which would have left a man-raised dog helpless for a fortnight was a mere scratch on the surface of White Wolf before the third day had ended.

On the fourth day they were gone. For, on that day, they saw a boat drift down the stream, slowly, touching at every one of the little islands above them, while the men on board went ashore in each place and searched eagerly. No doubt as to what they were searching for, and no doubt but that the point of rocks would not escape from this pair of systematic hunters. So, when the dusk descended, White Wolf and La Sombra faced the waters and swam to the shore.

They headed straight up the stream, keeping to the rocks along the shore where the splash of the spray would wash out the scent and the sign of their tracks before they were half an hour old. They kept to this slippery path for four or five miles before they ventured to leave the Winnemago's edge and strike inland, and after that they headed steadily towards the upper mountains.

They travelled slowly, led astray often to the north and to the south in following the chase from day to day, but on the whole the direction of their travel was east, and the course pointed towards Spencer Mountain, which grew greater and greater until it dominated the sky, with Mount Lomas huge also to the south and Table Mountain's flat top in the north. Each of them knew, without word spoken, that they were bound for the familiar old valley of the Seven Sisters. And each felt, no doubt, that they were approaching danger such as that from which they fled more than a year before. But the particular species of danger which existed that winter over the entire mountains was what White Wolf had no conception of until they turned the corner of a boulder, on a day, with a terrible crossgale cutting straight across their path, so that no scents blew either up or down, and so they came literally nose to nose with a mangy red fox which was hurrying west. It bounded back and stood lightly posed, ready to fly, but like any fox, unwilling to waste unnecessary effort.

"Shall I take this little brute by the throat and let him roll down the side of the cañon?" asked White Wolf. "He is at such a distance that I can catch him in the first sprint, before he has a chance to stretch away from me. Tell me, La Sombra!"

The wolf answered: "Look again. The creature is unclean. I would not put a tooth in that hide unless I were starving. What now, little red rat? Where do you travel to-day and what has dug the hollows in your sides?"

The fox grinned with purest malice and hatred, and his grin was made peculiarly ominous and ugly by a broken fang.

"I have come from what you are going to," said he. "I shall not tell you to turn back, because all wolves are headstrong fools. But when you cross the mountains, you will feel the pinch in your bellies, my friends. The very mice have died for the lack of seeds to feed on, and the rabbits have died of a plague, and without mice and without rabbits, what manner of a country is left for us who must have flesh? Adios, my friends. As for you, White Wolf, I have heard of you even here in the mountains. But I give you this warning—that when you come among others who are true wolves, they will see that you are really a dog, and they will dine upon you, my young friend! Farewell!"

He bounded to a higher rock, to another yet above, and then scampered lightly down the trail once more.

CHAPTER XIX

THEY were not long in finding that the words of the sick fox were more than true. When they came up to the top of the box-cañons and found themselves on the old familiar ground of the higher mountains, with the evergreens bending their boughs under loads of snow and the ground heaped thick with it, they discovered that nothing was afoot, and the wide-winged hawks sailed some high and some low on restless wings, making good weather perforce out of every storm.

La Sombra noted and snapped her teeth in impatience.

"When the hawks are hungry," said she, "then the bare bones of hard times are sure to be ahead of us, my son. But we have our wits to eat before we starve, unless you wish to turn about and go to the lowlands again. There are still plenty of sheep there and there are plenty of cattle."

White Wolf was already cold with the wind that curried his short hair and drove the edge of the temperature into his very bone. But now he grew colder still, and closing his eyes he saw a level drift of long-legged dogs shooting across the ground faster than a wolf can run—dogs who were each almost as formidable as matured wolves, and who knew how to fight together as well as a mother and father wolf in defense of their young.

So thought White Wolf. That he had managed—largely by good chance—to kill three of these monsters in one ever-memorable struggle did not obscure the major truth which was, in his mind, that given a fair chance and good ground any two of these dogs would be able to kill him without a great deal of trouble. And he had no desire at all to return to the lowlands and face those long-legged brutes. What havoc he had wrought with that particular pack, and how he had broken the spirit of the survivors did not enter his head.

He said to La Sombra: "No, let us take our chance in the snow with hunger and the man in the valley of the Seven Sisters. It is better than facing the dogs on the lower Winnemago."

La Sombra stooped her head and licked up a bit of fluffy snow, as though she did not wish her son to see the light in her eye at that particular moment, but she could not keep the satisfaction out of her voice when she answered:

"Then it is not for my sake only, my white son?"

"It is for the sake of both of us," he replied. For he was perhaps a trifle more honest than any wolf could really be; and as he thought of the great dogs the scarcely healed wounds in his throat tingled with fire.

They made their home in the old cave at the head of the Dunkeld Cañon, but at the end of three days they had had, between them, a single half-starved old rabbit, too weak to get away from them, and the White Wolf began to show the tokens of ill-fare. For he needed to have food and plenty of it if he was to live and work. You may starve a wolf until it is simply a loosely strung frame of bones and sinews covered with clumsy folds of hide, and still the wolf will run almost as fast and as far as ever and he will keep it up until close to his death-day at the hands of famine. But a dog has not these resources. He has not the same patience. He cannot look nature in the eye, when she is in one of her fiercer moods, without beginning to worry.

All of this La Sombra could not know except by intuition, but her intuition told her clearly that this son of hers was a high-strung youth who needed high fare and a great deal of pampering. Back to the lowlands she would not and she could not go, but if she remained in the moutains, it behoved her to see that her guardian and provider had an ample table spread. And so keenly did she feel this that she made it a point to restrain the terrible pangs of her own hunger if, by that means, she could provide a little better fare for her foster son.

In the first place, they left the old cave at the end of the third day, and dipping into the valley of the Tomahawk River, almost the first thing that they encountered was a mother elk and her half-grown son. White Wolf would have attacked at once, but the wary old veteran held him back.

"These are not man-handled, pastured cattle," said she. "Do not think, my son, that in the midst of a fight they grow foolishly blind, but even as we do, their eyes are opened most when danger is nearest! It would need more than two wolves to pull down one of them. If we attack, the calf, we have the mother on us, and one blow of her foot will shatter your ribs. Trust me, for I have seen it happen to the wisest leader of the greatest pack that I ever saw run in winter. However, we may follow the pair of them and see what opening they will give us. If it is a young and foolish mother, perhaps—Ay, ay, what a bitter winter is this, my son! Now, if ever, there is a need for good wolves to run together. For if there were a pack of us we should already be picking the bones of the two—and there would be meat enough for all—meat enough for all!"

She licked her thin lips as she spoke and her famine-reddened eye wandered like a questing fire among the naked trees and the rolling hills.

For two more days they followed the trail of the elk which was marching vigorously, making for a well-known elk yarding ground on the upper Tomahawk River; but during day and night the vigilance of the mother did not relax, and once when La Sombra thought that she saw a chance of dealing with the calf by a blow across the hamstring, the startled cry of the youngster brought a furious charge from the big female and a lunge of the forefoot that well-nigh knocked La Sombra then and there into the happy hunting grounds where, of course, all good wolves go.

It would have gone hard with La Sombra and her foster child in that dreary march, but they found a frozen rabbit in the snow, and on the next day, two partridges in their little hoods of ice perched on a low branch of a tree to which White Wolf was able to leap. But on the morning of the third day there was a change. It was La Sombra who heard first and touched her companion, and when he raised his head, he, too, could make out a deep-throated, melancholy chorus coming over the edge of the northern hills.

"What devils are those?" asked White Wolf, shrinking.

"Wolves, my son—like me and like you! And by the mother who bore me and died before me, they are running on this same trail. Ah, we shall have full bellies before night if the leader of that pack knows how to make a kill! Now stop the elk, my son! Let us show the pack that we are willing to do our share of the work. Ay—ay! To have my four feet under me now. Never did I need them more except when the dog pack chased me into the Winnemago River. Play at the heels of the elk, my son, but not too close. Play for the calf rather than the cow, and that will keep them both standing! As for me, I shall attend to the heads of them!"

And, in another moment, she was making good her word. One would have thought, from her slavvering fury and the noise of her howling, that La Sombra intended to attack the pair then and there, and the big cow came to a halt. With little rushes she strove to drive La Sombra away, and had the ground been firm beneath their feet, such was her speed that she might have caught the crippled wolf—but over this soft snow La Sombra could manage with ease. The calf backed its rump against that of its mother and made what head it could—but here was the terrier barking in a sharp, yapping voice, ridiculously small and high-pitched, considering his size and his character. And so the cow and the calf began to mill in a small circle, keeping their heads to the two foes as well as they could.

The baying down the trail grew more loud, now, and the poor mother knew well enough what it portended. She gave a trumpet call to her calf, and breaking from the two assailants, she headed off up the valley at a round pace. But only for a moment. A snap of La Sombra close to the hamstring of the calf made the mother elk turn in dismay and charge in vain. And before she had finished that charge, the pack was in sight, swinging over the heads of the northern hills with such a burst of ominous music as the White Wolf had never heard before.

He saw a round dozen of thin-sided wolves come at full gallop down the slope with a brown monster running well in the lead and giving tongue in a note of deep thunder that dominated the cry of the whole pack.

He came fast, but when he saw that the quarry was already at bay, he slackened his gait and rumbled to La Sombra only a deep-throated: "Well done, La Sombra! You have held them well—you and the other. Now stand back and let the men work at this business.'

"It is as you please, El Trueno," said La Sombra obsequiously, and she shrank away with White Wolf following her.

"Courage, my son," she murmured at his ear. "Do not look on them as though they were mountain lions. They are our people—our people, White Wolf. Do you hear me?"

"My heart cries out against them!" said White Wolf, and he added sadly: "How can they ever take me among them?"

"Why can they not? Ay, and with pride. For are you not my son? Mark the leader, my child. See how he marshals his wolves and places them in order. He has wit as well as strength. He is called El Trueno, because he has a voice like thunder. You have heard it! And yonder is a grey wolf with a white streak across his breast. He is a known warrior. He is a little old now, or else even El Trueno would not be leading while he is present. He is called Marco Blanco and I have seen him hamstring a moose at a single slash. There are other wolves here whom I know, and never have they been more welcome to my eye than now. They are thin—and when such a pack as this is thin, it is ample sign that single wolves must starve! Ha—there is a fool—a young one, and of all fools they are the worst!"

The pack had scattered itself in a swift circle around the pair of elk and now, sitting down on their haunches in the snow, they took breath once more and examined the work before them in greater detail. They were stricken hard with the sharpest tooth in the head of famine, so that the occasional glance which they threw at White Wolf pried to his very heart of hearts with savage greed. There was no mercy in such hunger as theirs. And yet they are marvellously patient, waiting for the word of their leader, and for his known wisdom.

However, there was one young brave in the group whose courage was greater than his discretion. He it was who now sprang to the front jumping up and down on stiffened legs and howling a short phrase over and over again.

"It is my kill! The kill is mine! It is my kill!"

And suddenly he darted at the heels of the cow and leaped long and straight with fangs bare to try for the hamstring. It seemed to the bull-terrier a well-made leap, better and swifter by far than any he had ever seen La Sombra make—crippled as she was. Yet she had brought down cow and bull alike. He could see now that she understood her business well when she said this was quarry of a different stripe, for the cow elk turned ever so little and struck out with a single hind foot. The sharp toes struck in the midst of the youngster's ribs and seemed to drive half way through him.

So the young wolf fell, dead before he struck the ground, and all his companions swarmed thick upon him. White Wolf, his heart aching with terror and with digust, saw that body torn to bits and devoured with incredible speed.

"Ah," he groaned, "are there not devils in these wolves?"

There was no answer from La Sombra. When he turned he saw that she was gone, and when he looked again he marked her in the thick of the mêlée, securing her portion with the rest!

CHAPTER XX

THE cow elk and her calf had made off the instant their foes were drawn away by this diversion. But it was hardly two minutes before only clean-picked, scattered bones remained of the fallen lobo; then the pack swept away with a brain-racking yell on the old trail.

White Wolf followed at his best pace, but it was slower than that of the youngest and weakest of the lot except for three-legged La Sombra. And here she was as of old, running eagerly but clumsily at his side. He did not look at her. He could not force himself to do so, but from the corner of his eye he saw the blood upon her face and his whole soul shrank from her.

But there seemed no compunctions of conscience in La Sombra after that act of cannibalism. The red fire had abated in her eye, now that her belly was somewhat sated, and she laughed silently as she ran for joy of the pack and the work before them.

"A day for raw meat and all that we can hold!" she gasped to her foster-child. "Write it down in red, my son, for you shall never forget!"

They had the cow and her calf at bay again. Once more the circle formed, but now the taste of flesh had emboldened them all and the impatient yelling began at once: "Is our leader El Trueno? Let him kill, then, for here is meat and our stomachs are empty."

El Trueno was not one to let such a call go unheeded. He stood up in the pride of his place and the glory of his strength and shook the dry snow from his flanks, and paused to bite a clot of ice from between his toes.

"Some two or three of you play at her heels," said he shortly. "El Trueno will cut her throat if you do your part!"

Not two, but five of them were instantly darting and feinting at the hind legs of the big cow, and as she wheeled towards them, El Trueno sprang in and up. Another leap as true and as swift as a stone flung from a sling, but the cow was no sluggard. She stopped her whirling movement and jerked up a foreleg. An instant later and the teeth of El Trueno would have caught her throat. An instant sooner and her fore hoof would have driven edged into the body of the flying leader. But as it was, only her knee struck him, and sent him spinning over and over.

He was royal even in his fall, and landing catlike on all feet, he drew back a little blinking and coughing, while the starved pack showed their glistening fangs and boomed in gloomy chorus: "El Trueno has missed the kill. Who next? Are we children or grown wolves?"

But wolves, like Indians, fight with caution first and courage afterwards, and though they skirmished at a distance, they had had too ample testimony of the skill of that veteran elk in defense of her own life and that of her calf. So they kept from her reach, and so doing, they kept from biting distance, also.

White Wolf had watched all this. It was a harder game than that which he and La Sombra had played so many and many a time with the fat-fed cattle of the plains. It needed a faster foot and a sharper eye, and he who failed was exceedingly apt to die. But it seemed to White Wolf that these cunning slayers erred in one vital thing. They played at the heels, the flank, and the throat but his own instinct, like that of soldiers of Rome, was to play for the head—ever for the head. Of all the body of the elk, it was the farthest from her active hoofs and as for speed to get at her, he had seen them work at their best, but he had seen no actual lightning play of foot and tooth such as he felt himself capable of.

And now he stood up and spoke for the first time among the pack.

"Wolves of El Trueno," said he, "I have seen you work bravely and well. But for you and for La Sombra and for my own sake also, I shall try myself at this game. Speak to the cow from the heels again. Take her eye, and let me try for her head!"

They bated their yelping for a single instant.

"Is it a wolf-dog, or a dog-wolf?" sneered El Trueno. "Will your cub strike home where El Trueno has failed, La Sombra? But let the young fool taste the sharpness of her heels if he will. Play with her again, brothers. Yet I think that this is a braggart and a coward. Does he not tremble as he speaks?"

For with the cold, and above all with excitement White Wolf was trembling in every fibre of his body, and the voice of La Sombra pealed above the rest: "Mark him, El Trueno. You may mark him now. By the mother who bore me, you shall see hunting, now. Now, for my honor and your own, little son of mine! Strike home!"

There was a flurry of active forms at the heels of the tormented cow again, and again as she swung about, danger flew at her. But not at flank or throat or leg. It darted in a gleaming white streak straight for her head, and the teeth of the terrier sank home in the tenderly nerved flesh of her broad nose. Then the eighty compacted pounds of his weight jerked whiplash fashion at her head and neck, with such a leverage that she was flung a staggering step sidewise.

She was unbalanced for a moment only, but that moment was more than enough for the hungry pack. It had waited long enough for this meal, and now a dozen strong bodies launched forward as though driven by springs released at the same instant. Haunch and flank and throat, those tearing fangs entered her flesh.

"Flee!" she bellowed to the calf. "My life for yours. It is the law! Flee, my darling——"

And she sank dying to the snow. There was no help for the calf, however. It struck valiantly away for liberty, but one wise old warrior lurked in its path—La Sombra, and the slash of her teeth snapped a hamstring of the calf as neatly as a frayed violin string parts under the bow. The calf was down also, and now there was no sound save the breathless snarling of the pack as they ate, and then the grinding powerful teeth upon the bones of the dead elk.

"Is it a wolf or a dog, El Trueno?" cried the happy mother. "Let the leader speak, and we will know the truth!"

White Wolf raised his head from his feeding. He was red from breast to toe, but he was happy, and he marked well that the leader pretended to be too busy with his meal to hear the taunting cry of La Sombra. There would be mischief ahead between him and that big-shouldered leader or the still small voice in the heart of the terrier was no prophet.

However, in the meantime there was food for all, and more than all. They ate to deep repletion, and then each took distance a quarter of a mile or more from the others —from the natural protective instinct of beasts who feel a great sleep coming upon them—and curled up in the snow. The restless wind raised clouds of snow dust and buried them warmly, and White Wolf, close beside his foster mother, slept with the rest.

For three days they remained there, feasting. And what poundage of meat went through the stomach of every one of the pack no man would believe.

The fourth day they gnawed the bones.

And the fifth day they turned to the trail again, a pack transformed. Their hollow sides were filled. Their sunken heads were high and their tails carried proudly straight behind. Every ounce of that meat seemed to have been transformed and added to the actual substance of their bodies, so that White Wolf marvelled at them. He himself felt fit enough, but he had not a tithe of the wonderful digestive powers of these rovers of the mountains.

On the fifth day, then, the call of El Trueno rang across the snows: "The time has come, my brothers! The time has come for the hunting trail again, and who but El Trueno shall lead?"

The wolves who were sleeping waked, indeed, and sat up in their places, but not one stood up to follow El Trueno, where he stood sending his mellow thunder across the valley, until the soft and melancholy echo came flying back from the southern Dunkeld hills. They waited, and they turned their heads a little and looked askance at the terrier. And he, in turn, said to his mother:

"What is it, La Sombra? Do they hate me? Will they not take the trail while I am among them? Why do they grin and show all their teeth and look askance at me in this fashion?"

He heard the snort of La Sombra's astonishment and disgust.

"Oh my son," she said, "surely there is no voice of a wolf in your heart! Do you ask why they will not follow El Trueno, and why they look to you? It is because you, son of my loins, flesh of my flesh, blood of my blood, have led at the kill where El Trueno failed. Do you understand?"

"Not I," said White Wolf. "It is true that I held the head of the elk while they pulled her down. But what of that?"

"Modesty," said the mother stiffly, "is well enough in cubs. But you are a cub no longer, but a grown wolf. Speak to that tall braggart, my child. Tell him that he has led them for the last day, and that you, oh my boy, are now king of the pack."

"I?" gasped White Wolf. "Shall I lead them, when I cannot tell the trail of an elk from that of a bull, hardly? Who am I to lead them?"

"You are my son, and that is enough," said La Sombra stiffly. "But tell me this: Do you feel fear to face El Trueno in fair fight, body to body and tooth to tooth for the kingship of the pack?"

"Ay," said White Wolf, as he scanned the hundred and ten or fifteen pounds of the tall frame of the old leader. "I feel fear, La Sombra. The joints of my legs are weak, and the hinges of my jaws are numb. Let him lead, and I shall follow willing, as before!"

He saw a green light of scorn—almost of hatred—in the eyes of La Sombra. "I had sooner see you dead and help the rest of them pick your bones than to see you shamed. Do you hear? And shamed I shall not be through you!"

CHAPTER XXI

SHE stood forward among them, hobbling on her three legs, but her mane bristling with her emotion until she seemed, for the moment, almost her old self, a queen among wolves.

"You wolves of the Dunkeld Hills," said she, "hear me! If my son has not spoken at once, it is not because his heart is weak. You have seen him proved at the kill and you see him proved hereafter, but the gift of words is not his. He leaves such matters to yonder brown thief, El Trueno. And he bids me speak for him in this fashion:

" 'I am not old in the ways of the mountains and I am not wise on the mountain trails, O brothers, for I have been long in the lowlands where men hunted for me as coyotes hunt for a mountain lion. But if you will have a heart without fear for your leader, accept me. As for wisdom, I have an ear for the council and a heart willing to listen to my elders. Rash blood shall not rule the pack that I lead.'

"Wolves of the Dunkeld, do you hear?"

They bayed with one tongue—save for the bristling silence of El Trueno: "We hear, La Sombra, and he speaks well from your mouth."

"As for El Trueno," went on La Sombra, "he bids me say that that clumsy coward is unworthy to be king. But my son will be king in his place by the power of tooth and claw, as the law holds in these mountains."

"The law holds and is strong," they yelled. And they stood up and chanted: "Do you speak, El Trueno?"

If El Trueno had failed at the kill and had seen the White Wolf perform a deed of singular derring do, nevertheless his heart was none the weaker in his breast. He came and stood close to the foster child of La Sombra.

"I have heard this chatter, like the foolish talk of a chipmunk," said El Trueno in his deep voice. "I have heard it and smiled, for it comes from the mother of a white dog, as it seems to me, with the scent of a wolf on his pelt. Now hear me, youngster. This much grace I shall grant you, to take a start from here to the blasted pine on the edge of yonder hill before we begin to hunt you. But if your heart is stronger and you will fight, you will sleep to-night in the bellies of my pack, nevertheless. Behold—I give you the first chance!"

And he dropped his massive head and pretended to be busied in licking up the snow at his feet.

White Wolf—be it spoken to his shame—looked askance at the blasted pine on the edge of the hill and the heart of La Sombra turned to water in her breast. For she knew what her fate would be if her son turned dastard or died in the fight. She had spoken much, and too much, and at the next touch of famine it only needed that the leader should murmur to the pack: "What have we to do with a lamed wolf in our midst?" and the teeth of the Dunkeld pack would worry her bones on that day! So she watched the ears flatten along the neck of her foster son, and she saw him cower and tremble, and her heart ached with a great pang as she strove to throw a little of her own dauntless spirit into the soul of the terrier. It was the first time that White Wolf had stood to a grown lobo in battle and the odds seemed great indeed against him. If El Trueno had charged in this first moment of shrinking, no doubt the end would have been sure and swift, and he delayed until White Wolf stood to his full height and shook himself.

"I am ready," he said in a voice that was almost a whine. "Begin, El Trueno."

"Shall I take the first step against a cub that is not yet grown to his first coat?" sneered El Trueno. "Not I!"

But that speech was mere shamming, and the next instant he had launched himself straight at the bull-terrier. He was an old and practiced fighter, and his leap was famous through the valleys of the San Jacinto Mountains, but the side rip of his fangs cut empty air. For White Wolf had jumped to the side, and now whirled and leaped in turn.

It was very strange to El Trueno. In all the battles he had fought and seen, a valiant wolf cuts and does not bite until the enemy leaves a wide opening. And he tries for throat or flank at once, but White Wolf drove straight at the head.

There was a sharp clash of teeth, and both recoiled deftly from the shock, while the pack howled with delight.

"Are these the ways of the lowland wolves?" snarled El Trueno. "A good way to die, then, in the mountains. Prepare yourself, White Wolf, for I am coming!"

And he came indeed, a brown streak across the snow. Once more the terrier danced to the side, but just a fraction of a second too late to avoid the knife-edge of those reaching fangs. They slit his tender skin down the shoulder and the blood gushed freely.

"The end!" bayed the Dunkeld wolves. "El Trueno conquers again!"

"Peace!" growled old Marco Blanco. "The first blood is not always the last, and the White Wolf is a tower of iron on his legs. Look, my brothers!"

El Trueno, charging again to follow up his first advantage, this time managed to strike his shoulder fairly against that of White Wolf, and the latter was flung a dozen feet away by the shock, but he landed on his feet, and the following slash of the leader encountered tooth for tooth.

And then the pack heard the fighting voice of White Wolf for the first time. How different from the throat tearing snarl of a battling lobo! For it was a shrill yelping whine that sounded like the complaint of a cub, and a rumble of wonder and amusement ran from throat to throat in the circle of spectators. Yet it was not the work of a cub that they were seeing.

White Wolf had taken wings, it seemed. He danced

from the path of El Trueno's lunge. He dipped under the darting head of the tall leader and wrenched away a brown tuft of fur. And then flinging himself at El Trueno again he secured such a grip as the Dunkeld wolves had never seen before. His muzzle was thrust into the gaping mouth of the leader, and his grip was fastened with all his tugging weight upon the lawer jaw of El Trueno.

A marvel indeed, but a marvel that many a man had seen in the pit, where bull-terriers struggle for life or death. No cunning could teach the use of that grip. No training could teach the lightning skill which was needed to get the deadly hold. Only instinct could do these things, and instinct of a long ancestry of warriors was rich in the blood of White Wolf.

It seemed the bare beginning of the struggle, but in truth it was the very end. With that hold fastened upon his nether jaw, El Trueno could not bite except by lifting eighty twisting, jerking pounds of bull-terrier. His jaw muscles were paralyzed with effort, and as he gasped in desperation and struggled hither and yon, the Dunkeld wolves stood stiff and straight and silent in wonder, for they realized that a new power had come upon the range. Only La Sombra was transformed with noisy joy. For she had seen that grip used once before by her foster son and she knew right well the meaning of it.

El Trueno had fought well and bravely but now his spirit wilted like the courage of a big man when the science of a smaller antagonist masters his strength. The ears of the leader fell. His tail drooped. He was wrenching eagerly as ever, but wrenching to get free and turn tail from the struggle—if only that grip would relax. Relax it did, when El Trueno was dizzy and sick with effort and the bloody froth of exhaustion was thick around his mouth and dropping on the snow. The grip relaxed and shifted faster than a hand could move to the throat of the doomed wolf. Deep and true the long punishing jaw sank through loose fur and rolling flesh and found the windpipe—and the life.

And then—through the red trance of White Wolf's joy, he heard the joyous voice of La Sombra:

"Stand back, my son. Let the pack see that the thing is

ended. The quicker his death the greater your glory. Let them see, for El Trueno will never call the Dunkeld wolves to the hunting again!"

So White Wolf rose from his work and stood back, trembling still. But the eyes of El Trueno were glazed and his long red tongue was lolling. One glance sufficed the pack—and then they swarmed in upon the kill.

"Come!" cried La Sombra.

"Faugh!" said White Wolf. "As you are truly my mother, do not join that horrible feast. He is an enemy and he is dead—but he is our own kind. When you and I grow old and weak, shall we go to the same death? It sickens me, La Sombra!"

But she merely stared at him a wondering moment or two, with the same strange green light in her eyes that he had seen there once before. Then she was gone to the banquet with the rest.

As for White Wolf, he drew back a little from the snarling circle. He wanted to have time and peace to lick his wounds. They were not many but they were deep. Skin and muscles had been shorn far in by the trenchant teeth of El Trueno, and the ache of pain throbbed against his brain.

He wanted to think, too.

No doubt it was happiness to lead these strong fighters and tireless runners on the trail. No doubt it was a glory to be ruler where all were kings. But what if he, in his day, should fail as El Trueno had failed and die as El Trueno had died?

A shudder ran through the very soul of White Wolf, and he closed his little triangular black eyes.

But he was young; his strength was great; he had learned such battle lessons on this day as would stand him in stead through a long future of combat; and after all, the taste of an enemy's blood was sweet in his mouth.

Yonder lay the gleaming bones of what had been El Trueno, ruler of the pack, and now the Dunkeld wolves sat on their haunches and with their tongues lolling from their mouths they stared on him with the fond eyes of admiration and deep respect.

So White Wolf stood up and shook the clinging snow

from his body. The sun was a small red disk, drifting down towards the western horizon behind dun-colored clouds, and the cold breath of the evening was already in the air. He pointed his nose at that sun and from his shuddering body there rose a howl that was hardly a single note from the true cry of a hunting wolf.

"Do you hear, brothers of the Dunkeld?"

Deep and true in a chiming chorus he heard them answer: "We hear the voice of our master. Speak to us, White Wolf, for all the ways of the conqueror are wise ways, in our seeming. Speak to us, and tell us what to do."

"Follow!" cried White Wolf. "Follow, and let no wolf come at my side saving only La Sombra."

And he added with a borrowed wisdom: "It is not the fastest four legs but the sharpest wit that keeps wolves fat in winter, and you shall not starve. My brothers, do you hear?"

"We hear, White Wolf!" they sang behind him.

So he jogged on the western trail, with the Tomahawk River flashing like a naked sword behind the thin screening of the winter trees. La Sombra hobbled swiftly at his side. But even she was changed from what she was, and she ran half a yard behind him, saying:

"Did I not say it, child of my body, flesh of my flesh? Did I not speak for you? Tell me, then, when was the heart of a mother ever a liar?"

CHAPTER XXII

"WHAT'S lying south, there? What's on the Dunkeld Hills?" asked Tucker Crosden of his daughter, for she stood at the back door of the cabin and peered intently to the south. "Is there a streak of black clouds, Molly?"

"No," said Molly Crosden. "There's ain't any streak of clouds. Only——"

"Only what?"

"Oh, it ain't nothing."

He finished his coffee and banged the tin cup on the table.

"Come here!" growled Tucker Crosden.

At that she crossed the room and stood before him, half frightened and half weary. And he dropped his broad elbow on the table and pointed a forefinger like a gun at her.

"Keep that fool look out of your eyes!" said Crosden.

"I dunno what look you mean, dad."

"Don't you? I say you do! And keep it out of your eyes. It's the way that your ma looked when she thought that I was gunna hit her. And I ain't gunna stand for it from you. I can take it from my wife, but I don't have to take it from my child, and I ain't gunna take it. You hear me talk?"

"I hear you," said Molly as firmly as she could.

"What if I've done a murder?" he growled. "Do I have to see that murder all over again every time that you look at me? Do I got to find it in your eyes? If I'm damned, should you look at me all the time as if you was seeing me in hell-fire?"

He had worked himself into a fury and now he beat his other fist on the table so that the heavy legs of it clattered upon the floor.

"What drove me to a killing except you womenfolks? What drove me to it except you, hey?"

"I?" cried Molly.

"Yes, you—or your ma—which is the same thing. It was you that put the murder into my hands. You and your ma yellin' for help to the neighbors and sayin' that I was murderin'——"

"Dad, I swear that I never——"

His great right hand fell upon her shoulder and drew her towards him.

"Don't you be lyin', Molly. I mean you nothin' but good. You're a tolerable faithful daughter and you take care of me, and I love you, Molly, but I would rather see you lyin' dead than to see you lyin'!"

She struck her hands together in desperation.

"I won't lie, dad," she cried to him. "I'll try to tell you the whole truth if you'll just gimme a chance."

"I give you the chance now."

"When I heard ma and Aunt Abbey yell out, that night, I got up and dressed and I went to the kitchen and I seen——"

"Don't talk about it. It makes me see red. I ain't gunna hear no more about it. But you tell me why you was lookin' at the Dunkelds like a dyin' calf, will you?"

"Because Mr. Gannaway went over them, going south."

Here big Crosden slumped back in his chair.

"It ain't missing your ma that makes you lonesome, then? It's Gannaway!"

"I ain't said that I was lonesome."

The fierceness slipped away from him and left him only sad.

"You ain't said it, but I've seen it. I ain't complete blind, Molly. I can see what I can see, and of course I know that you ain't a bit happy up here with me. Not a bit!"

"I am happy," said the girl. "In part, I'm mighty happy."

"What part of the time are you happy? The part of the time when I'm away."

"No, no!"

"Because I ain't the kind of company that would make a daughter happy."

"You are, dad, and I love you!"

"For what would you love me, then? Because I make games with you? Because I know how to talk to you about the things that you like?"

"Because you're my father, and there ain't any need of any other reason."

He laughed, and his laughter was like a groan.

"Didn't you say that you was gunna tell me the truth? Then tell it straight out. Gannaway is a gentleman. Gannaway, didn't he sit and tell you stories about the mountains and the storms and things? I never tell you no stories! Wasn't it Gannaway that thought to make you the frame for a doll—and damn badly he made it, too, but doggone me if Tucker Crosden had the sense to think of making you a doll, Molly. No, sir, I never thought of that! Because I ain't the kind of a man that Gannaway is—so good nor so generous nor so kind. Ay Molly, I understand why life is just hell for you here, and why you are looking over the hills for the hope that maybe Gannaway would be coming back."

At this, she could stand it no longer, and she burst into sudden tears and flung herself down on the bunk. The shadow of her father fell across her, and his voice, like a saddened thunder.

"It ain't that I blame you, Molly. I ain't the kind of a man that kids would be fond of."

She reached out blindly and clutched his coat.

"Dad, believe that I love you."

"There is only one thing that ever loved me, really— The King!" said Tucker Crosden. "I tell you, Molly, that when I held him in my arms when he was dyin', and he was smashed up cruel—cruel—his jaws was set and his eyes was glassy already, and he was using all of his strength to keep from yelling with the pain. But when he heard my voice and felt my hand, I tell you, Molly, that he plumb forgot his pain. He lifted his head and he licked my hand; and his head fell on my breast, and he died like that. *He* loved me, and remembering him is how I see that there ain't nothing like love in the other folks and the other dogs that I know. That's why you don't have to lie to me, but tell the truth only. Why, maybe it was worth everything even to have the knowing of a dog like The King! And besides, who knows but what he might come back to me?"

The tears of Molly stopped, and an icy pang went to her heart. Usually it was only in the weariness at the end of the day that the mania seized upon her father, but now he was slipping swiftly into it.

Ay, for he was thundering above her: "What's keeping him back except you, Molly? What's keeping him back, but you, the same way that your mother kept him back before you—God forgive me! What am I talkin' of now?"

For a stroke of daylight sanity seemed to be let in upon the mental confusion of the giant. He lunged through the open door into the snow beyond, and then he lumbered off along his trap line.

What he had said and done hung like a cloudy mirage in the rear of his memory and the brutal exactness of the truth was mercifully shrouded from him.

His trap line presently was taking most of his attention. It wound from the end of Pekan past Silver Lake and to the margin of Lake Gun, a distance of about twelve miles, counting its windings from hill to river and lakeside and back again, and over meadow and bog and forest-heart on the way. He had many traps out for a great variety of game. Mink, marten, fisher, otter, skunk, wolf, and fox were all expected and welcome in his traps and, all required a different finesse, and carrying bait.

Along the upper shore of Lake Pekan, he had several traps for mink, just awash at the edge of the lake, where the bloodthirsty little mink is apt to be hunting, keeping his eye out for the musquash as he runs, or for lesser prey whatever its feather or its fur. Those traps were empty. But he paused to freshen the scent on them, and strode on.

Twelve miles through woods and over deep snow or

slippery snow would in itself have been a day's labor for an ordinary man, but it was nothing for the swinging stride of the big man. He could cover that distance, visiting all of his traps, and skinning the victims where he found them, and then he would make the return not very long after the early winter dark began. Such tremendous journeys—considering the ground—were enough to weary even Tucker Crosden. But for that matter, he was glad to be wearied, because it lifted a dreadful weight of thought and reflection from his mind and made the haunting ghost of The King float farther away in dreams. To work to exhaustion and then sleep without dreams had become his one hope from life. So, on every day, he went the twelve miles through forest and hill and along the edges of the river and the lakes until he came to Lake Gun, and then he turned and swung back by the more southerly route among the taller hills, where there was not such a depth of snow, as a rule, to hamper him, so that the last half of his journey was usually the swiftest. Such a line of traps in such a country, freed from all competition, was bringing him in a rich reward even in such a bad winter season as this.

Yet he could not afford to lose the prey that had been robbed from a trap near the side of Silver Lake. The trap was sprung, but all that it held was a single small foot, above which the leg bone had been bitten off, and the ground was liberally sprinkled around the place with blood and with rich dark fur, like down streaked with frosty tippings. A silver fox, the chief dream of the trapper, had been in this trap, and the enormous, light track of a lynx, printed here and there, told the identity of the murderer.

Tucker Crosden re-set the trap and strode on, cursing, but not a mile away he had his vengeance. Those fluffy tracks of the lynx crossed his way again. Why had not the fool gone to sleep, with the whole of a fox in its belly? No, it had rambled on, and here it had its reward. Between a little creek, whose edges were deeply crusted with brittle ice, Crosden found the destroyer, couched with baleful yellow eyes burning through the winter gloom. He shot the beast and skinned it hastily. His enormous strength enabled him to almost rip a pelt bodily from the dead flesh and soon the body of the lynx was flung on top of some shrubbery, and the trapper went steadily on.

The lynx, a red fox, and a marten were his reward on the outward journey; and if he counted the lynx at eight dollars, the marten at twelve and the fox at seven, he had already a handsome profit for this half of his day's work. And money meant a good deal to Tucker Crosden. There was only one thing which had kept his industry and his patience from amassing a considerable little fortune, and that was the fatal inability to keep from spending all surplusage on bull-terriers. He had been "dog-poor" for many years, but still, he liked money and all that it would bring to his family and himself. So his spirits were rising as he came to the end of the round.

He was ready to turn back for the second and homeward half of his march when he heard something like the distant explosion of a rifle. That is to say, his ear felt the shock, and then distinguished the light ring of vibrating steel in the distance. He hung in his stride and listened sharply. He had many reasons for wanting no wandering hunters or trappers in this valley.

Presently, he made out the sound again, rhythmically repeated, and now he knew it to be a token still more ominous, an axman at work in the woods of the valley of the Seven Sisters!

He started forward at a long-striding run that carried him swiftly through the woods until he came in sight of two things at the same time—the gleaming waters of Lake Rooney in the distance, and nearby, a great mouse-colored dog, covered with curling hair. He had seen that dog before!

He went forward again with greater care, taking note of the musical duet of two axes which now filled the frosty air with their chimings. And presently he made sure of the calamity. A natural little clearing had been taken for a starting point, near a brook—for water—and under the shelter of a circle of low hills which would shut away the greater force of the mountain winds. In the center of this space Dan and Tom Loftus had laid the foundations of a small cabin and they were now felling trees to make their building. All was a wreckage of dead leaves, and fallen trunks, and boughs which had been slashed away. And the giant took note that this was the work of clever axmen and hard laborers! He admitted it even while his heart swelled with anger and jealousy.

Murderers cannot look kindly on any neighbor, he thought.

He went out and stood before them, at last, and they received him with a frank dislike. Tom Loftus picked up his rifle which lay conveniently at hand, but Dan contented himself with drawing a revolver and whistling. Two wolfhounds, and the odd-headed Grampus came swiftly in answer to the call.

"Friendly, ain't you?" said the giant, leaning on his own rifle and surveying them with an unwinking stare.

"We're as friendly as we need," said Tom Loftus. "You talk to him, Dan."

"I ain't got much to say," said Dan Loftus. "All I know is that we've picked out this place for the building of our shack and that we intend to stay here. We got a string of traps to put out. And we don't hanker to bother nobody—and we sure don't hanker to be *bothered!* You hear me talk, big man?"

"It was mighty neighborly," nodded the giant. "There wasn't more'n about five hundred thousand square miles where you boys could of put up your shack and strung your traps. You had to pick out this here valley!"

"Tell him, Dan," said Tom Loftus.

"I'll tell you this," said Dan, gripping his gun tighter. "Me an' my brother figger that you're a skunk, stranger, and maybe a crook! But we don't want none of your trouble and we don't intend to bother *you*. All that we ask out of you, big fellow, is that you keep hands off. We're here right in this spot not because we want to spoil your business or because we give a damn about your business, but because we've followed the trail of the lame wolf and the white wolf two hundred and fifty miles from the lowlands right here to the valley of the Seven Sisters. And he is the fur that we want to get and no other. We got wolf traps, and that is all!"

The scowl of the giant relaxed a little. Men who

marched two or three hundred miles in the search of a bounty on a wolf were not apt to act as informers, after all. As for their abuse of him, he did not resent it because he knew that he had deserved worse language than this from them. So, presently, he said to them: "You keep in your places and I'll not trouble you none. But if your dogs, there, bother my traps, I'll kill 'em! And if you two bother me in my trap line or my shack, I'll come for you. Mind you, I ain't talkin' to hear the sound of my voice. I mean considerable business. You two, you think it over."

And he turned back to complete his march around the trap line.

CHAPTER XXIII

ALL the days that followed were days of war, and therefore every day had its stories, but in such a mass, one must pick and choose, of course. Otherwise, the chronicles of that famous time when White Wolf led the Dunkeld pack would fill thick volumes, with no room for what came after that was, perhaps, more important.

First of all, it is necessary to know how the pack hunted. You have seen them on the trail, running in a compacted group, but that was after the game had been found, and the finding of the game was the hardest thing. The mere pulling down was comparatively simple.

You must consider, too, that the mountains were this year very barren of game. How such barren years come, no one can satisfactorily explain. But one year a district will yield fifteen hundred pelts, and the next year it may give a hundred, or less. There are some who have guessed that, after great plenty, the females grow too fat to reproduce, and therefore nature corrects her own prolificness and follows a swarm with a few scattering individuals. And there are others who declare that these alterations are caused by migration.

But the truth of it is, perhaps, that from time to time plague of one sort or another invades the ranks of the rabbits and the mice, which are to the flesh-eaters what grass is to the creatures of hoof and horn. Then the carnivora find their main source of supply withdrawn and the weaker themselves die of famine in their caves, while the more adventurous attempt a long and desperate journey to unknown regions where conditions may be more favorable.

At any rate, one of these scant seasons had come upon the San Jacinto Mountains, and in order to find living creatures, the wolves were forced to cast abroad a great dragnet which covered a huge territory.

This was the manner in which the net was cast.

When the line of the main direction was established, La Sombra, White Wolf, and Marco Blanco—the leader and the two wisest heads of the pack—ran along the central line at a leisurely speed. Beyond them, upon either side, scattered the rest of the tribe.

They ran at measured intervals of about a thousand yards, or a mile, and as they ran, they weaved from side to side a little, so that the ground was pretty thoroughly covered, what with the help of eye and nose and a wise wolf's consciousness of the best places to look for game of all kinds.

In this way, the net which was dragged was, when a pack numbered some fifteen or sixteen altogether, about ten or twelve miles across, from the tip of one wing to the tip of the other, so that a single day's run covered perhaps four or five hundred square miles of countryside, when the pack was very hungry and meant business.

When game was sighted or nosed, the lucky wolf at once gave tongue, which was heard and repeated by his nearest neighbors, so that in a very few seconds the signal had run along the entire line and the pack began to converge, not directly to one side or to the other, but slanting, along the line which the baying of the first indicated was that of the flight. And if the chase lasted for any length of time, the whole group was sure to be in on the kill. Or, at least, there would soon be plenty present to handle anything up to a grizzly.

Bearing this in mind, you can see why a big pack may keep fat while a small pack grows starvation thin. And those whom White Wolf led prospered exceedingly. Because they had at their head a leader who prevented all wrangling, and not a tooth was bared in his presence, so long as fortune ran well. In the second place, that young leader was using the brains of two exceptionally gifted wolves in the choice of the country over which he led the pack.

Moreover, running in a central position, the slowness of the crippled La Sombra and the short-legged terrier were compensated, to a certain extent, and usually they were up for the kill before the outermost members from the farthest wing of the pack had arrived.

Even with such cunning planning and careful work, they had many and many a lean day, and once their fast was broken in a strange way indeed, for while they were coursing slowly over the lower valley of the Tomahawk River, a wolverine was sighted by Marco Blanco himself —a wolverine busy on the top of the dam of a colony of beavers, digging up the surface with his powerful claws.

Marco Blanco gave one short cry, and this in turn was echoed softly up and down the long line which began to converge rapidly towards the point of information. So that, in a surprisingly short time, fifteen lean-bodied lobos lay in the naked autumn brush and looked down on the strange scene.

As for White Wolf, he wanted to leap down to the place at once, tear the wolverine to bits, and then continue the digging for themselves, but La Sombra checked him. She had only to point out that that beaver dam was thoroughly frozen, now, and the earth was as strong as hard wood. What could the comparatively feeble claws of a wolf effect in such a material? But the wolverine is equipped for the struggle with fate as hardly another animal in the world, not even excepting the omnipotent fisher. He has claws like the claws of a bear, with which he can chisel into anything but rock, and he has a positively gigantic strength locked in his hump-backed body and short arms. Yet even that wolverine was having a bitter hard job of it. His claws began to wear down, and even to break. His feet bled. But still the glutton continued for the wolverine is haunted by a dreadful devil of famine which never leaves the pit of its belly. And beneath that ridge of hard dirt he knew that there was a chance for filling his maw!

So he mined away, and the smell of the blood which he shed from his cut feet made the mouths of the watching wolves water, for the wind was blowing softly from the dam to them. They waited, then, until he was down to earth that was not frozen, and as soon as he reached the water beneath and they saw that the mud was beginning to fly, the whole flock came down at him with a sneaking rush.

They had a battle on their hands, then, that White Wolf, for one, would never forget. The wolverine was hardly a quarter the size of the least of them, but it had mysteriously condensed in its body the strength of any two lobos. It fought with the fury of the damned, but powerful jaws held it from every side, and it died, literally —in the air.

Wolverine is meat which only famine makes palatable to the most desperate wolf, but the Dunkeld pack was hard-pressed, and so the rank body of the glutton was devoured, and after that, they worked on down to the water of the dam and there they came to the soft-bodied beavers. Very valiant beavers, too, willing to wield their chisel teeth heartily in their own defense, but what could a beaver do with the teeth of a lobo in its back?

So the whole pack feasted until it could feast no longer, and slept that night the sleep of the blessed.

There was another adventure almost as strange. A strange animal was scented in the marshes of the upper Winnemago and followed over the Winnemago hills until, in the valley of the Seven Sisters, the pack sighted a seven foot monster with a huge head mounted upon long, spindling legs—a moose driven far south from its usual range!

They reached it on the edge of a lake, but they found it a more deadly foe than any elk. Two of the younger wolves went down before White Wolf made his flying leap and gripped the moose by the nose with jaws of fire. It could have split him in two with one blow of its splay forefeet, but the first instinct was to rear back from the painful leech, and in that moment the pack had closed on the foe.

Watching them as they swarmed upon the fallen giant and glutted themselves with the meat, a sudden disgust rose in the heart of White Wolf, a rush of aversion which he could not explain. He only knew that wolves and wolf-ways were to him utterly abhorrent and so he turned and trotted through the woods by Muncie Lake until, from the top of a low hill, he saw the narrow steel face of Pekan Lake before him, and near the head of the smaller body of water a smoke column that rolled south and south steadily through the trees.

It stopped White Wolf with a shock. It stopped him with a thrilling impulse towards temptation such as he had never felt before.

He could not understand it. What he saw was a drift of wood-smoke, made from the house of that man whose planted steel teeth had imprisoned La Sombra, one fatal evening; but what he thought of was the mellow lowlands of a summer's day, with many such drifts of smoke as this streaked across the face of the landscape, and the lowing of the cattle, and the scent of the grain fields, and the sweetness of drying hay everywhere in the air.

It was a most pleasant picture to the heart of White Wolf, but what pleased him most of all—no doubt because of the danger in it—was the thought of the houses of Man, and the revel and the play of the dogs, and their foolishly sharp, barking voices. And he thought, too, of the voices of Man himself—and sudden glimpses of the monster in the distance. Most of all, he remembered how the two who followed the six hounds on the edge of the Winnemago had roused their dogs to maddest courage by a mere shout or two.

Here in the mountains, it was very well, to be sure, and to be the king of a wolf pack was a triumph and an honor, considering his age. However, for this single moment he was wishing with all his heart to be back in the lowlands—and not with the Dunkeld pack trailing at his heels.

He had come this far in thoughts—not in his understanding, but in the pictures and the emotions—when he heard an evil, sneering voice of a fox behind him, saying: "look well, White Wolf! It is a sign of the slavery to come. Look well, White Wolf!"

He turned him about and saw that same old mangy red fox whom he and La Sombra had met as they were climbing up the valley of the Winnemago with the dread of the dog-pack in their hearts; the same fox, with the same broken-toothed grin. White Wolf shuddered with disgust and with contempt.

CHAPTER XXIV

HE felt fear, too, for there is no creature that runs the wild which loves the fox and is free from a sort of superstitious dread of it. For the excellent reason that even the wisdom of the grizzly may be understood, and the thoughtfulness of the lobo has its limitations, but the fox lives just beyond, and on that horizon line where the dim comprehension of all of two worlds is possible. So White Wolf felt fear mingled with hatred and disgust. This was not only a fox, but it was an unclean beast, weighed down with age and disease. Its eyes were red; and that pride of every self-respecting fox, the well-plumed tail, was a mere draggled rag, filled with dried mud and twigs.

The mockery with which it regarded White Wolf had a double edge, for a creature so near to a miserable grave should have had no thought except for its own wretchedness.

"You are not in the lowlands, after all?" said White Wolf.

"You see me here!" sneered the fox. "I am not what I once was, and after the dogs ran me once, I saw that the second time would see my finish. There is little left in me. Barely enough speed to let me scoff at those fat-sided fools, the wolves. Are you a wolf, my young friend?"

"I cannot hear you," said White Wolf, canting his head to one side. "For the wind blows from me to you. Will you come a little nearer?"

The fox grinned and showed its broken tooth again.

"Even when I was a young cub," it said, "I was not such a fool as to be taken in a trap as clumsy as this! Now, White Wolf, stay where you are and I shall sit here, for I know what speed you have for a hundred yards or so and this distance is just comfortable. No more, no less! so I ask you again: Are you a wolf?"

"Old scoundrel," said the terrier, fairly whining with rage, "ask your nose! What does it tell you?"

"It tells me a disgusting thing—wolf! But that may be a borrowed scent. And, taking you by and large, I must admit that I have never seen a wolf exactly like you before!"

"I have heard the same thing before," said the bull-terrier. And he wagged his tail complacently. "However, it seems that even an old fox like you still can learn what a wolf may be!"

"I am not complimenting you, altogether," said Red Fox dryly. "As a matter of fact, I have never before heard of a wolf with such an ugly head as yours or such wicked little eyes. And certainly I have never seen one with such a perfectly ridiculous tail which is never still."

White Wolf turned his head and looked back.

"Every wolf to its own liking!" said he. "I think that my tail does very well!"

"You *would* think so," said the fox. "However, it seems to me that you might have the sense to teach your tail dignified manners even if it hasn't dignified looks."

White Wolf licked his lips and strove to edge a little nearer, but the fox instantly took a greater distance.

He went on: "I have seen a wolf—a friend of yours, by the way—with a tail which even a fox might look upon with some toleration, although foxes, as even you must know, have the most beautiful tails in the world."

"I have noticed yours," said White Wolf with some point.

But the fox merely smiled, for his self-content was apparently an unshakeable world.

"My salad days are over," said he. "But I have seen the time when fifty dogs and almost as many men and horses have broken their hearts to get this same tail of mine."

"That," said White Wolf, "is absurd!"

"You would think so, of course," said the fox. "You are not very well educated, as even a cub could see. But culture in a wolf is something which I long ago gave over trying to find. However, I have a foolish partiality for you."

"I am not going to thank you," snarled White Wolf.

"I don't ask you to."

"But I should like to know what has made you presume to make an exception of me?"

"In the first place," said the veteran, tipping his head a trifle to one side, "in the first place, it is because you are such a caricature of a wolf!"

"So!" cried White Wolf, leaping up, bristling with impatient anger. "Have I not a pair of eyes and four feet and—a set of strong teeth, old villain?"

"You have, exactly," said the other with his evil grin. "And so has a fox—and so has a lynx—and finally, so has a dog, my dear young friend!"

He said this with such an innuendo at the close, and with such a secret smile of satisfaction, that White Wolf growled:

"You are talking the worst kind of nonsense, Red Fox. Let me tell you, in a word, that I know all about dogs, and they are a disgusting lot. I have studied them with eye and ear and tooth. And there is nothing to be said for them. Therefore, if you insist on comparing me with them, I shall listen to you no longer!"

"You cannot help yourself," grinned the mangy fox. "I can run behind you and shout my truths after you, so that you may as well sit still and listen to them! But what I wanted to talk to you about most of all, I haven't touched on, as yet."

"You may keep it to yourself," said White Wolf. "I haven't the slightest value for what you have to say."

"That is because you are sulky, just now. However, you will think it over in the little time that is left to you."

"What may you mean by that?"

"I mean, the little time that is left before the lone wolf takes you in hand and makes a meal of you—the Black Wolf, I mean, of course! It seems that I have touched you there!"

It was a very tender point with White Wolf. Now that he was grown to his full size and within an ace of his full strength, there were not very many things in the forest that he really feared, but the Black Wolf remained to him a phantom of dread—just as though he were still an unmatured puppy and the Black Wolf greater and huger than ever.

He said, gravely: "I have not done with Black Wolf. Long ago I promised him that one day I should take him by the throat and shake the life out of him. When you see him again, you may remind him that I am a wolf of my word and that I shall keep my promise."

"I have told him already," grinned the mischiefmaker. "And he promises to tear you to bits the first time that he can find you away from the pack. Yet he almost takes scorn, he says, to go out of his way for the killing of a wolf weak enough to need the help of a pack to make its kills. He himself hunts alone and stands alone. There is no other like him for strength and for beauty—among the wolves of the San Jacinto Mountains."

"I am glad of his glory," said the terrier. "It will be so much the more for me to win. I have fought three wolves, Red Fox, and three wolves are dead. May Black Wolf be the fourth."

"However that may be," said the fox, "there is still the matter of that smoke for me to touch upon."

White Wolf started.

"What devil has put the smoke into your mind?" he asked.

"Oh, you were watching it, just now. And you put a wonder into my mind."

"Will you tell me what that wonder is?"

"I could not help thinking that—which is most unlikely—if you dispose of Black Wolf, you will still have the Man to deal with."

White Wolf trembled with excitement.

"I have thought of that, too," said he, "and if his throat is ever in reach of my spring, he shall die, Red Fox!"

"So you say now," scoffed the old fox. "But let me tell you, my dear young friend, that if you ever have the courage to face him, you will never have the strength to endure so much as the mere weight of his eye. I, Red Fox, swear it. And I say, that I cannot tell which is the most dreadful end, to be buried in the belly of Black Wolf, dead, or buried in the house of the Man, a slave, which is a living death!"

"You do me too much wrong!" cried White Wolf. "I could never serve. Am I not a free wolf and the head of a clan? Yes, by the mother who bore me!"

"Ah!" said Red Fox. "And what mother bore you, pray?"

"Old fool!" cried the terrier. "Every wolf and coyote and fox in the mountains knows the truth. I am the son of La Sombra, and the very chipmunks would tell you the same."

"As for chipmunks and such other noisy idiots," said Red Fox, "they do not matter greatly. But still I cannot help asking if you have never wondered how La Sombra could be your mother?"

"Stuff!" said White Wolf. "I am going. You do nothing but irritate me, and that is your pleasure! Good-bye!"

"Stay!" said Red Fox, trotting slowly in pursuit and calling aloud. "I wish that you would stop for my sake at the edge of the lake and look carefully at your image in it."

"I have seen myself before," said White Wolf. "You think that I am blind?"

"Not blind in the eye but in the brain. Look again, oh White Wolf, and study the thing that you see, and then if you ever return to the pack, compare yourself with La Sombra and ask yourself how she could ever be your mother!"

"I shall send the pack to hunt you, you scoundrel!" cried White Wolf. "Be sure that I have not done with you!"

But the old fox showed his broken tooth again as he laughed, silently, and when White Wolf looked over his shoulder again at the edge of the trees, he saw the fox still sitting at the same place, still laughing—and deeply contented with the thing which he had performed on this day!

CHAPTER XXV

However, such speeches cannot fall on the soil of a young brain without bringing forth some fruit. And when White Wolf came to the edge of Pekan Lake, he jumped to a stone a dozen feet from the shore and examined himself with a scrupulous attention in the glasslike waters.

Of course, as he had said, he had seen himself many and many a time when he was swimming, but he had never before considered himself with care; and what a world of difference there is between a hasty glance and a well-considered scrutiny!

There was a vast gap between the things that he was and the things that composed the wolves of the pack. Certainly the mangy old red fox was himself far more similar to the heroes of the Dunkeld pack. For instance, except on the shoulders at times, who could see so much as a muscle through the long hair of a wolf? And here were his own lithe muscles scattered in an intermingling network across his whole body. Truly his tail was far, far from the tail of a wolf, and his long, wedge-shaped head with its little triangular black eyes was not like the noble head of a wolf.

"Faugh!" said White Wolf with a little shudder of disgust. "I am almost as much like a snake as I am like a wolf. It is no wonder that the pack does not love me. And even La Sombra—does she love me, except because I protect her and bring her to the chance of food? Who can tell? No, I am the ugliest brute in the whole range of the San Jacinto Mountains, and there is no doubt about it!"

It had been an old torment to him. When the kill was made and the flesh was eaten, each wolf went off and lay down by itself, and if White Wolf himself—leader though he was—came too near to the sleeper, there was an instant wakening, and a murderous growl. For his own part, he loved companionship, he loved talk, foolish or wise, and he delighted in ridiculous play, so that La Sombra had often said to him soberly: "Ah, my son, you are more cub than wolf! Is there no more dignity in the leader of the Dunkeld pack?"

But that was not all. The young wolves of the pack admired him and the old wolves respected him but they never opened their hearts to him, and if they yelled when he took his famous head-hold on an elk at bay, he felt that it was rather because they knew their appetites were about to be gratified than because they loved him and rejoiced in his fame. No eye brightened when he came among them. They remained critically aloof, and something in the heart of the young dog remained starved.

Now the wind ceased, and when he came to the next clearing, he saw the smoke column rising steadily like a thin arm stretched futilely towards the sky. Towards this he kept on his way, marveling what had told the red fox that this was the destination which he had had in mind.

The lessons of La Sombra were not forgotten. Approaching this dreadful objective, he came carefully up the wind, noting all the thronging and ominous scents—food raw and cooked, and iron, and the scent of the sharp voice that kills far off, and mingled with all this, the scent of Man.

But he would not turn back. If his hair bristled with dread, and if he stopped when he first heard the human voices, still he went on again, until he came to the very edge of the clearing and crouched behind a stump.

A rabbit rose before him and fled with frightened leaps to the center of the open space where Gannaway and Molly Crosden sat together on a fallen log. The rabbit took shelter between them, and the heart of White Wolf leaped into his throat.

For of course, the first and oldest law that had been taught to him concerning Man was that all the wild things dreaded him, and all that lived in the woods was his prey. Even the armored porcupine was an easy victim to Man, and the skunk died at his coming. How came it, then, that the rabbit dared to run to these two in the extremity of its terror and that it now took hiding between them?

The slender hand of the girl reached down—and the soul of White Wolf stood still to see that the little frightened thing put up its ears and brightened its eyes as though it loved the touch!

White Wolf closed his eyes tightly and looked again but the picture had not changed.

Behold, the rabbit, the common prey of all who run in the wilds, the tenderest and most foolish of all, with only the wit of its long hind legs to save it from easy destruction, seemed safe among all-devouring Man! Yes, it fled to them for shelter, and remained close to their feet!

Nor was that all that was strange to the bull-terrier. He vowed that he would report to La Sombra the big grey squirrel which recklessly flaunted itself across the opening and, at will, darted up to the shoulder of the girl, or to her lap, or stole a fragment of the peeling from the potatoes which she was preparing in the pan on her knees.

Ay, on the limbs of this child there was the skin of a fawn—a borrowed pelt to keep her warm. And yet the little rabbit was safe at her feet—the squirrel was safe in spite of its theft! All of these miracles must be written down in his heart of hearts and repeated. They would take much explaining from Mother Wolf, to be sure!

They spoke.

He had heard the voices of men before, but ever on a common key of harshness—shoutings of the hunters, as they cheered on the dogs, sounds to be dreaded by the fugitive wolves, and in the life of White Wolf the voice of man had always been the voice of danger. Truly, when from time to time he and La Sombra skulked near the houses in the lowlands by night, they now and then heard distant, musical fragments of speech. But though such music had never failed to bring up a stir of joy and sorrow in his heart, he had hardly connected them with Man himself.

But now he heard for the first time gentle question and gentle response and it was a miracle to be long brooded upon—stranger than the bravery of the rabbit, the confidence of the squirrel in the presence of these destroyers.

"There's this thing to think of, Molly," said Gannaway. "You're not happy here. You've confessed that yourself!"

"Oh, ay," sighed Molly, and the very heart of the bull-terrier softened at the tone of her sadness, "i'm not terrible happy here, but mostly folks don't seem to be so awful happy any place. There's always troubles around, someplace."

"For men and women. But not for children, I trust. I trust, not for children! No, no, Molly, let us be true to one another and speak frankly. Will you do that?"

She lifted her wise young head and smiled crookedly at him.

"I dunno, Mr. Gannaway. Sure, I'd like to talk. But I dunno that it would be a good thing. Most likely it's better that you should guess some things and not know them at all!"

He smiled in turn, but very sadly.

"I understand. If you were to tell me the truth of your unhappiness, then there would be nothing left to me, as an honorable man, except to get you away from these mountains and back to your mother?"

"Why should it be up to you? Why should me being unhappy mean that much to you?" asked Molly. "Why should it be your duty? You ain't no kin of mine?"

"I'm a man, Molly, and you're a child, and every man in this world owes a duty to every child in it, God knows. We owe you happiness, my dear."

She studied this speech with her lips parted a little.

"That's a grand thing to say," said Molly. "But supposing that I was to leave dad—why, when I was down yonder in the plains with mother, there wouldn't be no happiness for me, really. I would be thinking of how terrible lonely this here cabin can be. Lonesomeness is like a sort of another person in that house, setting in the corner when your back is turned, Mr. Gannaway!"

Gannaway made a turn up and down the clearing, and the terrier crouched lower as the man stood up and moved. Here was a man like any other that had ever been seen by the terrier, as tall and as strong, and with the old dreadful scents of iron and gunpowder strong on him, and a keen axe in his hand, for he had been chopping wood when Molly came out to him. Yet, armed though he was, every tone of his voice struck upon the ear of White Wolf like music and ran along secret, subtle nerves to his inmost heart, and opened unexpected doors in it, and hung there for a long, sweet, sad moment, like echoes in a deep ravine.

"I have to go off on another trip soon, Molly. And I hate to go. This is a thing that I've dreaded to talk to you about. Because you're a child. But I *have* to talk to you about it, because sorrow has made you something of a woman, too, my dear. And this is the thing that I have to say: Your father is not better now than he was a few weeks ago, when I came down from the Winnemagos on that other trip."

"Ay," assented Molly, "he's not better."

"The King is in his mind more than ever, I suppose."

"Ay, The King is in his mind—every evening!"

"And how many times in the day, too, when he's off walking his trap line?"

"I dunno," said Molly. "I don't like to think of it."

"And," cried Gannaway with a sudden great effort, "when that—excitement—takes hold of him, do you know that I'm afraid of him?"

She sat up a little straighter and stared with a white face.

"What are you gunna say, Mr. Gannaway?"

"Oh, you know what I'm going to say, Molly dear. I'm going to say that your father, on the subject of The King, is a dangerous man—dangerous to me, though I'm his friend. And dangerous even to you, though you're his daughter whom he loves!"

Molly made no answer, twisting the blind fingers of one hand into the blind fingers of the other.

"And that's why I'm going to take you away, Molly my dear. You're going away with me. You're going to go back to the house and take what you need, and you're going to start off with me. Quickly because we need every minute of time that we can get!"

There was a flash of light in the face of the child, but then she shook her head slowly.

"He would catch us," said Molly. "And if he caught us—"

Gannaway loosened his collar a little.

"It's a chance I have to take," he said huskily. "And it's a chance that you have to take. Molly, hurry to the house and get what you need—that pair of heavy new moccasins, for one thing."

She had made up her mind, by this time, and she could smile at him as she shook her head, so fixed was her determination.

"Jiminy, Mr. Gannaway," said she, "I know what dad meant when he said that you was a white man. Because you are—most awfully much. Maybe there is a mite of—danger. When he gets to talking about The King he sort of loses himself and thinks that everybody is against him—even me—even you! But still—if we was to go and even if we was to get away, what would happen when he come back to the cabin and found himself alone in it? Oh, I ain't much company for him, but I'm something. The things that I do to take care of him, they help him a little.

And if I was to go, he'd be lost for good and all. And he'd never come back to himself agin! You tell me man to man if that ain't right!"

And Gannaway, pale of face and stricken, strove to lie and found that the necessary words stuck in his throat.

A shadow stirred and slipped to the side of White Wolf, and he heard the ominous whisper of La Sombra:

"See if the dread that was in me was not a true thing and no foolish ghost! You are here! Oh my son, do you not know that the traps of Man are of many kinds and that he does not catch with teeth of iron only? Swiftly, come with me!"

The terrier slunk down-headed behind her, but with such a careless footfall that the noise called the eyes of the girl after them and she sprang up with a cry.

"What is it, Molly?"

"A wolf—and something white behind it—Mr. Gannaway, could it be the White Wolf?"

CHAPTER XXVI

THEY left the bones of the fallen moose on the next day and by the will of Marco Blanco they headed over the hills and into the lower Dunkeld valley, swimming the River of the Seven Sisters on the way.

They were defiling through a narrow pass among the Dunkeld Hills when a sharp, querulous voice rang from a rock on the edge of the cañon, and looking up, White

Wolf saw Red Fox sitting on a crag, perilously near to the edge, but contemptuous of the danger of falling, so it seemed.

"Are these the wolves of the Dunkeld pack?" cried the fox.

"These are they," howled Marco Blanco. "What will you have of us, oh mangy devil?"

"Are these the wolves, then, whose leader runs last on the hunting trail?"

"Come down, little one," answered La Sombra in a snarling rage, "and look into the mouth of that slow-footed leader. For he carries the reason for his leadership in his mouth and in no other place."

"It is the lame wolf and there is her bastard son beside her," said Red Fox, peering down at them, with half his old body seeming to hang over the ledge. "Tell me, wise mother, did you not find him with the new scent of man on him yesterday?"

"May the buzzards pick your bones before night!" howled La Sombra. "Do not heed him, brethren. Let us go on."

But the wolf-pack had paused, and now they sat on their haunches and pointed their noses upwards, with their bright eyes fixed upon the red interloper above.

"So—you are like a circle of cubs ready to receive wisdom from their father. Then listen to me, little ones! Is it wolf-dog or dog-wolf who leads you? If his mother is La Sombra, look at her face and look at his. Does his tail save him from the cold of the snow when he sits on it? Does his tail keep his nose warm of a night? Speak to me, little ones, and tell me if you are wolves, and blind also!"

They answered him with a yell of indignation, and one or two of the younger braves attempted stupidly to mount the sheer face of the rock-wall. Red Fox merely laughed from his perch high above them.

"It is well!" said he. "I have planted the seed and it shall grow. Look on him, wolves, and speak truth and see clearly. But one thing more, to teach you that I am your friend in all things, and the picker of the bones which you leave behind you in your kills—the heavy-headed liar and braggart, the Black Wolf, thought the wind was in his heels and he chased me this morning, because even my mangy skin looked like food in his eye. He chased me, and may he die and rot for it. He chased me, but now I am here, and he is lying in a little cave on the bank of the Dunkeld River—a shallow little cave where three could come at him at once! Do you hear me, brothers?"

"We hear you!" they yelled in ecstatic answer, for the Black Wolf was a lone monster whose evil saying concerning the pack had sent a ripple of laughter through all the wild folk who hunted over the mountains of the San Jacinto range. "We hear you, and we are gone."

"As for what I tell you of your leader, brethren of the Dunkeld, I give it in charity out of the fullness of my wisdom. Come to me when you would learn more, and I shall tell you all. It is a tale worth the knowing. And so, farewell!"

And White Wolf, quivering with rage, looked up as the pack swept down towards the throat of the cañon and saw the broken fang of the old fox as the latter smiled.

"Have you heard?" asked La Sombra bitterly as she hobbled at the side of her foster son. "Ah, that ever such words should be spoken by a cur of a fox about a son of mine—a son of my loins, my flesh, my body and blood! And that the pack should have heard it—and listened as if they half believed! What differences are there between us that my love for you cannot swallow? Tell me, White Wolf?"

In that moment of tenderness, he edged a little closer to her.

"Let the fox talk and the pack listen. They need me still for the kill and they will keep me, unless old Marco Blanco edges me from my place. Have you seen him talking with the young wolves?"

"Am I blind?" gasped La Sombra, laboring heavily in her stride. "I have seen it. And I have heard him talk in a great way of the other days, and of the kills he has made running at the head of a greater pack than ever was that of the Dunkeld Hills! The traitor has evil in his heart towards us, my son. But trust in me, and all shall yet be well. Now run, for the goal is Black Wolf, to-night!"

Truly he ran with all his power through the pinewoods

and the cedars below, and leaping ditch and creek in the trail of the pack, while the moon rose high above the black mountains and piled the snow-heaped boughs of the evergreens with loaded silver out of fairyland.

They reached the broad lands of the valley beneath. They crossed them to the woods beside the Dunkeld, and then down the river itself, running softly, without voice, and heading full against the stiff wind.

But, struggle as he might, in the course of that hard run the White Wolf was far behind, and all he knew of the first view of the quarry was a chorus of yelps and snarlings and one loud howl of pain from far ahead.

When he came up with the place, he saw a dying member of the pack lying in the mouth of the cave where, as Red Fox had promised, they had found the monster. From thence, the trail carried him across the river and through the water, to the farther lofty bank. There stood Black Wolf with the moonshine gilding him, on the top of the bank, and with his mane fluffed up in his fighting fury he seemed greater than a mountain lion.

The Dunkeld wolves had waited for their white leader at this unpleasant pass, but now they charged en masse up the slope of crumbling gravel and sliding sand. They reached the topmost edge with their impetus gone, and they were met by a whirlwind of destruction. White Wolf had seen great fighting since he first saw the light of day, but never any like this. There was twice the bulk of an ordinary wolf in the great black lobo, and there seemed to be threefold the strength. He fairly tore out the throat of the first of the pack to reach the ledge and sent it choking and dying to the bottom of the rise. He reached the jugular vein of the second—and the rest recoiled in terror from the destroyer—all except White Wolf, who clambered hard up the yielding face of the slope, clamoring in his foolish, thin voice: "Give room to me! The White Wolf is come! Black devil, this is the day of your death—"

"It is the day of death for one of us!" growled the monster. "But do you dare to face me alone?"

White Wolf, staggering on the edge of the upper slope, saw destruction rush at him. There was no chance to dodge. All he could do was to take the blow, and the sharp fangs of the giant ripped along his neck and through the cushioning muscles of his shoulder.

Such a stroke had never been received by the terrier before. Such a stroke he had never dreamed in the power of any wolf. And the force and the pain of it tumbled him disgracefully, head over heels, to the bottom of the rise.

What a yell of dismay and rage rose from the Dunkeld pack at that fall! And White Wolf, struggling blindly to rush the slope again, was blocked by La Sombra, who threw herself bodily before him and prevented him from coming at his goal.

"Are you mad?" she panted. "Do you wish to give yourself to his jaws? He has killed three, and this is not his day to go down. Will you make yourself the fourth?"

Her foster son was half-blinded with rage, but not blinded altogether, and he saw that there was truth in what she said. So he danced up and down, regardless of the blood that streamed forth and then caked upon his shoulder.

"Come to me, Black Wolf!" he yelled. "Or give me a chance to climb the bank and meet you on fair ground."

"What talk is this of giving?" snarled the giant. "When I give, I give death, and your turn almost came to you tonight. Have you heard me, White Wolf? I see your young wolves climbing yonder to take me in the side while the rest of you take me in the front. So I am gone. Remember me, wolves of the Dunkeld. I leave three dead ones. Come to me again, and I shall claim still more. What? Are you wolves? No, but coyotes! I scorn you. See if there is so much as a scratch upon my front? And then turn and see your dead and see your white leader. Is he white now? He is the color of mud and of blood. Farewell!"

He was gone, and La Sombra, licking the shoulder of her son till it was clean, whispered at his ear: "There will be trouble. You have missed in the kill as El Trueno missed in the kill before you. Be prepared. There is hunger in their eyes—not for food but for mischief. There may be more fighting, White Wolf, before the dawn."

He looked across at the pack. There were eight left

alive, and they sat together in a close mass, facing him, with old Marco Blanco in the center and pushed a little to the front. He lay down, now, and licked his paws, and when he spoke it was with a cruel sidewise glance.

"How many are dead to-night?" he asked.

The others looked full in the face of White Wolf with unwinking stares, but they answered Marco Blanco with solemn voices:

"There are three dead to-night, Marco Blanco."

"Ah," said the old wolf, "three strong wolves! And they are dead. But surely they are the first in a long time. It is a long, long time since another has died from our brothers!"

Still they stared solemnly at White Wolf as they answered: "Marco Blanco, two died when the moose fell. They paid for the meat which is still in our bellies, and they paid with their lives!"

Marco Blanco stood up and shook his hide savagely. "What?" cried he. "Is is true? Have you a leader who feeds you on your own flesh?"

"What shall I say to them?" asked White Wolf anxiously of his mother.

There was an ominous growl for answer.

"Tell them—that their own rashness caused the loss. And it was the steepness of the bank that allowed Black Wolf to destroy the two—say that and—"

But White Wolf strode a stiff-legged step or two towards them and then sank upon his belly with his legs strongly set beneath him and ready to launch him into the air. He looked down the line of savage faces, one by one, and their glances shifted away from him, and they shrugged the loose skin along their backs. Plainly they dreaded him still.

"Now," said he, "I shall not speak to defend myself. That I have led you into many dangers I know, but I have kept you fat. Where is there a rib to be seen in the Dunkeld pack? However, I shall not waste much speaking on wolves who listen to the voices of mangy foxes and of outcasts. This is the thing that I say: There is a law in these matters. I have missed in the kill. And therefore I am no longer worthy of leading. But you will fight me one by one and not two by two. Stand up, then, the best of you. What, Marco Blanco, do you not hear me?"

But greatly as Marco Blanco might have yearned for the sole leadership of the pack, he wished no single combat with this dreadful fighter. So he lolled his tongue and muttered: "Are we to have a law for the son of the lame wolf, who sneaks to the houses of men and comes back with the stink of man upon his pelt? Tell me, brothers, is there to be the law for this, also?"

There was a dangerous stir in the pack, so that La Sombra winced to the ground and bared her fangs, ready to leap to the battle and fight to save the rear of her foster child from attack, at least. They should not die without exacting tribute and great tribute from the Dunkeld wolves.

But White Wolf did not shrink now from the naked face of danger.

He stood up and walking to the place of Marco Blanco, he snarled above the head of that veteran warrior:

"Evil fall to the lot of your belly, Marco Blanco! I have honored you and make you great in the pack, and you have used my kindness to destroy me with them. But if you will not fight, call for the best and the bravest of your friends and let him come with you. You are old, though your teeth are still strong. Stand up, then, and let your best comrade stand up with you. I, the White Wolf, shall fight you together. For I tell you, wolves of the Dunkeld, that my heart is big with scorn of you. Look, now, I give you my side and my flank to jump it. I walk here before you and I invite you. Who moves? Who leaps? What, not one? Is the red fox a true speaker? Are these only the souls of coyotes in the pelts of wolves? Faugh! I leave you, and I despise you. Let no one follow me. Marco Blanco, take the pack, for I give it to you freely. Farewell!"

He passed to La Sombra, and she whined before him: "Are we outcasts, also?"

"Peace, La Sombra," said he. "It is no time for much speaking. Let us go, for my heart is sick in me!"

CHAPTER XXVII

LA SOMBRA was sick, and very, very sick, otherwise perhaps nothing that followed would have taken place. It was the change in her situation and the shock to her pride as much as anything that brought this sickness on. She had been like a queen in the pack while White Wolf ruled those warriors of the Dunkeld Hills. Now they were thrust out, and she was never weary of whining:

"If you had stayed, all would have been well. There was nothing to make you go. Could Marco Blanco have driven you? No, and the others would never have been willing to pay the price in fighting the two of us. But you, like a young and proud fool, would not stay. Was the mere fact that they were discontented on that day enough to send you off? Would you have them think you perfect every instant of your leadership? Tush, White Wolf! What would have become of you and the rest of my litter if I had left you when you all complained? Ay, and howled at me if I came home without raw meat for you, and bit at my face and pinched my fur and tugged at it!"

"This is all very well," answered her foster son stiffly, looking gloomily around him on the wretched little cave where they had taken shelter near the foot of Pekan Lake, on the southern face of a hill. "This is all very well, but you speak of children, and I speak of grown wolves."

"Let me tell you a thing that is worth much knowing. Wolves have died young that might have died old if they had only dreamed of it, but I shall tell you, that if one strong wolf is wise and brave and noble, ten strong wolves all gathered together are just ten cubs—foolish, easily angered, easily frightened, and with no real sense. And that is why, when they come together, they appoint one wolf to do their thinking for them. It is not, perhaps, that he is much wiser than the rest. Perhaps he has nothing but a strong pair of jaws, but it is better to have one stupid mind controlling affairs than it is to have ten muddlers all speaking at the same time, and that is why I say that the Dunkeld Pack will come to ruin, now. Marco Blanco is not only a traitor, but he is too old to lead. He will miss every kill and they will laugh in his face. They will all come to ruin—and this might all have been avoided if you, my son, had swallowed your pride and switched your tail in their faces——

"But now we are outcasts. The winter is long and cold. And ah, how the wind moans! I am sick. I fear that I shall never live to be strong again, for the heart is gone out of me!"

He regarded her helplessly. But since she persisted in lying with her body curled up and her eyes closed, shivering not so much with the cold as with the thought of the cold, he knew that there was nothing he could do except to leave her to her will, while he went out and did his best to hunt for two!

To hunt for two when there had never been food for one, even, before they joined the pack! That, too, had been in the early winter. Now that the cold season had reigned for many weeks, what chance was there that they might escape starvation? For no game seemed to be moving except what was too strong for all but a gathered pack to pull down. However, there was no use in lingering in the cave and freezing and starving by degrees. He stepped from the cave into the open air.

In the deep recesses of the cave they had seemed to hear a moaning of the wind, but when he came into the open it developed into a mad roaring, and he found that the world was filled with a dazzling brilliance, and the wind screamed out of the north with such a vibrating fury that the ground seemed to quiver beneath him.

White Wolf crouched and with flattened ears took stock of what he could see. A dreadful sense of calamity approaching was in his soul. He sneaked around the shoulder of the hill to the farther side, and as he turned the corner of the outermost rock the gale struck at him with the violence of a reaching hand. He dug in his toes and, stretched along the ground, looked out upon the wildest scene that ever his eye had seen or dreamed. For the plunging north wind shoved stiffly out from every mountain peak a long flag not of boiling mist and rain-cloud, but of crystal snow itself!

The sun was not half an hour from the time of setting on this December day and every translucent banner of snowdust was flooded and writhing with rosy light. All the snow in the world seemed to be feeding into some northern hopper and the air was filled with its dazzling particles. The winter gloom had lifted. The Seven Sisters were seven rosy, quivering faces in the valley. A vast light like the end of the world beat down on river and creek and naked trees, and the tall evergreens bowed far over. Ay, now and then with a boom like an exploding cannon, the back of some great tree burst and its upper half was buoyed in the gale as though floating for a moment in swift water.

White Wolf crouched in deep amazement until the rosy snowdust flags turned a deep crimson, and then lavender, and blue, and at last with the coming of the stars the wind fell suddenly and left only a moaning echo here and there through the mountains.

Then, numb and crushed in spirit, he began his hunting to the west. He stumbled up the shore of Lake Pekan until he reached its head, when his ear was caught by a furious little splashing on the shoreline ahead of him, and a catlike spitting. Even his nose could tell him that this was mink. He stood above the raging little demon which had been caught while at its fishing by one of the traps of Tucker Crosden. Unless he wanted to receive the two needle-like fangs in his head, it behoved him to attack with care. But the mink was blinded with such rage in fighting with the trap that it paid no heed to the other enemy above it. White Wolf, when he sprang, by good luck closed his teeth on the back of the mink's neck. And one shake tore the life from the lithe, snaky body.

He had only one impulse, and that was to carry the prey to Mother Wolf, where she waited in the cave. But the trap held it firmly in place, so he ate the mink on the spot, standing in the icy water, and then resumed his hunt.

He was on the trail of the trapper, now, well-marked from trap to trap, and that was the trail that he followed. He came, from time to time, to the deadly scent of iron, and he knew that Man had planted teeth in the ground at these places, such teeth as had maimed La Sombra. So he made a brief detour about each trap and went on cautiously until he saw the glimmer of eyes before him and then, under the stars in a thicket of naked brush, he saw the old red fox, watching him with the broken-toothed grin.

Something like a sense of approaching doom sent a chill through his body as he saw this mangy seer of the wilderness again before him.

"So the leader has left the pack?" said Red Fox softly. "It is no matter, my son. They were not worthy of your leading. But I shall tell you that they are in trouble already. Marco Blanco has twice missed the kill and the others murmur. They have not eaten flesh in five days, and their bellies begin to shrink and their hides grow loose. They gnaw at the moss and the bark of the trees and they yearn for the White Wolf to lead them to fatness again. Go back to them, White Wolf. You will find them to-night prowling between Mount Spencer and Lomas Mountain, but they will not travel far for they have no great hopes to carry them along. Go, and good luck go with you."

White Wolf licked his thin lips and smiled as only a bull-terrier can smile.

"You take me for a stupid cub," said he. "But I read your mind, Red Fox. You wish to turn me from this trail —why, I cannot guess. But I shall go on, and see what I can see."

"Keep you from the man's trail through the woods?

Not I, brother; not I! But I tell you this for the safety of your skin: This trail is thickly planted with traps. It is a trapper's trail that you follow, and sooner or later, that is death!"

"As for traps," said White Wolf calmly, "I know them of old from my own experience and from the teachings of La Sombra. But what deviltry is in you? I know that you hate me, Red Fox. Do you think that I would take advice from an enemy?"

He strode forward, and the veteran slid a little backwards into the brush.

"This in your ear," said Red Fox, panting with eagerness. "Believe me, for it is the truth. Black Wolf has not forgotten the lucky blow by which he wounded you—how my heart aches to see that the cut is still fresh in your shoulder!—and now he feels that he has only to meet you in order to destroy you. He has not left your trail since you went from the Dunkeld pack. No doubt he is following you close, even now."

"It is a lie, and the father of lies," said White Wolf. "There is nothing that would please you more than to see me in his jaws. It is a false warning, Red Fox."

"It is true, by the mother who bore me and the father who taught me hunting!"

"Let it be. There is something on this trail that you would hide—and this is it!"

For passing through the brush, he saw, between two saplings, a magnificent dog fox with a hind foot caught in the trap; and there was a moan of grief from old Red Fox behind him.

The prisoner stood up and faced White Wolf with bristling hair. And there was never a time when a cornered fox was not a desperate enemy. Besides, from the rear Red Fox was snapping: "Leave him, White Wolf, or while you leap at him from the front, I shall leap at you from the rear, white devil though you are!"

"Will you do so?" said the terrier, and he leaped straight at the older of the two. Red Fox fled wildly from destruction, but the dog did not try to send that charge home. Instead, he turned and rushed at the prisoned fox. A blow of his shoulder, wolf-wise, took the teeth of the poor fox and stretched him helpless. And the long, punishing jaw of White Wolf crunched out the life in the neck of his victim.

On the edge of the shrubbery he could hear Red Fox moaning: "May the man find you! May he stretch your pelt before his cave! Or may Black Wolf come on your traces! Be sure that I shall take him to your hiding place! And I shall help him in the battle! White devil, white devil, did I not see the evil in you when I first saw your bald, narrow face? Nothing so hateful was ever in the San Jacinto range; but you will not stay long!"

This talk went unregarded by White Wolf. Fox flesh was not all to his liking, but famine had provided him with a most catholic taste. Now he completed the meal of which the mink had provided the first portion. After that, he chewed the hind leg of the victim clear of the trap, and then taking firm hold on a rear leg, he threw the body across his back—after a fashion which La Sombra had shown him early in life. In this wise, he started on the homeward journey, tasting beforehand the joy of the mother wolf when she saw such ample fare brought to her.

He left the curving line of the river and the lake, however, and cut inland, to take the straightest path for the cave where he had left La Sombra mourning. And so it was that for the second time in his life he came upon the clearing where the cabin of Tucker Crosden stood.

At that moment, the door opened, and Molly Crosden came out, leaving the door ajar so that the following light would give her some illumination more than the stars on her way to the edge of the lake for water. The terrier, listening to the creaking of the pail handle as she went, laid down the body of his fox and stole forward.

For, now that the mouth of the cave of Man had been opened and left wide, what better time was there for looking into the mysterious deeps of it?

CHAPTER XXVIII

FIRST he gave a guilty glance around the edge of the door; but he saw the back of the Man was turned to that door, and the monster leaned over a gun, cleaning it busily. And ah, how many miraculous matters were gathered into that one cave! And how the scents thronged to him —from the bear skin and the great mountain-sheep skin on the floor, and the smell of the wood itself, crossed by ten thousand trails of Man, and the faint odor of many and many a pelt of captured beasts from the rear of the ogre's cave—of which he could distinguish only marten and skunk, at that instant.

For his brain was flooded with tidings and his nose drained startling news deep and all the wits of White Wolf were in a whirl.

Yonder on the wall were such teeth as Man buried in the earth, now hanging on oiled, but rusted chains; and there was a rack of guns, some of them still rank with the biting scent of gunpowder; axes were in yonder corner; and next to man himself, there were two focal points of interest and admiration.

From one corner a structure of stones and iron gave forth a steady rush of heat, like the sun at noonday. And on the top of this a thing that seemed iron panted forth steam, like one's breath when it blows over one's shoulders on a frosty morning. And there were other iron things from which the deep, rich scent of food poured forth towards the terrier.

Man had eaten. Upon a creature of wood, standing upon four stiff, wooden legs, there were scattered bits of food. And all was poisoned by the scent of Man, to be sure, and yet the mouth of the terrier watered, even though he had eaten not long before and been filled.

And he began to be filled with fear, too. For great as was his knowledge of the danger which lurked here, he felt working in himself a mad desire to step inside—even though the mouth of the cave should be suddenly shut behind him and he made a prisoner in the trap!

He would have shrunk away, but he could not turn. No, not even when the Man suddenly stiffened in his chair, White Wolf could not leap into the friendly blackness which waited for him upon either hand. Nor even when the Man began to swing around in his chair could the dog stir. Nor even when the dreadful face of Man was fully before him, could White Wolf leap for the shelter of the night!

He remembered, then, what La Sombra had said, of the miraculous strength of the eyes of Man, and he felt that strength, too. It fastened upon his soul through his eyes, it reached his inmost strength and mastered it, and yet that sense of mastery was hardly greater fear than joy. La Sombra had wished to flee, when the eye of Man was fixed upon her. But White Wolf felt in himself only a dreadful impulse to crawl forward into the cave and lie stretched at the feet of Man!

Such an impulse had come to him sickeningly, dizzily, when he had run on some perilous mountain trail—a temptation to hurl himself from the height into the abyss.

And yet there was less power of sense and resistance in him, now. He did not even shrink back when Man stretched forth his two terrible hands and whispered: "The King!"

No, for still he was hypnotized with dread, with wonder, and with ridiculous joy that rooted in his heart.

"The King!" said Man again, and rose from his chair, until it seemed to White Wolf that he would never have done rising—until his head brushed the top of the wooden cave, and still with his hands stretched forth he moved a half-step towards the terrier.

He wanted to flee, now, but truly it was a spell that held him and it seemed to White Wolf that the sound of the voice of this creature—this note which was deeper than the baying of a great wolf—ran in through his ears to his heart. It seemed to White Wolf that listening to that voice was like tasting food of a surpassing sweetness, saving that it was more than food. And strange waves of delight passed through him.

Yes, all at once, leaping upon his mind from every side like enveloping waves, he felt that he had known this voice before, and the face, and the magic power of the eyes of Man, fixed upon his own.

That instant, the spell was broken, for he heard the noisy creaking of the handle of the pail, as Molly Crosden came head down, laboriously into the path of the light from the door. And the noise behind him enabled White Wolf to turn his head and then to flash away into the kind blackness of the night.

In the very nick of time he had leaped, it seemed. For a terrible cry rang behind him, and as he leaped to the fallen body of the fox the monster Man rushed forth into the night with his arms past out and shouting in a frantic voice.

White Wolf waited for no more. He forgot the body of the dead fox. He forgot the hunger of La Sombra. All that he wanted was the comfort of her presence and the assurance that her ready wits would give him. So he fled like lightning through the blanketing dark. And still, before his eyes, the third miracle of the cabin seemed to be floating—the dazzling image of the lamp, whose brilliant white shade danced before White Wolf like a false moon, playing between him and the trees.

So he crossed the creeks that lay between, and flung straight forward. The true moon was rising, now. He was grateful only because its light helped his running, and so, with his lungs bursting with effort, he reached the cave—and found that others were there before him!

Two huge lobos stood at the entrance, but as he streaked forward from the trees and then checked himself on stiffened legs, they drew to either side.

"Enter, White Wolf!" said they. "And have no fear. For we are of your pack!"

Then purred La Sombra from the thick shadow at the mouth of the cave: "Is it so? What is his pack? Has he not denied it and left it? Shall he go back to you when you would have betrayed him once?"

"It is true that we were fools. But all of us are not very old, and the tongue of Marco Blanco was a wicked tongue, was it not?"

"It was a wicked tongue," said the other ambassador.

"Has even Marco Blanco sent to invite White Wolf back?" asked Mother Wolf, taking the matter into her own charge.

"There is no need," said the second ambassador, showing all his snowy teeth as he laughed in the moonlight. "Marco Blanco is dead."

"Good!" said La Sombra. "This is much better! You, my young friend, no doubt had a hand in his end?"

"My teeth were in his flank, it is true. Of the old pack, there are only five left, and all of us grow thin. Three more came to join us to-day; which makes us eight in all."

"Are none of them strong enough to lead you?"

"We want no leader but the White Wolf. In the days when he led us, we were fat. Is it not true, brother?"

"There was not one week of famine in all the time that he led us. Now we have nothing but hollow days. Consider, White Wolf!"

"Go back to the pack," said White Wolf. "I shall come, no doubt, in the morning. Wait for me on the shoulder of Spencer Mountain. I shall not fail you there in the dawn light."

They snarled with veritable joy and then stole like soft shadows away beneath the skeleton trees. White Wolf threw himself down beside La Sombra, and before he could speak, for panting, she had read half his story with her nose.

"Mink!" cried La Sombra. "You have had strong meat to-night, have you not?"

She added in another moment: "Fox, too! There is the blood of fox in your mouth and the rank smell of him is in your hair. Ay, you have eaten well, my son, but have you forgotten your sick mother?"

"No," breathed White Wolf. "Wait, only, till I can speak."

"Tush! But what is this? Your feet are rank with it—Man!"

"I only stood at his door and looked into his cave! Oh my mother, do you know that he prisons fire within stones and that he carries a moon in his cave to give him light?"

"Is this true?"

"It is as true as that I am your son, La Sombra."

"Ah, would one believe it? You will be a wise wolf, my child, unless you die young. But young you will surely die, unless you leave the caves of men far up the wind from the trails which you run! Now tell me what you have seen, besides, that makes you tremble, still?"

"I have seen the face of Man!"

She leaped back from him and spat like the mink which he had killed in the water of Lake Pekan.

"Pah!" gasped La Sombra. "Is it that? And do you not tremble in pure dread of it, now?"

"Dread?" said White Wolf. "I do not know. It is like a sickness in the stomach, the thing that I feel. It is like an empty stomach, La Sombra, when other wolves are eating, and you can see them kill! No, it is not like fear."

"Here is a wonder!" said she, sourly. "There is no wolf in the mountains that has seen Man without fear."

"He ran out to catch me, but I ran away very fast. I am going back——"

"Never, White Wolf! He sets other traps than steel ones for us, be sure!"

"I go back, only for the sake of bringing you the fox I left when Man frightened me away."

"Come straight to me, thereafter?"

"Straight as a hawk for the nest."

"I shall wait for you at the foot of the hill, or perhaps nearer. Good hunting, my son!"

CHAPTER XXIX

It had been a dreary day for Molly Crosden, for in the morning Adam Gannaway had said good-bye to her.

"I have told your father that I am heading for the lowlands and better weather," said Gannaway. "But, between you and me, I am simply going to see if his legal position is as bad as he considers it to be. It may be better, Molly. One can never tell. When a man is barred from his own door by a fellow who has no authority to stop him, and whn he strikes that man down not in malice but simply to clear his path—I don't know. Certainly it can't be a very terrible offense, if there is any common sense in the law. I am going where I can find out exactly what is what, and incidentally, I am going to learn whether or not the long arm of the law is really searching so very feverishly for your father. It seems to me that it is not. But, whatever happens, no harm can be done if I find out exactly what your father's status may be in the eyes of the law. And if he were free to return to the lowlands—would he not return, Molly?"

"I know he would go back," said Molly Crosden.

"I would try to persuade you to go with me, but I know that words can't budge you from this idea of your duty, child. But I'll be back before ten days have passed. And I trust that he'll not have another attack while I'm gone. Are you afraid, Molly?"

She wrinkled her eyes shut in thought.

"It ain't so scary—the idea of staying with him—as the idea is of going away from him and leaving him here with only himself for company. So—good-bye, Mr. Gannaway. You been tremendous kind to me, and I ain't gunna forget you!"

Gannaway took her hands between his own and pressed them hard.

"You beat all womenfolk ten ways from the ace," he said quietly. "But you talk as if I'm not coming back almost before you can turn around, Molly? Why, honey, I'll be back here in no time!"

She looked askance, past him and into her own thoughts, and found there something that brought a tear to her eye. But she said nothing, and Gannaway marvelled at the woman's patience and the woman's strength in this child.

"If you was my father," said she, "I would walk a ways with you when you start."

"You'll walk a way with me then, and tell me what's bothering you most, as we go along."

But, as far as she went with him, she did not say a word, and at last she stopped and held out her hand.

"Look at me, Molly," said Adam Gannaway. "Confound it, but my heart is aching in a frightful way! Poor kiddie, aren't you really frightened almost to death at the thought of staying here alone with him?"

A snow pile slipped from the limb of a pine tree and fell in a white, brilliant shower past them.

"When things are gunna happen," said Molly, "there ain't any stopping of them, is there?" And when they ain't gunna happen, they ain't any need to worry. Only—I'll be powerful glad to see you back, Uncle Adam!"

He thought of her wistful upturned face as he hurried down the valley of the Seven Sisters, and all was not well about the heart of Gannaway. If she had been his own daughter, he would not have felt a sense of desertion more keenly. Exactly what he could have done to solve this strange situation he did not know. But in some way he was confident that a really strong man would have mastered the dilemma, and saved Molly from the danger of her father's tottering reason.

His way to the lowlands led up the valley of the Seven Sisters, and he passed the shack of the Loftus brothers, whom he had not seen in some ten days. So he paused to stop at the closed door, and Dan Loftus, revolver in hand, opened it a little and peered out.

He did not invite Gannaway in, but stood there scowling and nervous, fingering the butt of the gun.

"What's wrong?" said Gannaway.

"Did I say that anything was wrong?" asked Loftus, eying the tall man without friendship.

"Why, man," said Gannaway, "I've simply stopped in to pass the time of day with you on my way to the lowlands. Is this the way to talk? Where's your brother?"

"About his business," said Dan Loftus. He added with a gleam in his eye: "Maybe you're leavin' the Crosden shack because you and the big feller have fell out?"

Gannaway smiled.

There had been no trouble of that sort, he assured young Loftus.

"And the White Wolf?" he asked

Dan Loftus grew darker of eye than ever.

"The damn critter ain't been seen," said he. "But we've spotted his trail here and there in this here valley, and we'll get him yet. So long!"

And he closed the door in the face of the meteorologist.

So Gannaway perforce continued on his trail, shifting his blanket roll to ease his shoulders, and cursing all underbred curmudgeons the world over.

He slept that night in a dell on the side of Mount Spencer, well sheltered from the wind. In the morning he had his breakfast of smoked meat, and strode on again, pulling his belt one notch tighter.

He was keeping well to the side of the main pass, for the good reason that the bottom of that pass was three and five times as deep in snow. And therefore he was at a considerable distance from the straightest line through the mountains when he saw a body of five horsemen marching through the light of the dawn.

He thought of hailing them, at first, but he checked that eager impulse because it is far better in the mountains to know your man a little before you hail him. And, unslinging his strong field glasses, he turned them upon the straggling file and centered them on the leader of the group, who was a little distance ahead.

He knew the thin features at once, even though they were partly obscured by the turned-up collar of the overcoat. It was Tom Loftus, with his rifle balanced across the pommel of his saddle.

What was he doing there at the head of such a body of men? It did not need much probing of the mind of Gannaway for him to decide that this errand was not concerned with the capture of the White Wolf or any other hunting business that Loftus and his brother might have on hand. Horsemen were not used in such pursuits.

He scanned the other members of the group one by one, and as they rode into the great circle of the glass, made bigger than human by the magnifying power, he saw that each was a grim-faced man, and that each was armed to the teeth, with rifle and revolvers. And it seemed to Gannaway that even a child would have known that there was only one good explanation for such a body of riders.

They were either fugitives from the power of the law, which was most unlikely at this season of the year and in these mountains to which all the passes could be easily blocked, or else what was far more likely, they were riding at the behest of the law itself. That explanation fitted in with a fear which had burst full-grown into the imagination of Gannaway when he saw Tom Loftus's face. There was no love lost between the Loftus brothers and big Crosden. And might not one of the pair have slipped down to the low-lands to see what he could discover concerning the identity of Crosden, and why the big man chose to live the life of a hermit trapper so far from all other men? This was the answer—five staunch riders come to seize Tucker Crosden in the name of the law. And perhaps some small reward would then slip into the calloused palm of the wolf-hunter.

It was too logical an explanation to be wrong, thought Gannaway.

He gave up all thought of the way to the lowlands and the long marches ahead of him. Instead, he turned sharply around, and he wondered if, by pouring forth all of his strength into the effort, he might not be able to distance the horsemen as they drove their tired beasts floundering through the snow, and so to bring warning to Crosden of the coming danger while there was still time.

He did not dream that such strange events had happened at the cabin that all thought of his murdered man, and of the power of the law, and of all the world, indeed, had been shut from the mind of Tucker Crosden.

CHAPTER XXX

MOLLY, head down, the loaded bucket straining at her arm, did not look up, as she approached the door of the cabin, until she heard the inarticulate cry of her father and then she saw his great bulk dash out the opened door and into the night.

She ran up the step and into the room, heedless of the water that sloshed from the bucket onto her dress, for she guessed that the thing which she had dreaded and which Gannaway had expected had come to pass at last, and the reason of Tucker Crosden was quite lost. She caught hold on the door in a frenzy of terror, but she realized at once that there was no use in closing her father out into the cold of the night. When he decided to return, the bolt of that door would never hold him out.

She heard him cry: "King! D'you hear me? King!"

And there was such wild joy and sorrow in his voice that Molly wrung her hands; one would have said that the dog was before his eyes.

There was no doubt that this was perfect madness, and when she heard his step returning, she shrank behind the table in spite of herself and watched him come with dread in her face. He stopped at the door and cast at her one look of sorrow and hatred.

It made the strength slip from the body of Molly.

She set about the work of washing the dishes with all the haste that she could muster, but her fingers were stuttering and the dishes clashed one against the other; and each clash brought a side glance from Tucker Crosden like the lash of a whip.

He stood in front of the photograph of The King, poring intently upon it, and her heart stood still as she heard him mutter: "There ain't any difference. Except that he looked bigger. But how would The King come back, except bigger and better than ever? How would he come back, except that way?"

His muttering stopped, and he began to pace up and down the cabin, his hands locked behind his back and his head bowed, as though he were wrestling with a great agony of spirit. She saw his excitement increasing, until his face turned crimson, and a purple, swollen vein was beating in his forehead.

At last he stopped by the table and said in a voice of terrible quiet:

"I would like to have you tell it to me, Molly, why you done it? Will you tell me that?"

"What, daddy?" said the child. "What have I done now?"

The madness leaped straightway into his eyes, and yet he fought it down with an effort that left him trembling.

"I ain't gunna say nothin' to you," said Crosden. "I'm gunna keep a grip on myself, only I ask you, man to man, have you been stayin' up here all the time pretendin' to care for me, but really just waitin' for the time to come when you could send The King back if he was to come to me?"

"I don't know what you mean," said Molly, her eyes growing great.

He caught her suddenly by the wrist and dragged her to him across the table, scattering the piled dishes in a noisy cataract upon the floor. She was thrown upon her knees, and when she looked up to his face she made sure that it was her time to die.

"Will you tell me," said Tucker Crosden, "that you didn't see him standing right there at the door?"

"Who?" asked Molly, when she could make herself speak. "Who was standing at the door?"

He cast up an arm above his head. She thought it was to dash the life from her as it descended, but it was only to call God to witness.

"I'm calm," groaned Tucker Crosden. "I don't want to do her no harm. I only beg her for the truth—and by God, she lies right to my face! Molly, I beg you here on my knees beside you—will you tell me true—what makes you lie to me and why did you do it? Why did you drive him away?"

A sob rose in her throat, but something told her that tears would be fatal. She choked it back and stammered: "I don't know! I——"

"When he was standing there in the door——"

"What was in the door, daddy?"

"If you love your life, Molly, don't you try to play with me! It was The King that had come back from the grave to me, d'ye hear? It was The King, and you knew it, and your ma sent you here to keep him from me, because—Oh, God, how am I gunna stand it?"

His voice had leaped up to a scream and with the last words she felt his great hand fumbling at her throat—it would need only one grip of that hand to end her life, she knew.

"I didn't see that it was The King standing there," gasped Molly, for his tightening fingers were nearly stifling her. She reached for them, but then she remembered that resistance was worse than useless. Gannaway had inculcated that lesson over and over again.

"You lie!" screamed Tucker Crosden. "There ain't nothin' but lies in the whole of you womenfolks. Because he was standin' there with a bright light shinin' through him and out of him—he was like he was cut out of the living moon, he was that bright. And you help from seein' him——"

"I was sort of dazzled, daddy," breathed Molly Crosden. "I didn't make out really what was in the light in the doorway, d'you see?"

"Are you gunna try to lie forwards and backwards?" groaned Tucker Crosden. "Then I tell you that there ain't a place in this here world for you. There ain't room for you and me in the valley of the Seven Sisters——"

She saw the active devil rising in his face and glittering in his eyes.

"You ain't gunna murder me?" screamed Molly. "I'm your own girl! You'll—you'll go to hell for it—if——"

All breath was shut from her throat, and spinning blackness swung before her eyes. Then she found herself lifted and pitched bodily through the doorway. A cold drift of snow received her like a bed of feathers, and above her she heard the vague thunder of Tucker Crosden's voice.

She raced blindly away. She crossed the clearing and fled west through the cold quiet of the moonshine, for the moon was brightening, now. She had no reason for selecting that direction except that towards the west she had seen the last of Adam Gannaway that morning. She ran with a nervous frenzy that defied exhaustion and through blind instinct only she followed the path of the trapper from set to set. Hurrying as she did without regard for where her feet fell, it was a wonder that it did not happen sooner, but presently a mouth seemed to gape at her from the ground, sharp teeth seized her leg, and she was jerked upon her face.

When she wakened, she was very cold. She thought at first that she was in the cabin, again, and that the covers had merely slipped away during her sleep. She reached vaguely for them and her hand touched the icy surface of the crusted snow.

Then Molly sat up, and ranged around her she saw the naked trees, with dark evergreens here and there like standing shadows, and strips of silver birch like gleaming metal in the moon.

After that, she felt the pain in her forehead. And still later, as she strove to stir, the numbness of her leg was replaced by a long, thrusting pain that reached through her flesh to her heart and to her brain.

She knew, then, that a wolf trap of the largest size had caught her, and the instant she examined it she saw that it was futile even to attempt to open it.

More than once she had tried with might and main to budge those ponderous springs, but she had never been able to handle them, whereas her father moved them without an effort. Moreover, this trap was thickly rusted and must have been long rusted.

She saw, then, that there was no hope of budging the trap and there remained to her only the dubious possibility of reaching the ear of her father with her call. Even if he heard, would he come? And, remembering the distance from the cabin to this spot, she was more than reasonably sure that he would not hear.

However, she brushed panic away from her patiently and cupping her hands at her lips she sent out a long, screaming cry, pitched high and held into a dying wail. Her father himself had taught her that cry to pierce the wind to a greater distance than a whistle, even, and it was a long familiar signal between them.

A dozen times she threw all of her strength and all of her art into that call, and each time she listened vainly for the great siren call of Tucker Crosden in answer. It did not come, and finally she set herself to face the last possibility of all, and that was the chance of sitting through the night without perishing.

Pain, at least, would not wear her down, for the numbed leg in which the trap was fastened had ceased aching and did not trouble her unless she strove to move.

And she thought of a wolf, straining vainly and patiently against this infernal machine.

But she could not last through the night, she saw at once. The chill was eating to her heart, and a sense of drowsing weakness increased each moment, which she knew to be the fatal sign.

She was perfectly familiar with the wilderness, however. When the great wave of hysterical fear welled up in her, she told herself what all woodsmen and plainsmen know—that panic in the wilderness may be as mortal as a rifle bullet. So she kept her wits and set about maintaining her circulation as well as she could.

To sit in the snow was making her chances worse,

every moment, and since there was a little small brush near her, she set about pulling it up, and succeeded soon in gathering a sufficient quantity to weave with it a criss-cross pattern of brush across the hard crust of the snow. On this she sat, and then wrung out the water where the heat of her body had melted enough snow to drench her to the skin.

Her hands were numb before she had ended that task, however, and the outer clothing was soon frozen stiff as wood by the stir of the icy wind that blew over her and through her.

She began to work her arms hard and fast. That seemed to pump the blood hot and fast through the upper half of her body, but in the lower half the frost sank deeper and deeper, and when she strove to rise to her knees, the teeth of the trap sickened her with pain.

She tried to estimate the time by the position of the moon. She could remember that it had not risen when she went out for the bucket of water, and yet the moon had flashed through the forest after she left the cabin, a little later. Now it was a good distance up the sky, but it would be long, long hours before even such an early riser as Tucker Crosden would get up.

And when he went his rounds and found her here, what would stir in his heart?

She turned sharply about in the midst of this thought for she felt something colder than the wind prying at her body, and there she saw, half in shadow and half in the moon, a wolf as large as a bear, well nigh, a terrific monster in a jet-black coat.

She lifted a stick, with a shout, and threw it with such good aim that it struck the wolf across the face. But he did not so much as wince. He merely took two or three rapidly gliding steps towards her, and then paused again. And she saw that his belly was drawn fine with famine!

CHAPTER XXXI

Now, when White Wolf left the cave of his foster-mother and started down the valley, he ran easily and strongly. He had eaten enough for strength; he had seen enough for strangely thrilling happiness. And he was gladder of one thing than of all else—that the way to the body of the dead fox lay near to the cave of Man, for what would prevent him from looking into the place again, and if the Man monster were there, perhaps of hearing the magic of his voice again?

So he reached the edge of the clearing and breathed himself for a moment, while he took stock of his surroundings. The door of the house was still open and the lamplight shone forth, but now it went only a pallid step from the door before it was lost in the bright shining of the moon.

He resisted the temptation to go to the doorway again. Duty called him first to the fox, but as he hurried across the clearing, a great soundless shadow rose from the spot where he had dropped the fox. An enormous owl floated on whispering wings above the treetops and slid out of view. And when White Wolf came to the spot, he found that the fox was represented only by a few bloody tufts of fur.

He paid the thought of the prowling owl with a silent baring of his teeth, and then in his anger he ran a few short circles sniffing at the snow.

In a trice he had come upon the only power which had

a greater attraction for him than the door of the man's house—the faint scent of Black Wolf upon the crusted surface of the snow, and instantly he remembered the warning of Red Fox that he would never rest until he had brought the monster to the terrier's trail.

He had lived up to his promise then—and at the thought the wound in the terrier's shoulder burned like fire.

He had no wish to retreat. For how sweet it would be to go back to Mother Wolf with the tidings that Black Wolf was dead—with the blood of the great beast upon him for proof of his deed. How sweet, too, to go back to the Dunkeld Pack with the proof that he had revenged his overthrow!

Instantly he was darting up the trail, and found it freshening each instant beneath his nose. It diverged from the straight line along the bank of a creek. Then he found the spot where the wolf had leaped across and presently the bull-terrier heard before him a sudden snarl, and after that the sharp cry of a human voice. He did not need to be told that it was a cry of utter terror.

He leaped through the screening brush before him—and the old fox jumped sidewise to escape his coming.

But the terrier had not so much as a glance for the malignant fox. In the center of a patch of moonlight he saw a thing that turned his blood to ice—the Black Wolf, looking more monstrous than ever, and a yard from his slavvering jaws the crouched figure of Molly Crosden!

The man scent was on her. It blew clearly to his nostrils, and yet she was so little formidable, that she cowered before a single wolf! Oh that La Sombra, with all her wisdom, should be able to see this picture and then explain it if she could!

What a voice, now, of terror and of wonder as she called the same words that the Man had used on this very night: "The King!"

Black Wolf jumped thrice his length backwards and whirled to face his old enemy, snarling:

"Is it the bastard child of La Sombra again? Look, fox, for there will be meat for both of us this night!"

And the red fox answered: "Is it not as I swore, my

lord? I have brought you to him. His pack is far away. He has no speed to escape you. No, and the fool does not intend to run."

"What is this, Black Wolf?" asked the terrier. "Have you grown so mad that you think to lift a tooth against Man? Has the last wisp of sense left your heavy brain? However, I have come in time!"

And he made a leap that placed him between the girl and the monster.

"Look!" snarled Red Fox. "All is as I have said. For what beast except a slave of a dog would risk his life for the sake of Man? It is a dog, and the son of a dog, and when has a dog dared to stand to a wolf, and a king of wolves like you, my great master?"

"He shall not stand long," said Black Wolf, "if he dares to face me, or will you crouch at the feet of the Man's child, bastard son of La Sombra?"

"It is the time which I promised you long ago when you hunted me at the edge of the lake. I swore to you then that the time would come when I should hunt *you*, oh eater of carrion. And it is now that I take you by the throat, so!"

He rushed, checked himself mid-charge, and then dived long and low for the legs of Black Wolf. He took a punishing cut across the back, but he found a grip on a foreleg, and as luck would have it, that was the very spot where the teeth of Nelly, long before, had gripped the monster and brought him near to destruction.

Even her strength had been enough to trouble and then to madden the big fellow, but what a difference was here, when the fighting jaw of White Wolf closed and his teeth gritted on the bone?

The howl of Black Wolf rang above the trees and made the drifting owl dip and stagger in its flight, with surprise. And old red fox cowered in the snow with astonishment. And Molly Crosden clasped her hands against her breast and could not utter even a whisper at the miracle which she was seeing.

For she knew what her father and every other woodman had always told her, that no single dog could ever stand against the tearing jaw-power of a wolf. And yet here she saw a giant of the race yelling with fear and pain as he flung about the open, striving with all his might to drag himself free, tugging until the whole body of the terrier came clear of the snow and whirled with resounding thumps against the trunk of pine or naked birch. But no buffeting could make him free his grip and though the repeated slashes of Black Wolf covered his back with flowing crimson, he held to his work.

"Red Fox!" snarled the maddened wolf, "do you leave this battle with a devil to me alone? Help me now, if you wish for meat or for revenge."

Red Fox heard, and grinning his broken-toothed grin, he stole up behind. He had not the courage to try for a vital hold, but he sank his time-worn teeth in the hip of White Wolf.

Surprise did what pain could not have done. White Wolf shifted from his leg hold and whirled to take Red Fox by the neck. He snapped at a jumping shadow, for Red Fox had gripped once, and then leaped for safety. While Black Wolf, staggering on three legs but nerved with a fury, drove wildly in and beat the terrier headlong in the snow with the blow of his massive shoulder. He tried for the throat as the dog went down and tore it across, but by the least part of an inch that slash was too short, and when he whirled again, as White Wolf struggled to his feet, an unexpected check delayed him.

Molly Crosden had forgot the trap that held her leg, sawing deep into the flesh, but like another boy watching a schoolyard fight, she rose to her knees and shouted for The King, until her cheerful voice rose above the savage snarling of the two warriors, and the eager whimperings of Red Fox, as he danced in circles around the pair, anxious to make his teeth tell, but dreading the teeth of the terrier like death itself.

She saw Red Fox make his contribution to the cause, at last, and at that she grew half blinded with fury. She had no weapon, nothing but the heavy root-end of a dead bush, but this she flung with all her might. It struck Black Wolf just as he was wheeling in to beat his half-risen enemy into the snow again, this time surely to finish him.

It landed fairly in the broad arch of his forehead, with

a double weight of surprise, and knocking a bit of earth into his eyes. It was a mere nothing—like the slap of a girl to a prize fighter, but it delayed the wolf for a space as long, say, as the winking of an eye—which was enough to permit White Wolf to gather all his feet beneath him and encounter the charge.

What instinct taught him first of all, what long practice at dog and cow and elk had made him perfect in, he used again now, driving straight at the head. The lofty front and towering majesty of the black monster had kept the terrier from trying those well-proved tactics at the first; there had seemed no way to topple the giant except to undermine him from beneath. But now the fight was too hot for thought or cunning and as Black Wolf came in, his teeth clashed against teeth—and ugly shock!

He gave back, in order to spring again, but White Wolf was not waiting for sparring room. He heard the voice of the child behind him and he knew that she was calling to him; he saw a flung stick from her hand strike Red Fox and send him to a distance with a yelp of fear. That instant the stage was cleared for him, Black Wolf was backing up—and in a trice the teeth of the dog were locked across the foreface of the wolf.

Have you seen a wrestler stand up and whirl his antagonist through the air? Even so, Black Wolf rose and wheeled to shake off the terrier. But the dog's hold was locked home and would not give. Through the underbrush leaped the great lobo until he seemed to be rushing away with a white lamb in his teeth, but he staggered back into the moonlit open, half exhausted, weakened by pain and by exquisite fear of the unknown.

Given any wolf on the range and in brave wolfish fight of charge, shock, slash, and cut, Black Wolf would prove the master. But here was a leech, like the white dog in the trapper's camp, long tens of weeks ago, only with thrice the power of that other leech.

"Help, Red Fox!" cried the monster.

"I come, great brother!" snarled the fox. "I peril my life for thee; and be it written thus in thy mind forever!"

He flung himself in, therefore, and sank his work-shortened fangs in the haunch of White Wolf again.

It made a sore wound, but this time it did not serve to make the terrier loosen his grip. The pain which it cost him, he put into his jaws, and forced his struggling teeth through the flesh of Black Wolf, until they grided against the bone.

It was an agony that drove Black Wolf insane. He flung back regardless of the effort that forced the fangs of the dog to cut through his flesh and so, though it left him half blinded and with the flesh of his face turned into a tattered mask, pouring blood, he lurched back, to freedom, turned a somersault, and plunged blindly away from the terror behind him.

He was given an instant's respite, for the tug of the fox at the hip of White Wolf delayed the latter, and when he had freed himself with a snap that sent Red Fox squealing away, Black Wolf was far off. Moreover, the hind leg of the terrier buckled under him when he tried to put weight upon it, and though a dog can run fast on three legs, it is only when the missing one is in front.

He took a staggering step or two in pursuit, and then he turned back and sat calmly down to lick his wounds.

Behold, the man-child held out hands to him and spoke in a voice that entered his soul like the sound of running water—cool running water in the summer of the year when the trail has been long and dusty. He forgot to lick his wounds, and raised his head to listen to her.

CHAPTER XXXII

THE frenzy died slowly in the breast of big Tucker Crosden on this night, and the last embers of the madness were burning in his brain as he sat in his doorway, his rifle across his knees, and wondered in what direction he should attempt to follow the trail of his daughter. But he had not yet come to the full realization of what he had done—so much so that the haze was still across his judgment. He only knew that there was peril of actual life in the cold of this winter night and that he must find some method of bringing Molly back to the house. He decided to try the power of his voice, then, and he stood up and sent a great bellow ringing through the cold air.

"Molly! Oh, Molly!"

Then he listened, but he only heard the echo flung loudly back from the nearest hill and it suddenly came to him that this was a desperate crisis indeed, for she had retreated beyond the reach of his voice!

That call accomplished one thing, however. For the flinging echo, striking from the hill against the ear of the fleeing Black Wolf, drove that monster from his course and so brought him, still more than half blind with pain and blood, straight across the clearing and into the view of Tucker Crosden.

He forgot Molly, at that, and remembered only that this was a thing for which he had almost given over actual hope. He pitched the rifle to his shoulder and fired. Black

Wolf left the ground in a last convulsive spring, and sent his death howl ringing and echoing over the trees and far away. Lying crumpled on the snow, he bit once at the place where the bullet had entered his body, then he straightened and died.

So Tucker Crosden strode out and stood exulting over him in an utter silence until, faint and far on the western wind, it seemed to him that he heard a shrill barking, as though a dog, yonder in the distance, were answering the cry of the wolf with another challenge.

He did not wait to hear again. He turned like one stricken with joy and plunged off up the western trail, and he stopped a quarter of a mile away to shout: "King! D'you hear? King!"

There was no response, but the heart of Crosden was still big in him, for it seemed that he could not be wrong. There are a hundred notes in which a dog may bark, but only one for the bull-terrier—an absurdly high-pitched, piercing note. And certainly that was what the night wind had brought to his ears.

He ran on again until shortness of breath stopped him, and again he sent his call booming around him until a night-hawk, dripping up above the trees, slid off hastily through the pallid moonlight.

But this time, as he listened, he heard a response distinctly enough—Molly Crosden, crying sharp and high: "Daddy Tucker!"

He reached the place in hot haste and there he found Molly sitting with a monster bull-terrier in her arms. She became a misty form in the background; the crystal white body of the dog, slashed across dreadfully with red, was all that he could see.

"The King!" cried Tucker Crosden, fairly staggering with joy, and he would have rushed straight upon them had not a murderous snarl stopped him.

For White Wolf was in doubt. He had kept this soft-handed child from death once, that night, and he was not ready to render her again to the first comer. Here was a Man, indeed, with a gun in his hand, but he defied the warnings of La Sombra to stand his ground and stop the monster.

"He don't know me," said Tucker Crosden, as though

the miracle were too great for his senses. "He don't know me, Molly. And if he come back to me—how could that be?"

"I don't know," said Molly, "but this here is what I *do* know—that he fought off the Black Wolf and made him run for it and saved my life—God bless him! Oh, dad, he fought like a hero. And now he's been sittin' here like a lamb, keepin' me warm!"

Tucker Crosden was on his knees in the snow, that he might the better conduct his examination. White Wolf no longer snarled. The scent of the very same cave was on man and child, as he could tell, now, and plainly it was folly to try to keep the father from the cub. However, in his last lingering doubts, he still stood his ground and curled his lip away from his fangs to show his willingness for battle.

The wildness had been shocked from the brain of Tucker Crosden. The mad preconceptions which had obsessed him were rudely scattered, and now he saw that the ghost which he thought poor Molly had frightened away from him was more the child's dog than his own. And the science of the breeder asserted itself, also. These were not the inches of The King. Neither was it his bulk, but a veritable giant of a warrior.

It crushed the very heart of Tucker Crosden, but it freed him from illusion. And with a cleared brain he kneeled beside Molly and freed her leg from the deep-sunk teeth of the trap. He raised her in his arms.

"Molly," he said. "it ain't The King. There ain't no mystery, after all. There ain't no coming back from the grave. But I've been a fool, and a terrible brute to you. How are you gunna forgive me?"

She lay back against his broad breast and smiled faintly up to him.

"I dunno," said Molly. "Forgiving you ain't hard, dad. But I dunno that there ain't a mystery, because it sure looks to me like God sent him here to-night."

"He's follerin' us on!" said Tucker Crosden. "Look at him come! Lord, Lord, how that wolf chawed him up! Is the leg hurtin' you bad, honey?"

"I'm too happy to feel no pain. Only tell me, dad. Him having come to me, like that, is he my dog?"

Her father drew a great breath. To give up all claim on this beautiful giant was like giving up his hope of heaven.

But he said at last: "What difference does it make? I didn't breed him—I didn't make him. Ay, he's yours, Molly. And a grand dog!"

He hurried on, but before he reached the cabin exhaustion, and fear, and bitter cold, and long-withstood pain, and the all-relaxing joy that followed, had dissolved the strength of Molly. She cried softly on the shoulder of Tucker Crosden, and as he reached the cabin, she was murmuring vague, wild things.

So he worked over her, feverishly, washing the wound, and softening the frozen flesh, and then swathing all in a soft, deep dressing. He gave her a taste of coffee, black, and strong as lye, and this seemed to clear her head, suddenly, and he could stand back and smile down at her, satisfied, while she smiled back to him, with joy in her eyes.

"Are you sufferin' a lot, Molly?"

"Nothin' but a heart that's bustin', Daddy Tucker, it's so happy. Look yonder how he's watchin' and understandin' everything!"

The white giant stepped a little nearer, and growled very softly, and wagged his tail, saying with all his might: "You are better, now! I, too, know what cold is in deep wounds. La Sombra has licked them until they grew well —but the man knows a better way!"

"He's grand!" said Tucker Crosden. "He's simply grand, Molly. And may I be struck blind if he ain't got the very look and the very turn of The King's head. D'you see it?"

"I see it," she nodded.

"Them things ain't by accident. How could The King's blood be up here?"

Inspiration darted into the mind of Molly.

"Dad, there was one of Nelly's litter that you didn't find when you come back to her."

He stared, unable to comprehend. "Could a pup like that of lived?"

"I dunno," said Molly, "but the blood of The King was in that litter, and here's The King all over again—but bigger and finer! Where else could it have come from?"

Logic will beat a way into the very most stubborn mind.

"Ay," said Tucker Crosden. "But *how* could it of lived, unless there was something to mother it!"

"And maybe there was," said Molly.

"Mother a pup like that? What could it be? It don't sound likely or natural."

La Sombra had waited long for the return of her foster-son. She had gone down to the foot of the hill. She had even hobbled across the brook. But finally her patience was exhausted and she sat down and pointed her nose to the moon and sent a long bay wavering across the forest.

"The woods is full of lobos to-night," said Molly, shivering with her memory. "Oh, but it's mighty good to be in here in the warm. But—look at him, Dad!"

The terrier had slipped to the door on feet he could make noiseless. Now, he squatted there and raised his head, and the bristles of his hair raised and sparkled in the lamplight along his back. All this Molly and her father watched; and then the long, smooth howl issued and rose and hung far off in echoes above the trees.

"I hear—but I cannot come, La Sombra!" said that call.

It was no perfect wolf's cry, no doubt, but to the wonderstricken pair in the cabin it seemed the voice of a lobo to the life.

"Them that taught him how to talk that way may of raised him, too," said Molly Crosden. "And ain't it likely, dad?"

"Raised by a wolf? Raised by a wolf?" repeated Tucker Crosden faintly. "If I thought it, honey, I'd never shoot another—I'd never trap 'em! But is it any ways possible?"

"Suppose," said Molly, "that the puppy got away and besides the Black Wolf, there was a female that had lost her litter, say—why, dad, ain't it more likely?"

Truth has a certain ring which false coin can never give, and this partial truth which Molly had worked out sank freely home in the mind of Tucker Crosden.

If this were truly one of Nell's litter, saved by miracle —then how great a joy was his! What he saw, in that flaming moment, was a judging ring in Madison Square Garden, and the eager crowd bending above the ropes all around, while above the bull-terriers a white giant towered, and amazement filled the face of the judge.

CHAPTER XXXIII

He took a scrap of cooked venison steak and held it out.

"We got to have a name for him. Come here, old timer, and sink a tooth in this."

White Wolf canted his head upon one side and observed with glistening eyes. It was a tasty trifle, no doubt. But it came from the hand of man, and had he not been taught by La Sombra that the very smell of man was the same as poison?

"He won't come near it," said the giant regretfully. "You try him, honey."

So Molly stretched out the bit of meat and called to him in a gentle voice. All the wisdom in his brain fought against it; all the new softness in his heart urged him forward. But, after all, he had seen that same hand strike in his behalf, in the desperate middle of the battle when Black Wolf had him down, and he had never forgotten.

He reached the hand. The fragrance of the meat made an instant passage to his heart, and suddenly it was down his throat.

"My gad!" breathed Tucker Crosden. "Did you see that snap? No wolf could be quicker than that. Now he's gunna see if the thing poisons him!"

For White Wolf had leaped back to the doorway and crouched there, studying the symptoms in his stomach. There were no bad ones. If this were poison, let him have much of it! So he stole back when the next bit was offered and picked it daintily and deftly from the slim fingers of the girl with a wolf-like slash of his fangs. He did not leap back, this time, but merely crouched a little.

Presently, his head was beneath her arm, he was eating from her hand, all the man-joy of which his life had been robbed was gleaming in his eyes. As long as the big man remained at a sufficient distance, so that he did not need to be on his guard every instant, all was well.

Tucker Crosden passed the pan of hot water to Molly. It was she who washed the wounds of back and haunch and throat, and as the warmed water soaked out the caked, hard blood more effectually than ever La Sombra's tongue could have done, and as the pain slipped swiftly from him, he raised his eyes to the face of the girl and worshipped her silently, tremendously, with an eternal love.

Neither was the washing all, but the water was dried away by a light patting with a hot cloth, and then salve was rubbed in, and the very last echoes of the pain seemed to have disappeared.

All this had ended when a faint sniff was heard under the crack of the cabin door and White Wolf turned in a flash.

"There's something there!" said Molly. "You never should of closed it, maybe. Let him out, dad!"

"Let him out? Look at him! Maybe it would be the last of him!"

For White Wolf was crouched at the doorway tensed and desperately eager.

"It we make him hate us by keeping him here, he'll sure find a way of getting loose. Let him go, dad—and then he'll come back, I think."

"Would you take that chance?" asked Tucker Crosden, with the picture of Madison Square Garden and the greatest dog show in the world growing dim before his eyes.

"We got to take that chance."

"He's your dog!" said her father almost bitterly, "and I

ain't got the right to say how you should handle him. Old timer, good-bye!"

He jerked open the door, and White Wolf was a mere flash of a dog as he darted through it; but far off at the edge of the moonlit clearing, the trapper had a single glimpse of a rangy wolf as it leaped clumsily, on three legs, into the brush. The next instant, White Wolf clove through the same spot of brush. And yet there was no snarling sound of battle between the wolf-killer and the wolf.

So sudden light descended upon the slow brain of Tucker Crosden. He went back to Molly and sat beside her on the bunk.

"Figure it out forwards and backwards, Molly. You think it out for yourself and then you tell me what you make of it. We hear a sniffin' at the door. We open it up. And the dog jumps out; and off at the edge of the clearin' I see a three-legged wolf snap into the brush, and the dog dives right in the same direction. And—"

"A three-legged wolf—dad, it's the White Wolf! And that's his mate—"

"Ay," cried Tucker Crosden. "His mate or his foster ma!"

So the truth was known, and being the truth, it rang like good coin in the minds of the two. They had no doubts thereafter, and there was no money in the wide world that could have tempted a gun into the hands of the trapper to bring down Mother Wolf!

She, in the meantime, stood half in shadow and half in the moon and gasped at her foster son:

"Of all the foul things in the world, there is nothing so foul as you, oh my son! The stench of man lives on you—issues from your breath—lies in your stomach—and the hand of man has rubbed grease on your hurts—is it not poison?"

"It tastes like the fat of good meat," said White Wolf. "You may see for yourself. And I tell you, my mother, that you are wise, and that you know far more of many things than your son can ever know. But of this one thing —of man—"

"His name chokes me!" said Mother Wolf. "I am half afraid of you, my son, and I half hate you! Were you not in his den? And did I hear you fighting to escape from him?"

"Let me tell you one thing. It will fill you with wonder, and it will say more than you could guess. When the entrance to the cave was closed, I hardly noticed, for many other strange things were happening to me then! But when I heard you call, I leaped to the place and bade them let me go. And they did! As truly as you are the mother who bore me, they opened the door, and I ran freely out to you, as you see!"

Mother Wolf stepped back a little and stared at him as though she would make sure that it was White Wolf indeed, and not his ghost that had come back to her from that den of many dangers.

"There is nothing but the scent of man upon you," she said gloomily. "The clean wolf-smell is almost gone. Alas, my son, a little more and only by my eye shall I know you from the village dogs which we have played with and slain in the lowlands. An evil day was that when we left the broad valleys. For this thing would never have come!"

"What thing?" said the terrier. "Am I not free? Am I not here with you, to go whither you will?"

"But will you go in happiness?" asked La Sombra.

"Why shall I not? Let us go to the cave."

"Have you forgot the pack that waits for you?"

"The pack, then," said White Wolf. "But do you go to them and call them here. You will find me not far from the clearing when you return!"

La Sombra asked no further questions and offered no more resistance, but she hurried off at her limping gait through the dark, and began to hunt for the wolf-pack which had been reported on the side of Spencer Mountain.

And so it had been, but restless hunger had driven it far away, and when La Sombra reached it, long after dawn, there was still a weary journey to bring the Dunkeld pack back to the place where she had left her foster son beside Lake Pekan.

When they reached that spot, no White Wolf waited for them, however, and the questing wolves could find no trail of him. For half a dozen trails of horses swept up to the door of the cabin and then turned back westward, once more, up the valley of the Seven Sisters.

All the house was closed. No sign of man was here, when La Sombra with her aching heart ventured close up to examine. But near the door she found the trail of her foster son, and thereafter all the tramplings of the horses could not suffice to blot out the scent for her. She hobbled steadily along it, until the trail freshened and the whole pack was able to pick out the significant sign of their lost leader. After that, they left La Sombra behind as they forged on, and the long swinging cry which they raised rang far and wide across the woodland.

Then, from the front, an answer came back to them. It was a howl which to the ear of a man would have been unmistakable wolf, only a little shriller and shorter than usual. But to the Dunkeld pack it was clear as day, and they knew that they had their lost leader before them.

La Sombra herself was not too far to the rear to hear the call, and now she labored up the slope, and standing between two close-growing shrubs at the top of the rise; she looked down into the shallow hollow beyond and saw a sight that made her grieve indeed.

Yonder were five horses. Four men rode, and the daughter of Tucker Crosden sat in the fifth saddle, her head bowed weakly. Gannaway and the two Loftus brothers walked, and with them was Tucker Crosden himself, with his monster arms tied behind his back.

All of this would only have gladdened the heart of the mother wolf, because it was a token that the men were leaving, perhaps never to return; but what lay like a load upon her eye was the sight of White Wolf, skulking from shrub to shrub in pursuit of the train. For she felt, as she saw this thing, that man had won and she had lost and that her strange son was being drawn from the mountains and the wolves forever.

The other wolves of the Dunkeld pack lay deep in the snow and peered down at the horse train, the men, and the three hunting hounds of the Loftus brothers, trotting meekly behind their masters.

"Go down softly!" said La Sombra. "Go down, Grey Wolf, and call my son back to us!"

CHAPTER XXXIV

Grey Wolf went softly, softly down, drifting from the shelter of bush to bush towards the terrier, but in the meantime, the caravan was mounting on the further slope and the eye of Dan Loftus flicked back and saw the mere tip of the tail of the skulking lobo as he glided into cover. That sight was enough for Loftus. He knew wolves so well that a glimpse of a single claw printed a picture of the whole body on his brain. Now his yell waked Grampus from his sleepy plodding through the snow.

"Hey. Grampus, hey, Pete, Doc. Go find 'em, boys—that way!"

Sheriff Larned halted the procession to see those famous hounds run, and even the sullen face of big Crosden lighted as he watched. It was a pretty thing to see their team work, as the tall fighting dogs dropped back on either side of Grampus and let that wonderful finder of game range swiftly down the hollow and up the farther side—

The lobo must have paused too long, undecided as to whether or no it could really have been seen behind its shrub, and when it started to run, the hounds were perilously close. It was bound to be a short run with such a start. Even Grampus, slowest of the three, caught up on the frightened lobo, and Pete and Doc simply ran over him in spite of efforts which made his lips grin tight back.

"By Gad!" cried the sheriff, "they'll have him in another six jumps! They're worth a treasure, Loftus. Hello—what's this?"

Whiter than the snow over which he ran, a gleaming streak showed from behind a tuft of shrubbery and darted straight for the race. What a joy, then, must have entered the heart of the lobo as he saw his great leader come like the wind to his help. His own heart was strengthened. He had thought of nothing but headlong flight, before; now he was ready to battle hard and long.

"Another dog—and a bull-terrier!" cried the sheriff. "Where in the name of all that's wonderful——".

"The White Wolf!" shouted Tom Loftus. "I told you, Dan, that it was a damned queer wolf! Lend me your rifle!"

"Leave the dogs try their hands!" yelled Dan Loftus: "Let 'em try——"

They tried, and their effort was over in a single second. White Wolf, reaching the line of the racing hounds, dove up and under like a seal through water. His teeth found their mark, and the heavy wrench of his body as it flung under the tall hound, tore the throat of Pete wide. He fell and slid on the crusted snow. Before he reached the bottom of the slope he was dead.

In the meantime, Grey Wolf had wheeled to stand at the side of his famous rescuer. Like a Polish saberer, he cut to either side, right and left, and slashed Grampus and Doc cruelly. They were good fighters. But they were hurt. Here was a deadly foe before them, and yonder, just picking himself from the snow, was a white devil which they had seen before and knew too well. They wheeled of one accord and bolted back down the slope far faster than they had come, but there was no pursuit behind them.

"Guns, young fools! Guns!" La Sombra was yelping frantically above them. "Do you hear me? Break for cover!"

They followed her orders at their best speed, but one of them, at least, would never have reached shelter, for Dan Loftus had raised his rifle and was following White Wolf with a slowly swinging gun, marking him down with a steady, practiced hand when Gannaway jumped out and knocked up the muzzle of the gun. It exploded high in the air; and White Wolf was gone.

The two Loftus brothers closed upon Gannaway like snarling dogs.

"There was twenty-five hundred dollars under my trigger finger!" groaned Dan Loftus, pale with anger. "We'll have that out of your hide, Gannaway!"

But Adam Gannaway was cool enough and big enough to smile in the faces of the brothers.

"The bounty is for a wolf, my friends," said he. "A small white wolf—not for a bull-terrier!"

"It's for the animal that's been butcherin' cattle," said Tom Loftus, edging in with hard-gripped hands, "and the county has published the prints of his feet. Dog or wolf, yonder is the critter, and you've skinned us out of his scalp, Gannaway! Get your rifle up again, Dan. He's in that bush, yonder, and if he starts out, we'll nail him."

He swung his own rifle to his shoulder as he spoke, and they started forward towards the shelter of the terrier.

No speed of thought and no courage of heart could have saved White Wolf now. He saw them coming, and he saw their ready guns, but when he looked around, a wide expanse of clear snow lay between him and the nearest woods. It was death to cross that open space, and he knew it.

"Larned," said Tucker Crosden, "no matter what the Loftus gents say, I say that that dog yonder is one of my breeding and he belongs to my Molly. Are you gunna stand by and see him murdered?"

The sheriff was a happy man, on this day. He had made a capture without loss of blood, without a gun being fired—a capture which he had expected to cost more lives than one. But, above all, he was an honest man, and he wanted nothing but justice for all, whether the state had put a price upon their heads or not.

"Hold up, Loftus! Hold up, Tom!" he called to them. "You can't shoot a dog that belongs to another man. Not without a warrant for it. A dog is property the same as money in your pocket."

Dan Loftus kept his gun ready for the mark, but Tom turned to answer.

"Let's have his proof!" said he. "You've seen that critter fighting *for* wolves, not with 'em. Is that the way of a man-owned dog? Lemme see the proofs of Crosden!"

"Ay," said the sheriff. "That's all reasonable enough. Talk up, Crosden. Can you call in your dog?"

"Molly," said Tucker Crosden, "go fetch him in."

She was weak from the wound in her leg and from the exposure of the night before, and the sudden, brutal coming of the posse this morning, but now excitement buoyed her up. She was lifted from the saddle by Adam Gannaway, and she hobbled slowly out across the snow until she was close to the bush. In her hand she carried leash and collar, and now she kneeled in the snow and held out her hands, and the breathless men up the slope could hear the murmur of her voice, as she talked softly.

"It's no good!" said Tom Loftus, grinning with pleasure. "She ain't gunna get no rise from him. It's one of Crosden's bluffs, sheriff—"

The sheriff looked at Tom Loftus and felt like nodding assent. He looked to the white, strained face of Tucker Crosden and knew, on the other hand, that this was something more than an affair of a man and a dog. It had to do with a man and his very soul. "We'll stay here," said the sheriff, "till we freeze the hosses into the snow. But the kid is gunna get her chance with the dog! That's final!"

It seemed whole hours, such was the tension of the long moments, but at last a bit of white glimmered through the brush, and then the faultless head of the terrier looked out on the valley, and shrank; and he looked out again, and came a step towards the girl. He knew that there was dreadful danger in the face of which he was standing naked, but the sound of the girl's voice came to him like utter peace and brought a soft content upon his heart.

He stood before her, at last, and her cold, slow hands buckled the collar around his neck, and gripped the leash. So that, as all the posse could swear thereafter, White Wolf voluntarily yielded himself into the hands of the law. And what law could be too hard upon the self-surrendered enemy?

No one could make out exactly what a bull-terrier had to do with the trial of a man for murder, but the truth was that of the people who crowded the courtroom only one in ten came to see the prisoner at the bar, and the other nine fastened their gaze upon White Wolf.

It was too good a story for the newspapers to miss, of course. A dog which had run wild with wolves and brought a bounty of twenty-five hundred dollars on his head—and which had been raised by a wolfish foster mother, so it seemed—and who had now returned to the man who bred him—such matters were not only "human interest" but they were headline stuff and they were used accordingly.

On the first bench sat Caroline Crosden, with her eyes never moving from the prisoner so that when he chanced to glance at her, now and then, she could catch his smile, and that smile never failed to come faintly and slowly on his face. For Tucker Crosden, on trial for his life, was at peace with the world!

What happened to him did not really matter for he had done his life-work, and that life-work appeared in the courtroom every day. Of course there was a rule against animals in the court, but the judge in that small town was an understanding man, and when he heard that the bull-terrier, on being left alone, went almost mad in the house, he allowed White Wolf to come with the prisoner's family. Molly sat next to her mother, and between Molly and the wall at the end of the bench the terrier sat up and looked the world in the eye.

It was all very exciting to White Wolf. Human faces were more interesting to him than ever a blood trail had been in the San Jacinto Mountains. He could feel the curiosity and the kindness in the eyes that watched him, and there was such gentleness in their voices that his tail wagged instinctively. However, they composed only a vague background in the front of which were two familiar faces—his master, and Molly Crosden. Even Tucker Crosden was not really important, for there was only room in the heart of White Wolf for one great love, and that had gone out to the girl for whom he had fought and who had fought for him in the snows of the valley of the Seven Sisters. Yet when Tucker Crosden looked that way, the terrier could spare a brightening of the eyes, now and then, and even a whine.

The district attorney, afterwards, declared that the dog had ruined everything. How could he stand up and make his denunciation of Tucker Crosden as a brute beyond human control, a type of the murderer, when an infernal dog sat on the first bench and let the jury see that he loved this destroyer? And Crosden's young lawyer was not fool enough to overlook that point, either. He made his summing up speech by dwelling on the man, the dog, and the child, and when he ended, the jury went out for the shortest session that was ever held in the jury room of that courthouse. It came back with a verdict of not guilty. And the court room cheered. Not for Tucker Crosden, but for White Wolf. And White Wolf seemed to understand, because he stood up and wagged his tail.

Said the Judge in part:

"When a man is barred from his own home by strangers—when God has placed more than normal power in his hands—is it his fault if he strikes home harder than he thought to do, or is it the fault of the unlucky man who stood in his path? I do not think that Tucker Crosden is a murderer by nature. I look upon him as a worker, and a worker who has accomplished a great task!"

And the eye of the judge dwelt upon White Wolf to point the moral of his tale.

CHAPTER XXXV

Go east, then, with the train that carried Molly Crosden and her father into the sight of Manhattan, where the roar of the city closed like an ocean over the head of Molly and made White Wolf crowd closer against her knee. Then through the long days of waiting until at last in the great, barn-like arch of Madison Square Garden the roar of a hundred kinds of barking dogs went crashing in endless volleys to the rafters and the deep murmur of happy human voices floated in placid currents underneath; go to the balcony where a densely massed crowd closed around the show-ring where were shown "Bull-terriers—American bred—Novice Dogs." A dozen fine specimens are here but the eyes of the crowd are fastened upon one only—a white monster fifteen pounds beyond his nearest rival. He stands on the central platform and the thin-faced priest who judges them puts one rival after another beside him and removes them rapidly, almost in despair.

He says, you would think in anger, to the young girl who holds the leash of the giant: "Newspaper talk and nonsense are not going to influence me in this ring but—good heavens, what a head! And where did he get such bone—and such muscle, like iron!"

The little girl lifts her head and answers with the faintest of smiles: "Wolf meat was a part of his diet, sir. Though it ain't recommended particular in the dog books, they say!"

Over in the corner a leaning giant and a little man with a withered face and eyes of fire.

"How far will he go, Newton?" says the giant.

"There ain't a bull-terrier to stop him, except Pinkerton Ask You. Pinkerton will take some beating!"

Pinkerton did take some beating, but he got it. The nervous hand of the priest hesitated on only one point, and that was some jagged roughness under the throat of White Wolf.

"What's wrong with this dog of yours here, young lady?" said he to Molly.

"A wolf done it," said Molly, "when White Wolf was fighting for me—when I was caught in the trap—I guess you never heard about it, though."

The priest *had* heard, however. He listened with a sort of distant joy in his eyes. Had he not been a priest, he himself would have been a fighting man. And White Wolf took the big rosette and the silver cup . . .

No other worlds to conquer among bull-terriers. But what of the class in which all terriers meet? For there is an Irish terrier straight out of a picture book and a wire-haired fox terrier that has romped to victory over his enormous class.

They walk the ring with dancing steps, and dancing eyes. All except White Wolf, who stands like a white statue clipped from marble, crystal clear.

"Let me see that dog move, my girl!"

This is how he moved up the trails, and this is how he learned to drift over the country with La Sombra, when they hunted in the lowlands.

"What more do you want?" growls one judge to another, almost sullenly.

"Nothing," says the other, "though a dog of a brutal fighting breed like that—"

And White Wolf is one of the few elect to go forward to the final ring. Who are here at this final mustering of the great? A Pekingese, which it is rumored cost twelve thousand dollars in England; and a greyhound that would have gladdened the heart of a knight of old; and White Wolf is the third in the ring—

"If he could only do it!" says the crowd. "But then, it

isn't in the books. A bull-terrier can't win the best of all breeds! Too many faults in the best of them!"

"Ay, but he's got this far," says the rest of the crowd. "And who knows? I'm ready to cheer."

For the crowd read newspapers, even if the judges didn't.

"Let there be no triumph for sentimentality!" says the cold-eyed sportsman.

"But," says the desperate judge—he of the white hair and the pale blue eyes—"where can we fault this white devil from the mountains?"

"Where can we fault him?" says the other two.

And, leaning at a corner: "Where can they fault him?" says Tucker Crosden in a sullen undertone.

"I see!" says the little man.

"What do you see, Newton?"

"It's in the eyes, old timer! Look at 'em again. We been blind, Tucker, because we know what he is and we know what his fighting can be. But he ain't got the look—the real look, old man. His eyes is too big—and too kind. He ain't got the battling look!"

Tucker Crosden stared like one enchanted. For, all these days, he had pored over White Wolf and studied him from nose to tail, and still the terrier seemed to his eye the perfect dog.

Said the white-haired judge: "The greyhound won't do. It won't live in this class with the terrier and the Pekingese. He has to go, gentlemen!"

The other two nodded slowly and sadly, for the greyhound was a glorious creature and seemed every moment about to take wings and speed away with the lightness of a blowing wind. So the greyhound was led from the ring, and a deadly hush fell upon the crowd, for now it was narrowed to the little soft-eyed brown lap dog which had cost the small fortune and the white statue which had been so mysteriously reclaimed from the wilderness. And for half an hour three grave and elderly men crouched and kneeled and walked about and looked far away to call up the picture of the perfect type, and then glanced back at the strangely contrasted pair in the ring.

Then—"My friends," said the white-haired man, "can

you fault that terrier? Because I cannot! Except for rough skin under the throat—new scars, sirs, brought by fighting a wolf for the life of that same girl who holds the leash! Gentlemen, I have to vote for the terrier."

They brought a great silver cup, and a flaring rosette, and when they went to Molly Crosden, the packed thousands who watched raised a cheer that boomed against the great beams in the roof of the Garden.

But Tucker Crosden hardly heard. He was saying—and every word came slowly, dragged from his heart of hearts—"Newton, you're right. He's off the type. And—we got to start all over again, at the bottom, and build up!"

One thing at least had been proven to Caroline Tucker—that her husband could make more money in the mountain cabin with his traps than in the lowlands, and when that point was decided, the family moved to the Valley of the Seven Sisters and found there the thing which they had missed so long together—happiness.

"But," said Tucker's wife, "what'll become of White Wolf up here?"

"Let him run where he ran before," said Tucker Crosden. "He lived through the mountains once, and he'll live through them again!"

So White Wolf was turned loose to go where he pleased.

During the first day, he remained close to the house, but when the evening came on, with a pale moon hanging in the east, and growing brighter every moment, he sat down beneath the trees and raised a long howl that echoed far away among the hills. He listened, but no answer came.

Then he started west up the valley and ran hard until the shortness of his wind gave him pause, for he had fallen off a good deal from the iron strength which was his of old. When he stopped he heard something stir behind him, and looking back he saw the old red fox with the mangy coat and the broken-toothed grin.

"Once more, brother!" grinned White Wolf.

"Do you hunt for La Sombra?" said the fox. "Go up to the old cave on Spencer Mountain. There you will find her, and she will tell you certain things that will be good for you to know!"

White Wolf would have waited to ask more, but his heart was burning with eagerness, and he ran on again with all his might and so, climbing the long and rounded slopes, he came to the little shoulder in front of the cave —the same opening where he had seen the fisher kill his foster-brothers and where he and the litter had romped and played together so often.

At the same instant the tall form of the grey lobo bounded out of the brush and, dropping a dead rabbit in front of the mouth of the cave, turned to block the way of the stranger.

"Ah, Grey Wolf," said the terrier, "have you left the Dunkeld pack? But what do you here so far from your old hunting grounds?"

"Faugh!" said Grey Wolf. "What is this that speaks in the tongue of a wolf and bears the form and the smell of a dog? Have you dared to come up here to face me, alone? Now, by the hills of Dunkeld, the day has come for the cubs to eat well, and for La Sombra's maw to be filled at last!"

And he dragged himself forward on his belly, crouched for the leap. White Wolf did not stir.

"It is well that I have come back, young fool," said he, "before my people forget me. It is not the scent which makes the wolf, but the heart, and my heart is true to my people forever. What? Have you forgotten me and the bull elk whom I killed to fill the bellies of the Dunkeld pack, and you among the rest? Have you forgotten, Grey Wolf? Or must I take you by the throat and shake sense into you again!"

Before the calm and kingly front, the lobo gave back a little.

"La Sombra!" he growled. "Here is a danger that may need two pairs of jaws to fight it!"

That instant the gaunt shadow of La Sombra appeared from the shadows at the mouth of the cave, and the hot scent of the litter which had been huddled about her rolled rankly forth to the nostrils of White Wolf.

"Oh, mother!" cried White Wolf, "I have come to you again!"

She stood at the side of Grey Wolf and her eyes glimmered with green light.

"A dog—with the filthy scent of man thick on him!" said Mother Wolf. "Have you called for help to fight such a cur as this? Have you no shame, Grey Wolf?"

"I have shame," said Grey Wolf slowly. "But there is a dim memory half awake in my mind, of the pack at bay, and a white leader who knew no fear—and is there not a legend out of the long ago of how the lone hunter, Black Wolf, was killed by a creature like this?"

"Ah," moaned White Wolf, crouching to the ground in an agony of grief, "have you forgotten that you nursed me and how I have hunted and fought for you?"

"Who is this that talks of hunting and battle?" snarled La Sombra. "I know one thing only—that the cubs cry for food!"

And she picked up the fallen rabbit and retreated growling into the cave, where White Wolf instantly heard the joyous voices of the litter, welcoming the scent of food. So he turned, as if Grey Wolf had been no more than a tree squirrel behind him, and returned slowly and sadly towards the valley of the Seven Sisters, for he knew that he had closed a chapter which he could never open again.

He reached the clearing. The door of the house was closed but when he scratched at it, there was a joyous shout inside, and it was snatched open before him, and the arms of Molly went round his neck.

He repulsed her with a dreadful snarl such as the Dunkeld pack had once known and trembled at.

"Has he gone mad?" gasped Molly, shrinking away.

The White Wolf glanced back, and at the edge of the clearing, facing the doorway with a broken-toothed grin, was the mangy red fox. But now the door closed, and the sense of emasculating warmth and laziness swept about him. Into the coldest corner he backed and lay down, and wondered at the wretchedness in his heart.

"What has happened to him!" breathed Molly and her

mother, clinging to one another. "Look at his eyes! They've turned green!"

But Tucker Crosden leaned and watched and nodded.

"Leave him be," said he. "There's some things that have got to be fought out all alone—by dogs and men!"

Max Brand is the best-known pen name of Frederick Faust, creator of Dr. Kildare, Destry, and many other fictional characters popular with readers and viewers worldwide. Faust wrote for a variety of audiences in many genres. His enormous output, totaling approximately thirty million words or the equivalent of 530 ordinary books, covered nearly every field: crime, fantasy, historical romance, espionage, Westerns, science fiction, adventure, animal stories, love, war, and fashionable society, big business and big medicine. Eighty motion pictures have been based on his work along with many radio and television programs. For good measure he also published four volumes of poetry. Perhaps no other author has reached more people in more different ways.

Born in Seattle in 1892, orphaned early, Faust grew up in the rural San Joaquin Valley of California. At Berkeley he became a student rebel and one-man literary movement, contributing prodigiously to all campus publications. Denied a degree because of unconventional conduct, he embarked on a series of adventures culminating in New York City where, after a period of near starvation, he received simultaneous recognition as a serious poet and successful popular-prose writer. Later, he traveled widely, making his home in New York, then in Florence, and finally in Los Angeles.

Once the United States entered the Second World War, Faust abandoned his lucrative writing career and his work as a screenwriter to serve as a war correspondent with the infantry in Italy, despite his fifty-one years and a bad heart. He was killed during a night attack on a hilltop village held by the German army. New books based on magazine serials or unpublished manuscripts continue to appear. Alive and dead he has averaged a new one every four months for seventy-five years. In the U.S. alone nine publishers issue his work, plus many more in foreign countries. Yet, only recently have the full dimensions of this extraordinarily versatile and prolific writer come to be recognized and his stature as a protean literary figure in the 20th Century acknowledged. His popularity continues to grow throughout the world.